AF473262

# An Independent Woman

Kate Loveday

1st Edition published in Australia in 2009 by Scribe's Ink Publishers, SA, Australia.

2nd Edition published in Australia in 2018 by Scribes Ink Publishers, South Australia



National Library of Australia Catalogue-in-Publication entry

A823.4

Loveday, Kate

An Independent Woman/Kate Loveday

2nd. Edition 2018

ISBN: 978 0 646 51431 4 (pbk)

Typeset in 12/16 Garamond

Scribe's Ink Publishers

Also by Kate Loveday

*Inheritance*

*Black Mountain*

*The Trophy Wife*

*Reflections*

The Redwood Series

*An Independent Woman*

*A Liberated Woman*

*An Ambitious Woman*

## Acknowledgements

I'd like to thank Jacqui Winn for her critiques, editorial suggestions and encouragement, to say nothing of her time spent over numerous cups of coffee.

Thanks to Janice and Roger, Kay and Melissa for their supportive assessments, and to Leonie Bell for loaning me her copy of 'The letters of Rachel Henning' which first sparked my interest in the early days of Bulahdelah.

I thank my publishers for help in getting it all right.

I must also thank Peter for all his listening, support and encouragement.

And last but not least to all my readers and particularly those who have told me they are eagerly awaiting my next book, thank you all

For Peter

# CHAPTER ONE

*London 1878*

Kitty Morland leant on the balustrade, watching the dancers below. The colours of the silks and satins of the ladies' gowns, the flash of jewels sparkling in the gaslights, all created a moving kaleidoscope of colour as the elegantly dressed men guided their partners around the floor. Her foot tapped in time to the music, but resentment simmered inside her. By rights she belonged down there, with them, not up here, an onlooker.

Looking down at her neat, grey governess's dress, Kitty smoothed it over her slim hips, and lifted her hand to touch the no-nonsense bun she was now forced to wear to tame the honey gold curls of her hair. How drab her appearance, compared to those she watched below.

She caught a whiff of something like cigar smoke and turned, but the gallery of the elegant Knightsbridge house was empty. The doors to the balcony at the side were open on this warm night, and the darkness revealed no one beyond.

She gazed at the portraits lining the walls of the gallery, her lips twisting. The owners of the house described them to all as their ancestors, but she knew better. The Arnolds, her employers, were nouveau riche, and their ancestors had no portraits. Turning back, she resumed her watching.

'Ah, Charlotte, I wondered why you were skulking around the house in the dark. Was it just to come and watch the gaiety, eh, or did you have something else in mind?'

Whirling around, Kitty saw Craddock, George Arnold's personal servant, standing close beside her. Tall, sleek and sharp, she mistrusted him, and had avoided him whenever possible since coming to this house. She narrowed her eyes as he leant towards her, and took a step back.

'Oh, Mr. Craddock, you startled me. I didn't hear you coming. I just came down to watch the dancing.'

'I guess you'd love to be down there with them, wouldn't you? You look lonely, standing here all on your own in the half dark. Now that I've found you, I'll keep you company.'

He moved closer, and she stepped back again. 'I can assure you I'm not at all lonely. I'm just enjoying watching the party.'

Craddock's eyes glinted. 'We could have a little party all on our own.' He sidled closer still and slipped his arm around her waist, holding her firmly. 'I have some gin in my room, good stuff, not your cheap rubbish. We can go up there and have a little drink and…'

Kitty cut him off before he could finish. 'Thank you, but I have no desire to go to your room...' her voice dripped ice, 'for a drink, or anything else.' She tried to remove his arm but he held her tighter.

'Come on now, don't be like that. We can have a good time together; you and me, and you'll find me a good friend to have in this house.' He spun her around. His hot breath fanned her face.

She struggled to free herself but found his grip too strong. Both his arms were around her, pinning her arms to her sides. He bent closer, pushing her back against the rail, and his mouth came down on hers. Revolted by his wet lips she twisted her face away, her heart thudding.

'Let me go.'

'Be nice to me, Charlotte. I'm not going to hurt you; we can have some fun together.'

Her breath came in gasps. 'Let me go, you pig.'

Craddock took no notice as she twisted, trying to escape from his grasp. His mouth slid down and he kissed her neck.

'You're lovely,' he muttered as his hand came up and fondled her breast.

Kitty took advantage of having one hand free and pushed him with all her strength, her pulses pounding, but she was still pinned against the rail.

He raised his head, fumbling with the buttons on her bodice, and moved back momentarily. Raising her free arm she hit him a stinging blow on the face and raked her nails down his cheek.

Uttering an oath, he released her and stepped back, his hand at his cheek. When he took it away he looked at the blood on it.

'Look what you've done, you little hell cat, you've drawn blood.' He raised his hand as if to strike her, but dropped it and reached into his pocket for a handkerchief. 'Think you're too good for me, with your hoity-toity manners, do you? Well, we all know you're poor as a church mouse, in spite of your airs and graces.'

Kitty panted, struggling to regain her breath. 'If you ever touch me again, I'll hurt you where it'll do a lot more damage.'

'You'll be sorry for this, mark my words. I'll see you suffer for it.'

Craddock spun around and hurried away, holding the handkerchief to his cheek.

Kitty crossed the gallery to sit on a bench near the open doors while she composed herself. Her breath came heavily as she checked her buttons were done up, and tucked one of her curls back into the bun it had fallen from in the scuffle. Wanting a breath of fresh air, she stood and walked towards the balcony, but as she neared the open doors she jumped back with fright. Someone was already out there.

A man in evening dress sauntered through the doors into the gallery.

'My, my,' he drawled, 'you do have a temper, but I don't think I'd go so far as to call you a hell cat, even if you did draw blood.'

'Who…who are you?'

'Just a guest for the ball.'

'What were you doing out there?'

'I went out earlier to escape the crowd for a while and smoke a cigar in peace. I didn't know I was going to witness such an interesting exchange.'

Kitty detected amusement in his voice, and her body stiffened. 'If you saw what was happening then why didn't you come to my aid?'

'You were managing quite well on your own, I thought.'

'Any gentleman would have helped me.'

'Ah, you English wouldn't consider me a gentleman, I'm afraid.'

'Obviously you're not. If you were, you'd pretend you hadn't heard the exchange, instead of trying to embarrass me.'

His eyebrows rose. 'Are you embarrassed?' His face held the hint of a smile.

'Of course I am.'

He laughed. 'I think not.' He dropped his bantering manner. 'Look, why don't you come downstairs and I'll get you a glass of champagne. I've always found there's nothing like champagne to raise a young lady's spirits.'

Suddenly, Kitty remembered her circumstances.

He was a guest for the evening, while she should not be here, watching the festivities. It would not be viewed kindly by her employers if they knew one of their guests had witnessed the scene between her and Craddock. If it came to that, Craddock would twist things around to make it seem as if she was in the wrong. Her stomach clenched, she was under no illusion as to who would be believed if it came to a confrontation.

Kitty looked up at the stranger. Even in this dim light she could see he was not what she called the 'usual insipid upper-class Englishman'. She judged him to be in his early thirties, tall and lean, with dark hair and eyes and regular features. He was clean-shaven except for a neatly trimmed moustache, and his skin showed he spent time in the sun. But it was something else that made him different; an air of self-confidence, of energy and vitality.

He was the sort of man she would enjoy getting to know, under different circumstances. But now was not the time. Regretfully, she shook her head. 'Thank you, but no. I must go.'

'At least come and have a dance with me.'

How she would love to do that. Her heart raced at the thought of this dashing stranger's arms around her as he swept her on to the floor. If only things were different. If only she could meet him as an equal.

'Surely you can see I'm not dressed for a ball.'

'You look beautiful.' He sounded as if he meant it.

Kitty shook her head again. 'I really can't.'

At that moment the music started again, playing a Strauss waltz.

'Then we'll have our own dance floor up here.' He took her into his arms and swept her around the floor of the gallery.

Her heart pumped with excitement as her feet followed his, bringing a flush to her cheeks. She relaxed for a moment or two as he held her close, allowing herself to experience the dizzying sensations before she pulled from his arms. Whatever was she thinking? If she was seen, she would surely be dismissed.

'I must go.'

He put out his hand to detain her. 'Stay just a while, please.'

She shook her head. 'No, I can't.' Turning, she moved away.

'Please, Charlotte, wait.'

Kitty heard him call her name as she sped across the gallery. He made no attempt to follow her.

For several days she was apprehensive, expecting some repercussion from the events of the evening, but there was none. The disturbing stranger had evidently made no mention of their meeting. Sadly, she realised she was unlikely to see him again.

Craddock kept away from her. Not knowing how he explained the scratches on his cheek, she didn't care. She knew she had made an enemy, but tried to put it from her mind.

Kitty received a summons from the mistress of the house late one evening three months later.

'Charlotte, the mistress wants you in the drawing room.'

'Thank you, Betsy.'

'You better hurry. She don't look happy.'

Why she was being summoned at this hour? Nanny put the children to bed earlier; they should both be asleep by now.

As she passed the study on her way down, Kitty heard loud snores coming from behind the partly open door. It sounded as if the master had taken a drop too much after-dinner port again.

Tapping on the drawing room door, she waited to hear the voice call, 'Come in,' before entering the room.

Mrs. Arnold sat in a chair drawn up close to the brightly burning fire. She wore the same green silk gown Kitty remembered from earlier in the evening. Jewels at her throat and ears shone brilliantly in the firelight. Kitty drew in her breath as she recognised the diamond and emerald necklace and earrings that had belonged to her own mother.

The expensive gown and jewels could not hide the plainness of her employer's pointed nose, thin lips set in a line, and steely eyes, glinting coldly as her gaze travelled over Kitty.

'You want to see me, Mrs. Arnold?'

'Yes. It has been brought to my attention that a vase is missing from the top of the bureau in the music room. A very expensive antique vase. What do you know about it?' Her voice was as cold as her eyes.

Kitty's cheeks flamed. Was she being accused of stealing the vase? Remembering her livelihood depended on this woman, she bit back a sharp rejoinder. 'Why, nothing. Why would I know anything about it?'

'I'm assured it was there when the room was cleaned this morning. I believe you were in there this afternoon?'

'No. I haven't been in there at all today.'

'The vase was broken, Charlotte. I believe you broke it and said nothing, thinking it wouldn't be missed for some time, if at all.'

How dare she accuse her like this? 'No, I didn't break it. I told you, I wasn't in there today.'

'You were seen coming out, holding something hidden in the folds of your skirt.'

Kitty's nails bit into the palms as she clenched her fists at her sides. 'That's not true. If someone told you that, they were mistaken.'

'It mightn't have been discovered if you hadn't kicked a piece under the bureau. I think you missed that piece when you picked up the rest and took it out to dispose of it. But when Hawkins went into the room this evening, he noticed it poking out from under the side of the bureau.' She paused. 'What do you have to say to that?'

'If someone broke it, it wasn't me.'

'Then what were you carrying out?'

'I told you, I wasn't in the room. If someone says they saw me then they're lying.'

Mrs. Arnold's eyes narrowed. 'I think you are lying. I think you're frightened to own up to what you did.'

Kitty's pulses pounded. 'That's not true. If I'd broken your vase, I'd have told you.'

'I suppose you're frightened I'll take the money out of your wages to replace it. Well, I know I'd have no hope, it would take years.' Her voice was cold. 'However, I will not have servants who tell lies. I expected better from you. You will leave first thing in the morning.'

Kitty remembered how dependent she was on her small wage. She almost choked as she brought out the words. 'I did not break your vase. I was not in that room today.'

'Don't lie to me anymore,' the woman shouted at her, her face livid, her jaw quivering. 'Your father would be ashamed of you if he were still here. He would expect you to own up to what you've done.'

Kitty's control crumbled. Rage seared her throat as she replied. 'How dare you bring my father into this? He would know I don't lie. Which is more than can be said for others in this house.'

'I think you'd better be careful what you say, Charlotte. You will leave in the morning. Under the circumstances, I will not be giving you a character.'

Kitty heard the satisfaction in her voice. She knew the woman was jealous and spiteful, resenting anyone younger or more attractive than herself, as well as those whose family background was better. But never had she expected her to carry her vindictiveness to such lengths. Shaken, Kitty turned and left the room without another word, slamming the door.

## CHAPTER TWO

In the hall Kitty leant against the wall, waiting until her fury subsided a little, and her heartbeat slowed. Who could have lied about seeing her come out of the music room? She didn't have to think long, it had to be Craddock. Her skin crawled as she remembered how he tried to maul her on the night of the ball. He had barely spoken to her since, biding his time. Now, this was his ultimate revenge.

Kitty headed for the stairs. As she reached the study, the snoring was still loud, the door ajar. Pausing, she turned and pushed the door open and looked inside. The master of the house sprawled in his armchair, fast asleep.

Moving into the room she stood looking down at him, hands clenched at her sides. This was the man she blamed for her father's death and her own present circumstances. George Arnold. How she hated him. Kitty stared down at him, filled with loathing. Middle age was upon him and his once muscular body showed signs of fat. He had slid down in the chair, with his flushed face slumped on his chest, and his legs stuck out straight in front of him. One arm rested along the arm of the chair, and the other hung limply across the front of his body. His slack mouth sagged open and his snores were loud and rhythmic. This was the man who had shattered her life.

Her chest tightened as she remembered, as clearly as yesterday, sitting with her parents in the garden of their home in Hampstead, three years ago, when the quiet of the afternoon was broken by the sound of an approaching horse.

The sound had drawn the attention of the four people seated beneath the branches of a large oak tree, their chairs alongside a table set for tea.

Charles Morland, a thin, silver-haired man with the look of a scholar, shaded his eyes with his hand as he peered down the driveway. He turned to his wife with a smile.

'Why, Bella, I do believe it's my friend Mr. Arnold come to visit us. What a pleasant surprise. Hopefully, he has good news of my investment, and our financial worries will soon be over.'

'What investment is that, Father?' asked the young man seated beside him.

'You know Mr. Arnold is a successful jeweller, Robert, with a shop in Bond Street?'

'Yes, I've heard you talk of it.'

'He's very successful and has told me many times of the big profits he makes by buying direct from his friend's diamond mine in South Africa. By cutting out the middleman and setting the gems and selling them through his own shop he makes a great deal of money. He offered to let me put up money for a shipment and we'll share the profits. It's very kind of him; he had no need to make such a generous offer.'

Bella frowned. 'I hope it all goes as well as he says it will. I must say I felt alarmed when you told me you'd raised such a large sum of money on the house, and given it to him.'

'There's no need to worry, my dear. It's a foolproof way to recoup our dwindling funds.' He paused before speaking to his daughter, who was sitting on the other side of the table. 'Kitty, will you please tell Jane there will be another one for tea?'

Kitty rose from her chair at the same time as the visitor arrived at the top of the drive and slid from his horse.

The new arrival was a tall, fleshy man with a sensuous mouth, rather red in the face now as he mopped his brow with a handkerchief and strode towards their table.

'Charles,' he called out, 'I am the bearer of unfortunate tidings.'

As Kitty watched Arnold now, sprawled in the chair, he stirred in his sleep, snorted, and flung his arm away from his body and out to his side. Perhaps he was about to wake up. Not caring if he saw her standing there, she stood her ground.

His arm fell onto the top of a small table standing by the chair, before he settled down again. His hand had just missed the half-empty glass of port standing on the table, but it had knocked over a small chamois pouch sitting near it. A stream of diamonds spilled out on to the table as the pouch toppled sideways.

Kitty stared at the jewels as they glittered in the lamplight. She drew in her breath sharply. Why, there must be thousands of pounds worth in the pouch. He'd obviously brought them home with him from his jewellery shop, and had fallen asleep with them beside him.

The past raced through her mind.

Kitty would never forget that day when Arnold had arrived at their house seemingly in a state of agitation. The shipment had been waylaid on its way to the ship and the bandits had made off with the diamonds, he told them. They had lost it all.

After listening to his friend's tale that day, her father, her gentle, scholarly father Charles, who spent most of his time in the library with his books, went into the library one last time, and put a bullet through his brain.

Their house in Hampstead, with its large grounds and handsome furnishings, had been sold over their heads, along with most of their possessions. Even her mother's jewellery, much of which had been left to her by her own mother, had been taken by the bailiffs, deemed, by law, to be her husband's property. They learned later that George Arnold bought most of their possessions for a fraction of their worth.

Kitty and her mother had been forced to move into two rooms over the top of a draper's shop in Bloomsbury, where her mother took in sewing and embroidery to earn a pittance to live on.

There was no money for her brother Robert, whom Kitty had adored since a small child, to continue his law studies at Cambridge. In desperation, he decided to go to Australia and seek his fortune. He had hopes of finding gold and then, he promised, he would send for them,

Kitty reluctantly accepted the offer of coming here as governess to the two Arnold children, giving her mother most of the small wage she earned towards the rent of the rooms. She never believed Arnold's story of the robbery, certain he had fabricated it to swindle her father out of his investment. But, much as she hated him, what else could she do? There were few ways for a young lady of nineteen to earn a living in England.

Now, here was George Arnold, still living in luxury. And tomorrow she would be forced to return to the two rooms with her mother. Without a character she would be unable to find another position. The meagre amount her mother earned could never sustain them. She trembled as she contemplated their future. What was to become of them?

Kitty stared at the diamonds winking up at her. Biting her lip, she picked one up. Turning it around in her fingers, she watched the changing colours as the facets reflected the light. How much would it be worth? She didn't know, but guessed it would be enough to keep the two of them in food for months, maybe a year or more. And there must be dozens in the bag.

Looking around guiltily, she put it back with the others. There was no sound apart from the snoring. Going to the door, Kitty looked out. No one was in sight. The servants would all be downstairs, hoping they were finished for the night. Moving back to the table, she stood there again, looking, her heart pounding. Slowly, she reached down and stood the bag upright again. A scatter of diamonds remained on the table.

Kitty watched the sleeping man, thinking how easy it would be to help herself to the spilt diamonds. If she took them, wouldn't she only be repaying a fraction of what Arnold stole from her father? She took a step back. No, she couldn't.

Then a picture of her mother, bent over her sewing in that cold and dingy room in Bloomsbury, flashed through her mind. Followed immediately by one of this man's wife, sitting by the fire. Wearing her mother's jewels. Abruptly, she leant over, scooped up the loose diamonds and slipped them into her pocket. The blood pounded in her ears.

Fleeing from the room, she sped along the hall to the bottom of the stairs. Pausing, she looked around. Was that the downstairs door closing as she turned? Had she really seen it, or was it her guilty conscience playing tricks on her? Turning, she hurried up the stairs to her room on the third floor.

Once inside, she closed the door and placed a chair beneath the knob to keep it firmly shut. Kitty sat on the bed drawing in deep mouthfuls of air. Taking the diamonds from her pocket with shaking fingers she examined them. There were twenty six in all, of varying sizes and shapes, gleaming brilliantly on her bed. If she kept them and sold them, it would replace some of what Arnold had stolen from them. It would give her and her mother a new start.

But what if Arnold woke and realised some of the diamonds were missing? A cold knot of fear twisted inside her. What would he do? Had he counted them before he fell asleep? Did he have a record at the shop of what he had taken home? If they were missed, would she be suspected?

Perhaps someone saw her come out of the study. Perhaps she would be searched.

Kitty looked around the room. Where could she hide them? And what if her case was searched before she left in the morning? How was she to get them safely out of the house? Her glance settled on the glass of water on her bedside table.

Drawing a deep breath, she picked it up. Very deliberately, she placed a diamond on her tongue, took a mouthful of water and gulped it down, then repeated it, one by one, until the diamonds were all gone.

As Kitty tossed and turned in her bed later that night she relived the moment when she put the diamonds in her pocket. She knew she would not have yielded to the impulse if Mrs. Arnold had not sacked her so unjustly, and in such a malicious fashion. Worry for their future, coupled with anger, had caused her to become a thief. Her conscience gave her no rest. She regretted her actions, but what could she do? It was impossible for her to return the diamonds; she must wait for Nature to take its course before they would be in her possession again. The only course left to her was to leave first thing in the morning and hope she escaped detection.

Kitty was up before it was light. Hurriedly she washed and dressed, her fingers trembling so much she had difficulty fastening her buttons. It took her only a few moments to pack her belongings into her case and she was ready to leave. She looked around her small room. She was not sorry to leave, she'd not been happy in the time spent in this house. Making her way downstairs through the silent house she shivered in the morning chill. The only person she met as she carried her case out was the housemaid, up early to clean out the grates and light the fires before the rest of the household stirred. When Kitty told her she was leaving, the maid shrugged her shoulders and went on with her work.

When she reached the street, Kitty looked up at the house with its imposing façade. In the early morning light it appeared dark and menacing. Its shadow leant towards her as if it meant to pull her back into its clutches.

Kitty hurried away, fear gnawing at her insides. She'd taken no breakfast, not wanting her body to try ejecting its unusual supper prematurely. It must wait until she reached home.

Would the loss of the diamonds be discovered when George Arnold woke? Or would they not be missed until they were counted at the shop? Would he connect her with their disappearance? Kitty felt almost certain he would, particularly once he heard the story of her dismissal from his wife, and the fact that she left so early this morning.

If so, how long did she have before he contacted the police? How long until they came looking for her? Fear lent urgency to her footsteps.

She had a long walk to reach the street where she could board a horse-drawn bus that would take her close to Bloomsbury. She eyed the hansom cabs waiting for hire by the kerbs, but knew she had no money to spare for this luxury.

Meanwhile, each bobby on his beat was now a possible source of danger, in place of being a reassuring sight as usual.

Kitty heaved a sigh of relief as she finally clambered aboard a bus, and settled back in her seat. She had plenty of time to think as it rumbled its way through the streets on the long ride home. Terror gripped her as she thought of what she had done, and what could happen to her. She was under no illusion that Arnold would show her any mercy if he suspected her. No, he would want his diamonds back, he would send the police after her, and, even if he got them back, he would still charge her with theft. And Kitty knew what that meant. Prison. She broke into a cold sweat. Perhaps it could even be considered a hanging offence.

Kitty drew deep breaths, trying to still her mind, but her thoughts chased themselves around like a dog chasing its tail. She had to get away from London. Go somewhere she wasn't known. Her mother would come with her; they would start a new life. But where could they go? Where would she be safe? They could bury themselves in the country, far away, in a small village. They could change their names. But she would be hard pressed to find another position in the country. The money from the diamonds wouldn't last forever, and she was going to find it almost impossible to secure another position anywhere, without a character. What were they to do?

Suddenly Kitty had the answer. She felt faint with relief. Of course. They would go to Australia. Robert was already there; they would go and join him. They would go immediately, before she could be found. She would book passage for them both on the first ship leaving, immediately she sold some of the diamonds. Then she would be safe, and they would start their new life in a new country, with Robert. Yes, Australia. In Australia she would be safe.

# CHAPTER THREE

*Five months later*

The Osprey's sails billowed, the canvas slapping in the wind as the pilot guided her through the Heads into Sydney Harbour. Kitty looked at the panorama opening up in front of her as she stood by the rail of the majestic clipper as it sped through the water. Her heart felt as if it might burst with excitement as she turned to her mother beside her.

'I can hardly believe we're finally here. We've come twelve thousand miles, from the top of the earth right down here to the bottom, but we've finally arrived, ready to start a new life in a new country.'

Bella took a deep breath, her fingers twisting the beads that hung at her throat. 'Let us hope it's far enough away for you to be safe.'

'Oh Mother, of course it is. Who would ever think to come looking for me in Australia? Besides...' she paused, her hand tightening on the rail, 'we're not even sure they are looking for me.'

Bella's brow puckered. 'It's certainly very probable.'

Shaking her head to dispel the sudden flicker of fear at her mother's words, Kitty grabbed Bella's arm, giving it a little shake as she pointed ahead. 'Forget about that for now. Look, just look at that!'

They were through the Heads now and a huge harbour spread before them. Kitty had never seen anything to match its beauty. The blue of the sky was reflected in the ocean. Where the waves splintered the rising sun's slanting rays, it bounced them up to dazzle their eyes. Cotton wool clouds dotted the sky above, scudding before a light breeze. In the distance, green wooded slopes surrounded the sea, tumbling down to little bays and inlets around the coastline, and dark rocks spilled out to encircle scoops of golden sand.

Small islands popped up out of the water here and there, and everywhere there were boats, all sizes and shapes. Ferry boats crisscrossed the waters, carrying early morning passengers, while yachts and fishing boats were already out and about. Another clipper passed them heading back out to sea, its sails swelling, about to start its journey. Tied up at the wharves ahead were more ships, their sails furled.

Directly in front lay the city of Sydney. Buildings lined the foreshore and spread around it, while houses stretched up the hills behind. And over all the sun shone, bright, clear and warm.

Kitty was relieved to see the tension fade from Bella's face.

'It's certainly beautiful.' She smiled. 'You're right, let us hope that it's the beginning of a new life. Let's hope we can forget the past and start afresh.'

'Poor Mother.' Kitty reached across and took her hand. 'I think these last years have been harder for you than they were for me.'

'Things haven't been easy, I admit.' Bella drew a deep breath and shook her head. 'And I could see little hope of things improving.'

'Well, that's all behind us now.' Kitty patted Bella's hand. 'And I'm glad I did what I did,' she added fiercely. 'It's what's given us this chance, to come here to Australia and find Robert, and start afresh.'

Bella's fingers sought her beads again. 'We must hope it never catches up with you.' Her voice shook. 'I still have sleepless nights thinking about the consequences, if it does.'

Kitty took her hand again as a little knot of anxiety twisted inside her. 'It's all right,' she insisted. 'We'll be safe here.'

'I hope so. Thank goodness we were able to leave London so quickly. If we hadn't…' Her voice trailed away as she took a deep breath and shook her head wordlessly.

'Don't even think about that. It's all behind us now. We're about to start a new life.' Kitty squeezed Bella's hand before releasing it, her optimism returning. 'And Mother, while we're certainly not wealthy, we have enough money now to be able to buy the necessities of life, and even a few luxuries. Like some new clothes.' Stepping back she studied Bella, thinking how elegant her mother looked in her soft blue dress with white lace trimming on the bodice. Her dark hair, piled high, emphasised her even features. 'You always look lovely, but it's years since we've had anything new.'

Bella smiled and, reaching up, tucked back one of Kitty's curls that had escaped in the breeze, then patted her cheek gently. 'Well, this dress has always been a good stand-by, but I know it's old. And as for you, you're so beautiful you look good in anything, but particularly so in that red dress. You must wear the beautiful hat you had made to go with it.'

'Ah yes, that was when we were affluent.' Kitty sighed, reflecting. Money. It all came down to money, didn't it? With it you could have what you wanted – without it you were at the mercy of others. She clenched her fists so tightly the nails dug into her palms, determined they would become affluent again in this new country. She would do whatever was necessary to get enough money so they would never be poor again. Her mother would never have to suffer again as she had these past few years. Kitty set her lips firmly. 'Don't worry Mother. We'll be affluent again, I promise you.'

Bella smiled at her. 'As long as you're safe. That's more important.' She paused for a moment before she went on. 'Kitty, I've been thinking – about William Barron. He's been most attentive to you on the journey. He's obviously very taken with you. Has he mentioned marriage?'

'No. I keep heading him off whenever I think he might.'

'So you think he will?'

'I think it's possible.'

'And if he does, will you accept him?'

Kitty sighed. 'He's very attentive, I know, and I suppose he's rather sweet really, in a hang-dog sort of way, but I don't want to be married to him, to have to spend the rest of my life with him…'

Bella interrupted her. 'My dear, I know that type. Once you were married you wouldn't have to put up with spending all your time with him. He would be at his club, or in his library.'

'He thinks reading is a waste of time.'

'Oh. Well then, hunting, or about the estate.'

'He would still be my husband, and I don't love him.'

'Love isn't everything in marriage. Once babies come you would be content.'

'Do you think that's all I have to look forward to, marriage and babies? Surely there's more in life than that.'

'It's what most girls look forward to.'

'Perhaps if our lives hadn't changed the way they did, I'd have been content with that, too, but now I don't know I want to marry anyone. I've been talking with many of the colonials who are returning home, and Australia sounds an exciting place. It seems not everyone follows the same old patterns out here. I don't want to be some man's chattel. I want to be independent. I want to lead my life the way I want – not bending to a man's wishes all the time.'

'Kitty, you're a woman. That's the way it is for us. How do you think you're going to live? The money won't last forever, and as for your brother Robert, we don't know what his situation is. First we have to find him.'

'We'll find him. And when we do, I've worked it all out. I'll dispose of the rest of our diamonds and we'll buy a business, with Robert. Robert can run it and we'll both help.' She paused, her lips tightening. 'I'm afraid Robert's hopes of being a lawyer died with Father, but at least now we can help him to create a good life in the new country. And it'll be fun to be involved in a business.'

'Kitty, aren't you forgetting the danger you could be in? You might not be safe, even out here. But if you were married to William no one would dare accuse you, wherever you were, even back in England. You'd be under the protection of the Barron name, with Sir Alexander Barron as your father-in-law. They're an important family. You'd be safe.'

Kitty took a deep breath, seeking to reassure herself. 'But it might never happen. Perhaps I was never suspected when the diamonds went missing. And we're twelve thousand miles away. I'm sure we'll be safe in Australia.'

'That might be so, but at least think about William. Promise me you'll at least think about him, don't say 'no' without some thought.'

'All right. He might never ask me, but if he does, I promise I'll think about it. But I wouldn't make any decision until we see Robert.'

'Very well, I agree with that. I must say I am worried about him, it's so long since we last heard from him.' An extra strong gust of wind tugged at their skirts. Bella moved away from the rail. 'Now let's go inside. I could do with a cup of tea, and it'll be breakfast time soon.'

'You go in. I want to stay here a bit longer, I'm enjoying the sights.'

Kitty leant against the rail staring out over the harbour, enjoying the spectacle. When she looked up and saw a sandy haired man with a smooth, pink face approaching her she was tempted to rush away, but it was too late.

She found William pompous and boring. Having enjoyed interesting conversations as a young woman with her father, who encouraged her to think for herself and form opinions of her own, and to discuss them with others, she had tried to draw William into serious discussions when they had been thrown together in the confines of the ship. But he always shied away, obviously believing it neither necessary nor desirable for young ladies to concern themselves with such things, an attitude she found annoying. She really didn't want to talk to him on this exciting morning, but he knew she had seen him, so she forced a smile as he stood beside her.

'Good morning, Miss Morland, I'm so pleased to have caught you early, we have time for a little talk now, before the hustle and bustle of disembarking.'

'I still have some packing to do. I should go back to my cabin.'

'Please.' He cleared his throat. 'I have something important I wish to speak to you about.'

'Very well, but I really mustn't be too long.'

'Of course, I understand.'

'Isn't it exciting to be in Sydney? I can't wait to begin our new life here.'

'Have you thought about when you'll return to England?'

Kitty turned to him in astonishment. 'I don't think I'll ever return. I've told you, we'll join Robert and we plan staying here permanently.'

'Perhaps I can persuade you to return.' He grasped her hand. 'Miss Morland...Kitty, have you not perceived my feelings for you?'

Kitty felt something near to panic; she didn't want to hear his proposal, now they were finally here. The future promised too much excitement. She pretended surprise. 'What do you mean, Mr. Barron?'

'Kitty, I'm overwhelmed with love for you. Surely you've realised, surely I haven't been able to conceal my feelings from you?'

'Why, no, I had no idea.'

'I've had eyes for no other since I saw you that first night.' His pressure on her hand tightened. 'Kitty, dare I hope you may reciprocate my feelings…that you may consider...' He paused to draw a breath, and then brought out the words in a rush. 'Kitty, will you make me the happiest man alive and agree to become my wife?'

Kitty bit her lip. Her promise to Bella meant she couldn't refuse him outright, as she wished. 'William, this is so unexpected. I had no idea of your feelings. I really don't know what to say. I'll have to give it some thought. You see, I have my mother to think of. We've so looked forward to settling here with my brother, I couldn't abandon her when we're just arriving. She depends on me for comfort, you see, now that my father is no longer with us, after we lost him to his sudden illness.'

'Of course, I can understand that. But I'm sure she wouldn't wish to stand in the way of your happiness.'

'I believe I couldn't be happy if I thought of her away over the other side of the world and fretting for my presence.'

'Perhaps she could come with us and we could find a house nearby for her?'

'You mean, on your estate in Buckinghamshire?'

'Er…yes, yes, of course.'

Surprised, Kitty thought about this. She would surely be safe, Arnold would hesitate to accuse her if she was part of the influential Barron family, and her mother would have the comfort she'd been used to. She supposed she should at least consider it.

'This has come as such a surprise; I'm not sure what to say.'

'You needn't give me an answer now. Take some time to think about it. I don't wish to rush you. We'll be staying here for some time while we visit my sister Anne and her husband. I understand your concern for your mother, being the sweet person you are.'

'You are understanding, William. I'll try not to keep you waiting too long. And now I must go and finish my packing.'

'I'll be in a fever of impatience until I hear you say 'yes'. I'll see you again before we go ashore.'

Kitty swallowed. 'I'll need longer than that.'

His face fell. 'I should have spoken earlier.' He looked around. They were alone on the deck. 'I'll have to wait but, Kitty, will you…will you allow me to kiss you.'

She decided she owed him that. 'Yes.'

He leant across and kissed her solemnly on the cheek.

It was another hour of smooth sailing on the calm waters of the harbour before the shouts of the sailors handling the lines told them they were ready to tie up at the quay. Immediately, all was hustle and bustle, as preparations were made to disembark. All about them people were laughing and waving to friends and relatives waiting on the quay below.

Kitty took Bella by the arm. 'Let's go down to the cabin and get our things. We know Robert won't be waiting for us, seeing we had no time to let him know we were coming. The sooner we go ashore the better. We're in a strange city; we have to find our way around.'

'Mr. van Mayen recommends that we stay at Petty's Hotel.'

'Mr. van Mayen, he's the passenger who came on board in Cape Town, isn't he? Has he been to Sydney before?'

'Yes, I had a few words with him yesterday, and he told me he travels extensively.'

After disembarking, they stood by their trunk on the quay while people milled all around. Kitty saw William and his parents greeted by a young matron, who looked like a younger version of William's mother, and a large man with a ruddy complexion and fair hair.

'There are the Barrons,' she murmured as she watched them walk over to a carriage waiting nearby. 'That must be William's sister and her husband that they've come out to visit. She looks just like his mother. I must say I'll be pleased to see the back of William.'

'Kitty, don't talk so. He's a very nice young man.'

'I know you think so, Mother. Now, more important, I wonder where Petty's Hotel is?'

'Mr. van Mayen told me it's in the city, but I don't know exactly where. We must find a cab.'

At that moment, a short, stocky, man with a lined face came hurrying over to them. 'Has your son arrived to meet you, Mrs. Morland?' he asked Bella, his voice betraying an accent that was neither English nor Australian.

'No, I'm afraid not Mr. van Mayen.'

'Then you must allow me to call a cab for you. Are you going to Petty's Hotel?'

'Yes, we are.'

'I, too, am staying there, while the ship is in port, but I'm being collected by a friend, who will be here at any moment.' He scanned the crowd as he finished speaking. 'Ah, here he comes now,' he said, raising his hand to attract the attention of a man who had just stepped down from a cab nearby. 'Cavanagh, over here,' he called.

The man turned towards them, a smile creasing his face.

Kitty felt as if the ground was slipping from beneath her as she saw that the newcomer was the stranger who had danced with her on the night of the Arnolds' ball. Gripping Bella's arm tightly she watched with a hammering heart as he turned and spoke to the driver. Would he recognise her? Although she still remembered him vividly, the last person Kitty needed to meet again was someone who could connect her to the Arnolds. She shivered with apprehension as he strode towards their group, holding out his hand to Jan van Mayen.

After they greeted each other, van Mayen turned. 'Ladies, allow me to introduce Rufe Cavanagh, a citizen of this great country. Cavanagh, this is Mrs. Morland and her daughter, my fellow passengers.'

'At your service, Mrs. Morland, Miss Morland.'

As he raised his hat to them, Kitty waited for him to recall their meeting, but there was no sign of recognition on his face.

'And are you ladies here visiting?' he asked.

'No, Mr. Cavanagh,' Bella replied. 'We've come here to join my son Robert, who is already established here.'

'Then I hope you're going to enjoy living here.'

As he flashed them a smile, Kitty noticed his eyes on her. He seemed to note every detail about her in one sweeping glance and she saw a slight pucker on his forehead, but in an instant it was gone, and he turned his attention back to her mother.

'I'm sure we will,' Bella was saying.

Swallowing a constriction in her throat, Kitty added a polite response as she tried to still her beating heart. It seemed as if he didn't remember her. She knew she'd looked different in her plain governess's dress, with her hair pulled back in a bun. And the light had been dim in the gallery. She felt the tension in her body ease a little. Perhaps she was safe from discovery.

'The ladies will be staying at Petty's Hotel,' Mr. van Mayen told Rufe. 'I was just about to find a cab for them.'

'Then they must take ours, we'll soon find another.'

'That is really very kind of you.' Bella smiled.

'Not at all.' He turned and signalled the driver, who jumped down and came over to help with the luggage.

At that moment William hurried up to them. After greeting them and being introduced to Rufe, William held out his hand towards Kitty. 'I hope I can have a word with you before you go, Kitty.'

Kitty shook her head. 'Oh, not now, William, we're just about to leave.'

'Please Kitty, just a word.'

Stepping a short distance away from the others, she remonstrated with him. 'Really, William, I can't talk now. Where are you staying?'

'At the Royal Hotel, but I had hoped…that is…have you...' he stammered.

'No, I haven't. I'm sorry, but I told you, I need some time. Everything is so chaotic at the moment. We'll be at Petty's Hotel. I'll send you a note and tell you when you can call on us.'

He stepped aside, disappointment clouding his face. 'Very well, Kitty. Please make it soon. I'll count the hours until we meet again.' Taking her hand, he raised it to his lips.

Kitty removed her hand from his with a nod and turned away. Bella and Mr. van Mayen had moved over by the cab where they stood engrossed in conversation, but Rufe still waited, looking down at her with a flicker of a smile on his face, his eyes twinkling.

'An old friend, Miss Morland?' he asked.

'No, Mr. Barron and I met on board the ship.'

'Then I see you've made a conquest.' He laughed.

Kitty stiffened. 'I don't know what you mean.'

'It's obvious that young Barron has fallen for your charms in a big way.'

'I think you are very impolite, Mr. Cavanagh.'

He laughed again. 'Forgive me, but it's not every day we see a gentleman kiss a lady's hand in Australia. We're less gallant than those from the land of our forbears, I'm afraid.'

Kitty lifted her chin. 'Surely civility is not frowned upon in the Antipodes?'

'You'll probably find us boorish and backward. I guess most of us have been too busy trying to tame the wilderness to have much time left over for the delicate social graces.'

'And which parts of the wilderness have you been taming, Mr. Cavanagh?'

'I go here and there, wherever my business takes me.'

Kitty forgot her annoyance as she became interested. 'So, are you a merchant?'

'Of sorts.'

'You must know a great deal about business then?'

'As well as most, I suppose.'

'Then perhaps you can tell me where you think would be a good place to start a business?'

His brows rose. 'Are you thinking of going into business?'

'I might be.'

'What type of business?'

'I'm not sure.'

'Have you been in business before?'

'No, not really.'

Rufe's eyes narrowed. 'Aren't you a little young and inexperienced to be thinking of going into business? Particularly in a country you don't know? Besides, I daresay you'll be married before you have time to set up a business.'

Kitty stiffened. He was insufferable. Why had she thought him so attractive? Coldly, she answered him. 'Why do all men assume every woman is just waiting around to marry the first man who comes along?'

Rufe laughed. 'Probably because it's usually true.'

'Well, I can assure you it's not so in my case. I have no intention of marrying anyone.'

His lips quirked. 'My dear Miss Morland, with your looks, I doubt you'll last six months. In fact, from the way young Barron was gazing at you a few moments ago, it might be very soon.'

Kitty tossed her head. 'Our talk has been most illuminating, Mr. Cavanagh. I'm sure you've given me an insight into the charms of Australian men. Perhaps I should now look for a cab.'

'There's a perfectly good one waiting for you now. With your mother already waiting alongside it for you, with my friend Jan.'

With tight lips, Kitty walked across to join Bella.

'I'm sure you'll be most comfortable at Petty's,' Rufe told them as he and Jan saw them and their luggage safely inside. 'I'm staying there myself, so I hope we'll meet again,' he added as he tipped his hat before moving back as the driver climbed up to his seat.

'What a charming man,' Bella remarked as they settled themselves in the cab.

'Hmm, perhaps,' Kitty muttered, knowing that, in spite of his insufferable manners, she would like to get to know him. But she could not run the risk of him remembering her. The danger was too great. 'And now, we have our first chance to see what Sydney is like,' she added, leaning forward in her seat.

The two women peered from the cab as it made its way from the quay, anxious for their first sight of the city at close quarters.

'It's busy,' Kitty exclaimed, 'I didn't expect the streets to be so crowded.'

'It's very much like a city in England. Look at the buildings. And the carriages. We could think we're back home.'

'Look, there's a drapery store. Farmers and Company,' Kitty read from the façade. 'We'll come back here when we're unpacked and buy some lighter clothing. It's so hot. Most of the women are wearing very light dresses, I see. Apart from that, it all looks very English.'

'Indeed, we could easily be back home. I must say I'm pleasantly surprised.'

'This is home now,' Kitty reminded her gently.

'Of course.' Bella settled back in her seat. 'Well, it all looks very civilised.'

'Oh, look, there's a park, and lots of people strolling through it. I see most of the women are carrying parasols to keep the sun off.'

'Very wise. We'll have to do the same.'

'Oh, there's another big store. Look at all the goods in the windows. We'll have great fun doing some shopping here.'

'Our first job is to find Robert.'

'Of course, I'm not forgetting, but this is so exciting. I think I'm going to like living in Sydney.'

After unpacking some clothes and freshening up they took a cab to Bourke Street in Surry Hills, to the address they had for

Robert. After asking the cab to wait they mounted the steps to a large terrace house.

The young woman who answered their knock had a small child clinging to her skirts.

'Robert Morland?' she said in answer to Bella's query. 'Yes, I remember him, a nice young gentleman. But he left quite a long time ago.'

'Do you know where he's gone?' asked Bella anxiously.

'No. He told us he was going to look for gold with another young gentleman who came here sometimes to see him.'

Bella frowned. 'Do you know where they were going to look for the gold?'

'Not really. I remember he talked a lot about Queensland, but I'm not sure if that's where he was going or not.'

'Do you know who the other man was?' asked Kitty.

'No, I'm sorry. I don't think I ever heard his name. If I did, I don't remember it. He was a friend, that's all I know.'

'Do you know where he lived?'

'No, I'm sorry.'

'Is there anything you can think of that might help us to find him?' Kitty persisted.

'No, I'm really sorry, but I can't think of anything.'

Bella sighed. 'Oh dear. We're staying at Petty's Hotel. If you should hear anything of him, would you be kind enough to let me know?'

'Yes, I will. I do hope you find him. He's such a nice young man.'

'Thank you. I hope so too. Good day.'

'So where to now? Back to the hotel?' asked Kitty as they turned and walked down the steps.

'Yes, for the moment.'

Back in their hotel room, Bella went straight to the chest of drawers and took out a small bag from which she extracted some letters. Selecting one she carried it to a chair, sat down, and started reading.

'Ah. Here it is. I knew Robert told me the name of the firm he was working for here. As you know, he was a clerk in a lawyer's office. It was Messrs Gordon, Fairfield and Hargreaves.'

'And does he say where they are?'

'Yes, in Pitt Street.'

'Then let's go there straightaway and see if they know anything.'

When the young man in the front office of the lawyers' rooms learned their identity, he asked them to wait, and returned in a few moments with a fussy-looking little man who regarded them through gold-rimmed glasses.

'I'm Horace Samuels, the chief clerk here. Please come through.' He ushered them into his office and offered them chairs, then sat behind his desk. 'I believe you're looking for your son Robert, is that so?'

Bella clutched her reticule on her lap. 'Yes, we've been to the lodgings where he was living, but he no longer lives longer there, and I'm hoping you might be able to help us to locate him.'

He pursed his lips. 'I'm afraid I'm not going to be able to help you. I really have no idea where he might be now.'

Bella's hands clutched the reticule tighter. 'Do you know where he was going when he left here?'

'I only know that he and another young clerk here decided they would leave their positions and go north looking for gold.' He sniffed. 'A most foolhardy undertaking, I'm afraid.'

Kitty smiled sweetly at him. 'Do you know where they were going?'

'I believe they were going north, more than that I can't tell you.'

'Have you heard from him since he left?'

'No.' He picked up a pen and tapped it on the desk. 'I made my displeasure known at the time. For two of them to leave at the same time like that seriously inconvenienced us, so I'm not surprised to hear nothing from either of them.'

'I see.' Kitty made her voice conciliatory. 'I can see that would've been a problem for you. Is it possible you can tell us the name of the other young man?'

He seemed somewhat mollified by her reply. 'Yes. It was Matthew Guilford.'

Kitty smiled at him again. 'I wonder if you know where he lived?'

'I can find his address for you. I believe he lived with his sister and her husband, somewhere in Surry Hills.'

'Oh, that's where Robert was living.'

'Yes, I believe they were good friends.' Opening a drawer in his desk, he took out a book and turned the pages, running his finger down the neatly written contents of each one. 'Yes, here it is. Matthew Guilford. High Holborn Street, Surry Hills. His sister's name is Mrs. Nash. I'll write the address down for you.'

Taking a slip of paper, he copied the address and handed it to Kitty. 'Here you are then. I hope this might be of help to you.'

'Thank you, Mr. Samuels. We're most grateful for your help.' They all rose as she took the paper. 'We'll go there immediately.'

When they reached their destination, Bella instructed the cab to wait, but this time there was no response to their knock. They stood back and regarded the house, another terrace, but there was no sign of life.

'Nobody at home,' Kitty said. 'We'd best come back tomorrow.'

Bella sighed. 'Yes, I'm afraid so.'

'Then let's go shopping. I'm so hot, I hope we won't have to wear these heavy clothes for another day in this heat.'

'Yes, I agree it's most uncomfortable. Where to, then?'

'To Farmers and Company,' Kitty told the driver as he held the door for them.

It was such a pleasure to be able to afford new clothes again that they put aside their worries over Robert for a while. They tried on a selection of light, summery muslin dresses. Kitty chose one in apple green and another, in deep rose, which set off her golden colouring to perfection. Bella chose the more sedate colours of deep blue and burgundy, as being more suitable for a mature lady. Then Kitty decided they needed a taffeta dress each for evening, Kitty's a deep ruby red and Bella's soft dove grey.

And, of course, they had to have hats and shoes to complement the dresses, undergarments and a parasol each for when out walking. Kitty laughed with delight as she twirled and pirouetted before the mirror.

They needed two juniors following them to carry all their parcels to a cab. Back at their hotel room, Bella sank into a chair, tired after the strenuous day, but Kitty tried everything on once more, relishing the look and feel of the new clothes.

Jan van Mayen approached them as they sat in the hotel lounge that afternoon after taking tea.

'We meet again so soon,' he greeted them. 'May I join you for a little?'

'Of course, please sit down,' Bella invited him.

'I hope you ladies are recovering from the journey. You must be glad to be on land again.'

'I must admit I'm pleased to have left the rocking of the ship behind,' Bella told him. 'But apart from that I enjoyed the journey. It was quite a holiday.'

'I'm pleased to hear that. You know, Mrs. Morland, I've been pondering something.'

'Oh, and what is that?'

'I've been wondering if you are related to Mr. Charles Morland, whom I met during a visit to England a few years ago. He resided in Hampstead, I believe.'

'That's my late husband.'

'Really? I'm so sorry. I remember him as a charming man. I'm unhappy to hear of his passing. Please accept my condolences.'

'Thank you.'

'I believe you said you're planning on staying here in Sydney?'

'Yes. My son Robert is here and we'll be joining him.'

'That's good, have you met up with him yet?'

'No, he's away from Sydney at the moment. And you, Mr. van Mayen? Do you visit Sydney often?'

'Yes. My home is in Cape Town, but I often visit Sydney. I have some business here.'

'And will you be staying long?'

'No, I need to conclude my business quickly. I'm not leaving the Osprey here in Sydney. I'll be sailing with her, up to Brisbane.'

'That's a very quick visit. And what business are you in, Mr. van Mayen?'

'I'm a diamond merchant.'

Kitty went cold at his words. A diamond merchant. Could he possibly know George Arnold? Had he, perhaps, delivered those diamonds? Would he know anything of the theft? Was he regarding her with interest? She swallowed and forced herself to sit calmly.

'You must lead an interesting life. Do you travel to visit clients often?' Bella asked, her voice betraying no strain.

'Sometimes, and sometimes my clients visit me. I was in England recently to deliver some diamonds that I didn't wish to entrust to a messenger, and to make some enquiries into a certain matter. And then I found it necessary to come on to Sydney. It means, sadly, I must be away from home for a long time, but that's business. As to it being interesting,' he shrugged, 'it's a business like any other.'

'But surely it's a glamorous world,' Kitty asked, managing to keep her voice level. 'One associates diamonds with beautiful women and lavish living.'

'I'm afraid that's not the case,' he replied with a small laugh. 'I only wish it were so. No, there's only one aspect that sets it aside from any other business.'

'And what is that?'

'The danger of theft is always present. One must always be alert for it. Diamonds excite avarice more than any other commodity, except, perhaps, gold.'

Kitty's heart jumped, but she forced herself to speak lightly. 'How interesting. You must need to be always on your guard.'

'That is true.' He rose to his feet. 'And now, if you'll excuse me, I have some letters to write. I look forward to seeing you again.'

As Kitty watched him walk away she wondered if one of his letters would be to George Arnold, disclosing their presence.

It was later that night, after Rufe Cavanagh and Jan van Mayen dined together, that Rufe suggested they retire to his suite to enjoy a glass of port.

'It's better to be where it's private,' Jan agreed, as Rufe opened the door into his room. 'Now we're alone we can compare notes. Have you discovered anything more about who could be behind the gem robberies?'

'Enough to make me sure the trail leads back to London, and to suspect that George Arnold is involved in some way. His name crops up too often for coincidence, I believe.'

Jan nodded. 'That's my belief. Were you able to learn anything else?'

'Unfortunately, no. How about you? Were you able to discover anything more in London?'

'Not really. As you know, I decided to make it known that I'd deliver the last shipment myself, hoping to provoke an attempt to relieve me of it, for which I was well prepared.' He patted his jacket. 'My little pistol goes everywhere with me, and of course I took the precaution of sending the main shipment in secret by the usual means. What I carried myself were gems of lesser value. But no one took the bait.'

'The fact that he operates on an irregular basis makes it more difficult to find him. We have no way of knowing when or where he will act next.'

'I don't feel good at having involved you. If they know you're trying to find them you will also need to be on guard. It could become dangerous.'

Rufe shrugged. 'I would have become involved anyway when my consignment of diamonds from Two Mile Flat disappeared. Seeing the local police made no progress, I had to take a hand myself. Whoever our man is, he seems prepared to operate in several countries. If it's the same person.'

Jan nodded. 'What I have learned is that he sets up agents wherever there are valuable gems. It was probably talk of the last discovery in the Bingara and Copeton areas that brought him to Australia. Incidentally, I find it interesting that the robberies have become more prevalent in Australia since Thomas Arnold set up his business. The word in London is that he was financed by his cousin George.'

'Ah.' Rufe narrowed his eyes. 'Interesting indeed. Perhaps another link to friend George?'

'Perhaps. By the way, I heard an interesting story about him before I left London. It concerned Charles Morland, the late husband of Mrs. Morland.' Jan's mouth quirked. 'You know, the lady with the oh-so-pretty daughter that you were admiring down at the quay?'

Rufe lifted a brow, deciding to ignore the jibe, knowing he had indeed found her attractive, and intended to make sure he saw her again. 'And what was the story?'

Jan related how Arnold's scheme had ruined Kitty's father, and resulted in his death.

'Poor Mrs. Morland. That's tragic. Do you believe the story of the shipment being waylaid and stolen?'

Jan shrugged. 'As you know, it's possible. Who knows?'

'I wonder if Mrs. Morland and her daughter know anything of Arnold that could help us?' Rufe frowned. 'Whoever our man is, whether it's Arnold or not, when he finds out you're in Australia looking around the latest fields, perhaps he'll decide to make another move.'

'It's all we can hope for. And if he does, we'll be ready for him.'

## CHAPTER FOUR

The next morning Bella and Kitty again took a cab, this time to the address in High Holborn Street. The door was opened by a maid, and they were shown into the parlour.

After introducing themselves to Emily Nash, a fresh-faced young matron, Bella told her they were looking for Robert, and hoped she could help them to locate him.

'I'm not sure where they are,' a cloud crossed Mrs. Nash's face, 'and I'm very worried about them. I haven't heard from Matthew for several months now.'

Bella paled. 'Oh, dear. Where were they when you last heard from him?'

'They were on the Palmer River, west of Cooktown. They went looking for gold, you know.'

'Yes, we've been told that.'

'I didn't want Matthew to go. My husband and I both tried our hardest to persuade him not to, but he wouldn't listen to us. Goodness knows what's happened to them, I'm sure he'd have written again, if he's all right. I believe conditions are still primitive, it's dangerous out there, even though Cooktown itself is relatively civilised now.' Mrs. Nash twisted her hands together in her lap as she talked. 'They never should have gone. They never should have listened to that man.'

Kitty's stomach clenched. 'What man?' she asked.

'A prospector they met, Harry Mulligan. Apparently, he told them there's still plenty of gold left on the Palmer River if you know where to look for it. He said he'd staked out this fabulous claim further up the river from the main diggings, and he was looking for a partner to help him share the costs and do the digging.'

'A partner? Just one?'

'Yes, but they decided to pool their resources and both go. He told them there was so much gold there'd be plenty for all of them, and with more capital behind them, it would be all the sooner they would all be rich.'

'Did you ever meet this prospector?' Bella asked.

'No. James asked Matthew to bring him here several times, but he always made an excuse. He had his heart set on going, and he didn't want James to find fault with their plans, I suppose.'

'Where is the Palmer River?'

'It's right up in Far North Queensland, in from Cooktown. It's nearly two thousand miles away from here. Almost to the top of Australia.'

'So far!' Bella's fingers went to the beads around her neck, twisting them.

'How would you reach it?' Kitty asked, apprehension making her cold in spite of the heat.

'By steamer to Cooktown. They went on the Lady Jane. Then by horse from there.'

'Do you think there really is gold there?'

'There was, plenty of it, but we thought it had mostly gone by now. That's what James tried to tell them, but they wouldn't listen. They said Harry had gone to a different place that hadn't been worked before, all very secret, they didn't know the exact whereabouts, and that's where he'd made this rich strike.'

Kitty bit her lip as she thought about this. 'Then why would he have needed someone to help him if there was so much gold?'

'That's what I said, but Matthew said the shaft had to go deeper, and he needed someone to help him. Of course, it is dangerous to work alone, in case of accidents, we know that, but…' her voice trailed off and she shrugged her shoulders, her face tight with anxiety. 'But why haven't we heard, if they're still all right?'

Bella sat forward. 'Do you believe this Harry was genuine?'

'He might have been, although James doesn't think so, but if he was, why haven't they written?'

'What do you think could have happened?'

'It's wild country up there, and there's always danger from the natives, or there might have been an accident, a cave in, or they could be sick. Who knows what could have happened?'

Kitty felt sick at her words. 'Where would they have to go, to send a letter from this place?'

'Back to Cooktown.'

'And to buy supplies?'

'The same, I suppose, or perhaps Maytown, that's a bit closer.'

'What did your brother tell you in his last letter?'

'Only that they'd reached Cooktown, the three of them, and had managed to buy horses and supplies and were setting out straight-away, and not to worry if he didn't write for a while. But that was eight months ago. Surely they couldn't stay out there that long without fresh supplies.'

'Could a letter have gone astray?'

'That's what James keeps telling me. Who knows how reliable the mail is from such a remote place?'

'Is there any way we might be able to find out about them?'

'James has already telegraphed the police in Cooktown to see if anyone knows where they are, but no one knows. I don't know what else we can do.' She spread her hands in a gesture of helplessness, shaking her head. 'It's such wild country up there, so far from civilisation – they could just disappear without a trace.'

Bella rose, her face pale, obviously struggling to retain control of her emotions. 'Thank you for your help, Mrs. Nash. If you hear anything from your brother would you please let us know? We're staying at Petty's Hotel.'

'I will, and if you're able to find out anything will you do the same?'

'Yes, of course. Thank you again.'

Mrs. Nash escorted them to the door. Kitty noticed tears in her eyes as they made their farewells. She was obviously fearful for her brother's safety.

As they rode back to the hotel, tears rolled down Bella's cheeks.

Kitty felt a lump in her throat threatening to choke her. *What if something terrible has happened to Robert? What if we can't find him?*

They sat in the lounge at Petty's Hotel to discuss what steps they could take to find Robert. Bella's tears had gone but her distress showed.

'Whatever could have possessed Robert to go off like that, without even writing to let me know what he was doing?'

'I suppose he didn't want to worry you.'

'Well, I'm certainly worried now.'

'Of course you are, and so am I. The question is, what are we to do?'

'What can we do?'

Kitty took a deep breath. 'I think I should go and look for him.'

'Up to this Palmer River?'

'Yes.'

'If you go, then I shall certainly come with you.'

Kitty wrinkled her brow. 'We need to find out more about where it is.'

'And here comes someone who might be able to tell us.'

Kitty looked across to see Rufe Cavanagh approaching them.

He smiled as he reached them. 'Good morning, ladies. I'm about to order some tea. Will you join me?'

'Thank you, Mr. Cavanagh. That would be delightful.' Bella gave a half-hearted smile as Rufe took a seat opposite and ordered tea from the waiter.

'And have you ladies been out sightseeing this lovely morning?' Rufe asked.

'No, actually we've been trying to track down my brother Robert,' Kitty replied.

'Were you successful?'

'No. We might have to go to Cooktown to find him.'

Rufe's head jerked back. 'To Cooktown? That's a long way and scarcely a place for ladies.'

'To the Palmer River, really,' Bella interjected.

He looked shocked. 'Mrs. Morland, you could not possibly go to the Palmer River.'

'We have to,' Kitty told him firmly.

He shook his head. 'My dear Miss Morland, you don't understand. The Palmer River is definitely not a place where a lady could possibly go.'

'Why not?'

Rufe took a deep breath and then spoke forcefully. 'For a start, there are few people left on the goldfields now, but those who remain are ruffians, men who've come from all over the world, to search for gold. And most of the men wouldn't have seen a woman in months. You wouldn't be safe, no woman would. You must understand that.'

Kitty swallowed. 'You make it quite plain.'

'Good.' He nodded, his face severe. 'Now, the other thing is that it's over fifteen hundred miles north of here. Apart from being a long way, the climate is unbelievable. If you think Sydney's hot, you haven't seen anything. Men find it difficult to survive there, let alone a woman. And the conditions are pitiful; there are no facilities there, no houses, no comfortable hotels. No one to cook meals or do anything else.'

'I see.'

'Good. I'm glad you do.' He sat back in his seat as the tea arrived. 'Now, let's enjoy our morning tea and forget this crazy idea.'

Bella sighed as she reached for the pot. 'Shall I pour?' she asked.

'Please.' Rufe sat back, watching them.

Bella's normally calm face was creased with worry and her hand shook as she passed the cups.

Kitty considered Rufe's words as she took her cup. Well, perhaps they couldn't go to the Palmer River, but if they went to Cooktown they might be able to find someone who knew of Robert's whereabouts, and send a message to him. Or they might find a guide who could take them to the diggings in safety.

'And what is Cooktown like, Mr. Cavanagh?' she asked.

'Cooktown is still a frontier town, even though it's trying to project a veneer of respectability these days.'

'I believe you travel there by steamer?'

'Yes, that's right. But I hope you're not thinking of going there, it's still no place for ladies on their own.'

'I see. And how far is it from there to the Palmer River?'

Rufe frowned at her. 'It's about another hundred and fifty miles, over a rough bullock track, through jungle and country still inhabited by wild natives who think nothing of putting a spear through you.'

Trembling, Bella placed her cup on the table. 'Mr. Cavanagh, I'm so worried about what could have happened to my son,' she said. 'I don't know how else we can find out if we don't go up there.'

Rufe's gaze softened. 'What makes you believe he's up there?'

'We've been told that's where he went.'

'Would you care to tell me what you've found out? I might be able to help.'

In a worried voice, Bella repeated their conversation with Emily Nash.

'So you see,' Kitty told him at the end of the narrative, 'it seems the only way to find him is to go up there and look for ourselves.'

'Let me think for a moment.'

Rufe sat back, pursing his lips. He felt sorry for Bella, she was a nice woman and obviously distressed. There was no way he could let them go up there by themselves, though why he should worry, he didn't know. They were a couple of women who foolishly came all this way without making certain they could find the son when they arrived. But he would like to help her. Besides which, he found the daughter attractive, and would like to get to know her better. He had the vague feeling he had met her somewhere before, but for the life of him couldn't recall any meeting. He made a decision.

'It so happens I have some business interests up that way. I have contacts there, an agent. I'll telegraph him and ask him to see if he can find Robert for you, or at least find out if anything has happened to him.'

Bella clasped her hands together, a look of relief on her face. 'Would you do that, Mr. Cavanagh? Oh, I can't tell you how grateful I am.'

Kitty added her thanks. 'It's very kind of you. How long do you think it will take for us to hear something?'

'I really can't answer that. I'll telegraph right away, but it depends on how easy or difficult it is to trace him. Now, I'll just check the details again.' Taking a small book from his pocket, he wrote it down as Bella directed. 'Let's hope my agent can find them for you, alive and well. It's unlikely we'll hear anything back for a few days, but I'll let you know as soon as I do. You'll be staying here in the hotel for a bit longer?'

Bella nodded. 'Yes. At least until Robert comes back. And thank you again.'

Rufe dared not utter the thought that sprang to his mind, that the Palmer River was so dangerous there was a chance Robert might not be found. And then what?

A quick knock sounded at their door and a well-built young woman with red hair and freckles, wearing a housemaid's apron and cap, entered their sitting room.

'Oh, sorry miss, I didn't think anyone was here. I'm just returning your clothes from the laundress. Would you like me to put them away for you?'

'No, it's all right, thank you,' Kitty replied. 'Those are our heavy clothes from England. We'll be packing them away in the trunk.'

'Yes, they're a bit too heavy for our weather, aren't they? Except maybe for a short time in the winter.'

'Oh, so it does get cold here at times?'

'Yes, a bit, but nothing like it does in England, so I've been told. Your first time here, is it, miss?'

'Yes, it is.'

'Well, I hope you enjoy it.' She smiled.

'Why, thank you...what is your name?'

'Mary.'

'Thank you, Mary.' Kitty smiled back at her. 'I take it you were born here in Australia?'

'Yes, right here in Sydney, but my mum came out from England.'

'Did she? Has she ever thought of going back?'

'No, no way. Wild horses wouldn't drag her back there, she says.'

'Really? Has she been here long?'

'Yes, since she was eighteen. That's over thirty years ago.'

'Then she must be happy here.'

'Oh, yes. Well, I best get on with my work. Just let me know if you need anything. Good day, miss.'

The servants here were different from those in England, Kitty reflected, as the girl left. Much freer in their manner. She recalled her time in the Arnold household. No wonder Mary's mother didn't want to go back, it certainly did seem to be a more relaxed way of life here, and all the better for it.

'So what shall we do now?' Bella asked. 'There's nothing more we can do towards finding Robert, until Mr. Cavanagh receives a reply.' She went to the window and stared out. 'I think I need to do something to take my mind away from what might have happened to him.' As she turned back towards the room, Kitty could see the worry on her face. 'Hearing Mr. Cavanagh talk about the dangers up there frightened me.'

Kitty walked over and put her arms around her. 'I know.' She hugged Bella. 'We need something to take your mind off this, and I know just the thing.' Releasing Bella she smoothed down her skirts. And now that I've packed away the clothes we brought with us we need more clothes, and it's time to see more of Sydney. So let's go for a walk.'

Once again, they were amazed at the busyness of the streets. Pedestrians bustled along the footpaths, while the streets themselves were crowded with every type of conveyance on wheels. Horse drawn buggies, delivery wagons, double-decker steam trams, cabs and carriages, all fought for space with riders on horseback.

They wandered along, discreetly inspecting the other pedestrians and looking into the shop windows as they passed.

'We could be back in London,' Bella exclaimed. 'There are plenty of goods in the shops and while the fashions seem to be a little behind London, the locals are every bit as smart in their dress as people back home.'

'Yes, I must say I'm pleasantly surprised. Sydney is certainly not the colonial outpost I expected. And there is so much building going on. It must be growing fast to warrant so many new buildings.' Kitty stopped to read the name as they came to an arcade. 'Royal Arcade, let's go in and have a look.'

There were shops that sold hats for men and women, boots and shoes, sturdy umbrellas and dainty parasols, saddles and bridles, a barber and tobacconist and a shop that sold scissors and knives. They paused as they saw a jewellery shop ahead, and checked that the name outside was not Arnold, before they continued.

'It brings to mind our goods,' Kitty lowered her voice. 'We need to find a bank with a safety deposit box. And to think of where we're going to find a buyer. We'll probably need to sell most of them if we're going into business.'

Bella looked around at the smart shops and bustling people. 'I don't think this would be the sort of establishment to approach, we'll need to look around for an area like the East End of London.'

Kitty pulled at her lip thoughtfully. 'That's awkward when we don't know our way around.' She brightened. 'Robert will know. If not, he'll find out.'

Bella stood silent for a moment, gazing into the window. 'And what if we haven't found Robert by the time we need money?'

'Then we'll just have to rely on ourselves. But we'll find him, don't worry. Now come along, we have to find a bank, and somewhere to sell one piece, we really need more cash now. And then I want to find that store I saw on our way from the ship, the tall one – it looked very new and smart, I'm sure they'll have all the latest fashions.'

They found a bank close to the arcade and went in.

Kitty had no trouble in opening an account and hiring a safety deposit box. Putting one diamond into her purse, she deposited the rest in the box.

Bella heaved a sigh of relief. 'At least that's one worry off my mind, now they're safe.'

They walked further until they found a pawnshop and entered.

'How much will you give us for this?' Kitty asked, producing the diamond. The proprietor looked at it then offered a figure that was less than half of what they had received for a similar stone in London.

'It's worth at least twice that,' Kitty objected.

He shrugged. 'Take it or leave it, lady. It's the best I can do.'

Bella nudged her and nodded.

'Very well then, but it's the last time I'll do business with you.'

'He handed over the money. 'Suit yourself.'

Kitty's heart sank as they left the shop. If this was all they could expect for each one, would they have enough for a business?

'I think that should do us for shopping for some time now,' Bella said as she looked at their purchases spread out across the bed back in their hotel room.

Kitty regarded her mother with affection, glad that the shopping had taken her mind off Robert for a while. 'Yes. We'll be able to hold our heads up in any company now. It's nice not to feel like a poor relation, and those days are behind us now. We need to look to the future.'

'The money won't last forever. We mustn't continue to spend it so quickly.'

'No. You're right. I've been thinking, we should look for a house to rent. It's too expensive to stay here for long. And as soon as we find Robert we'll see what sort of business he's interested in. Of course, if they've found gold, things might be different again. He might not need to go into business. But I'm not counting on that.'

'I should think not. From what Mrs. Nash said the whole venture was foolhardy. I just want to see him safely back here.'

'So do I. Let's hope Rufe Cavanagh's agent is successful in finding him.'

Over the next few days, Rufe made a point of spending time with Kitty and Bella. He felt concerned for the two women, in limbo here in Sydney as they anxiously awaited news of Robert. And, if he was honest with himself, he had to admit he wanted to get to know Kitty better. So he invited them to join him on sightseeing jaunts around Sydney in his trap. They found him a likeable and entertaining companion as he pointed out places of interest, with comments on history and amusing anecdotes of happenings in the city's earlier days.

Although Kitty knew that for her own safety she should have as little contact with Rufe as possible, she could think of no good reason to refuse his invitations, and so the three of them spent much time together, and she found herself enjoying his company.

Although he never attempted any personal conversations, she found he was willing to converse on any subject. Ah, if only things were different. If only she had never met him in London.

For his part, Rufe found her remarkably well informed and unafraid to voice her opinions. She became quite heated over subjects she felt strongly about and at times he opposed her views simply in order to see her eyes glitter and the colour come to her cheeks. Intelligent and spirited as well as beautiful, he thought admiringly, a rare combination in a woman. What a shame it would be if she wasted herself on that milk-sop Barron.

Bella and Kitty seated themselves in chairs in the lounge after they came out from breakfast one morning.

'I'm surprised you haven't heard from William,' Bella said. 'I hope you didn't discourage him too much by being so off-hand with him.'

'I hope I did, Mother. You know I'm not interested in becoming his wife.'

'That's all very well, but you need to remember your position. You could still be in danger of being discovered. We don't know what's happening back in London, what steps might have been taken to try and find you. With the telegraph making contact so easy these days, you might not be safe anywhere. If you marry William, you'd be under the protection of the Barron name, with Sir Alexander Barron as your father-in-law. They're an important family.'

'I know that, but, while Sir Alexander seems nice enough, his wife's a domineering tyrant. I realised that as soon as William introduced us back on the ship. It's obvious he's frightened of her. I don't fancy her for a mother-in-law. Besides, I've told you, I don't love William.'

'That's not so important. Surely it would be better to be married to William than to face the consequences of what happened in London?'

'A fine choice. With William I'd be married to a man I don't love and with the other…' her voice trailed away and her heartbeat quickened as she remembered her worry during their last days in England, and her fear of discovery.

'Well?'

Kitty took a deep breath, seeking to reassure herself. 'But that might never happen. Perhaps I was never suspected. And we're twelve thousand miles away. I'm sure we'll be safe here in Australia.'

'I'm not so sure. But you promised me you'd think carefully about his proposal.'

'I know, but until we hear from Robert, I'll make no decision. I told you that. Anyhow, I haven't heard from William since we arrived, so let's not discuss it now.'

'But what if we can't find Robert?' Bella's voice shook. 'What then?'

Kitty set her lips in a determined line. 'Then we'll dispose of some more of our goods, and decide what to do. Now, I'm going back up to our room. Are you coming?'

Kitty stood, and Bella sighed as she did the same and followed her daughter to the stairs.

Rufe waited a few moments before rising from the chair around the corner, where he had been sitting reading the morning newspaper. He hadn't meant to eavesdrop, but as he rose to reveal himself the two women had started what he realised was a private conversation. Rather than embarrass them, he decided to stay where he was until they left; he could always feign total immersion in his paper if he was discovered. What he heard astonished him. What had Kitty done in London? What were the goods she needed to dispose of? And would she marry a man she didn't love to save herself from – what?

## CHAPTER FIVE

Alexander Barron regarded his son keenly. 'William, I cannot understand why you want to stay in Australia now. I know your sister Anne is here, and she seems to enjoy the life, but you've never shown any interest in farming.'

William felt the old resentment return. 'Well, there's really nothing for me in England, is there? I mean, Rupert will inherit the estates and Hector will stay and help him, what is there for me?'

'There are other options. There's always the army, for instance.'

William had no desire for a regimented life. 'That's not what I want, and life out here rather appeals. Anne likes it, don't you?' He turned to his sister.

'Yes, but we like farming, don't we, George?' Anne looked at her husband, who nodded his agreement. 'You don't know the first thing about sheep.'

Her reply annoyed him; they all seemed to think he was good for nothing. 'I could learn. But perhaps I wouldn't go into farming. It seems like there's plenty of opportunities out here for an enterprising person.'

'I don't know that I'd call you enterprising…' his father began, but Anne interrupted.

'You're not thinking of going into trade, I hope.'

Before William could reply his mother added her voice. 'It's that girl, isn't it?' she asked, her eyes narrowing.

William swallowed in an effort to quell the butterflies inside him – his mother always frightened him. 'What girl?' he asked in a strangled voice.

'You know very well what girl. The one on the ship. The Morland girl.'

The blood rushed to his face as they all stared at him. 'I am indeed very fond of Miss Morland. In fact,' he blurted out, 'I hope she'll consent to become my wife.'

'Marriage.' His mother's ample bosom heaved. 'So it's gone this far.'

'Have you actually asked her?' his father interjected.

'Yes, I have.'

His father frowned. 'I can't believe you'd take such a step without discussing it with me first.'

'Never mind that,' his mother said. 'I suppose she's accepted? She's not likely to pass up such an opportunity.'

Now it was out in the open, William felt better. 'As a matter of fact, she hasn't given me her answer yet. She hadn't realised how I felt and needed time to think about it. She's concerned to leave her mother in a new country without her. She's such a kind and thoughtful person.' His mother sniffed. 'You could have no objection to her. She's from a good family.'

'Yes, the family would be acceptable enough, though there's no money there, if it weren't for the fact that the father took his own life a few years ago. Not something we would want to be associated with.'

William was shocked. 'Poor Miss Morland. What a terrible thing for her. I didn't know.'

'No. She's not likely to make it known, is she?'

'You can't hold it against her.'

'It rubs off. If she hasn't accepted, you can back out. Withdraw your offer,' she ordered.

William stiffened. 'I mean to marry her, if she'll have me.'

'Then it would be all for the best if you do stay in Australia. I wouldn't want the family to be associated with her back home.'

Alexander lifted his hand to his wife and addressed William. 'That's as may be, but it brings us back to the question of what you're to do, either here or in England.'

'I've made up my mind I want to stay here.'

'Perhaps the clubs here won't be gambling dens as they are at home,' his mother said, compressing her lips as she glared at her son.

William flushed. 'I don't…'

Alexander silenced them with a raised hand. 'Let's not go into past mistakes now, any of them. Now then, I'm prepared to finance you into a property. I'll give you enough to set up and to cover the first year, but after that you'll have to be self-sustaining if you wish to remain here. I don't know if you'll be a good enough farmer. You haven't shown much aptitude for the land.'

'I don't know. Maybe farming's not what I really want.'

'I suggest you make up your mind.'

George spoke for the first time. 'Look, there might be something else I could suggest. There's good money in timber. A logging business might suit you, William. You can have a manager who knows the business and you only have to oversee it and manage the business side. How would that appeal?'

'A logging business?' William turned it over in his mind. 'Where do you get the timber?'

'There are miles and miles of it in the forests. I happen to know of an established business that's up for sale. In Bulahdelah. The owner's returning to England. You'd just have to step in and take it over.'

'Where is Bulahdelah?'

'North of Sydney, on the Myall River. It's beautiful country through there. Plenty of trees, just waiting to be cut down.'

'How far north?'

'Oh, about a hundred miles, maybe a little more.'

'Does it have a manager?'

'Yes, and he's anxious to stay.'

'How do you know about it?' asked Alexander.

'I heard about it when I was looking at timber for a new shed. Here in Sydney, before you arrived. There's such a building boom going on here that I thought at the time it sounded like a good opportunity, but I can't take on any more. You'd need to be there to keep an eye on things.'

'Does that appeal to you more than farming?' Alexander asked William.

'Yes, it does rather.'

'Then we'll make arrangements to go and view the place as soon as possible. If it seems like a good proposition, we'll buy it.'

William was elated. Already he could visualise himself and Kitty sharing life together in a tranquil country setting, with himself riding around supervising the felling of giant trees and directing his employees while Kitty sat by the fire with her needlework.

As soon as he was alone he sat down and wrote to her, explaining that he had to leave town before he could see her but that he hoped to have some exciting news for her when he returned.

'Goodness, just listen to this.' Kitty held a letter in her hand and read it aloud to Bella. "My dearest Kitty, in anticipation of your answer to my proposal being the one I am so desperate to hear, I am making some plans for our future. Knowing how much you wish to remain in Australia, to be near your mother and brother, I am leaving early in the morning with my father and my sister's husband George Remington to inspect a timber logging business that is for sale at Bulahdelah, north of Sydney. I will be away for about two to three weeks and will tell you all the details on my return. I remain your faithful and devoted servant, William Barron." Kitty drew a deep breath. 'What do you think of that?'

Bella's eyes widened. 'That means he's willing to remain in Australia to be with you. He's a very determined young man, I must say.'

Kitty made a moue of distaste. 'Pity he's not a bit more interesting.'

'Really, Kitty, I don't know what more you want.'

'I've told you, I don't know that I want to marry anyone, not yet anyhow.'

'You could do a lot worse.'

'Mother, I don't love him.'

'For a woman, that comes after marriage. If she's lucky. The main thing is that he loves you, and William obviously does.'

'Let's not worry about it just now. I'm more concerned about finding Robert.'

'As William will be away for a while it gives you a breathing space. I wonder what this Bulahdelah is like.'

Kitty moved to answer a knock at the door, glad of the diversion.

Mary stood there. 'Good afternoon, miss. I just came to see if everything's all right. Is there anything I can do for you?'

'Why, no, thank you, Mary.'

'Just a moment, Mary,' Bella called out. 'Come in. Do you know anything about a place called Bulahdelah, north of Sydney?'

'Not a lot, but I have heard a bit about it. My young man, Tom, has done some timber cutting up that way. It's only a small place, on the Myall River, not far from Stroud, I believe. Very pretty up that way, so he says.'

'How would you go up there?'

'Well, you can go by steamer as far as Raymond Terrace, that's in a bit from Newcastle, and it's probably about a day or so's ride from there. Are you thinking of going?'

'No, no,' Kitty answered. 'We just heard about the timber up there, and we were curious. Thank you, Mary.'

'You're welcome, miss. Are you sure there's nothing I can do for you?'

'No, thank you.'

'Then good afternoon, miss.'

'Such a pleasant young woman,' said Kitty after she had left the room.

Bella was not to be sidetracked. 'So, this Bulahdelah sounds as if it could be an agreeable place to live.'

'Let's forget about Bulahdelah for now, shall we? Although...' Kitty paused as she thought for a moment. 'I wonder if Robert might be interested in timber logging.'

'Robert? I don't know.' Bella sounded doubtful.

'We saw so much building around Sydney, I wonder if there's much outside the city? If there is, then it would have to be a good business. We should go and have a look around the outskirts of town.' She noticed Bella's hesitation. 'We could look for a house to rent at the same time.'

'That would be a good idea. And it will tell us if the timber business will be good for William, too.'

Kitty rolled her eyes. 'That's settled then. We'll go in the morning.'

Bella woke with a headache.

'You stay in bed for a while,' Kitty told her. 'I'll be quite all right to go alone.'

'But you don't know where to go,' Bella objected.

'Neither do you. I'll take a cab. I'll be quite all right.'

Bella pressed her hand to her brow, obviously in no state to argue.

Kitty kissed her cheek before leaving. 'Don't worry. Go back to sleep.'

As she crossed the foyer she met Rufe. 'I don't suppose you've heard anything back from your agent yet?' Kitty asked him.

'I've had an acknowledgement of my cable and his assurance that he'll do all he can to find your brother. It might take a while, but if anyone can find him, he will.'

'I'm most grateful to you for your trouble.'

'Not at all.' Rufe smiled at her. 'And where are you off to this lovely morning?'

'We've decided to look for a house to rent. We were both going to have a look around, but my mother has a headache so I'm going alone.'

His brows rose. 'On your own? Where do you plan on looking?'

'Oh, I thought I'd just take a cab and drive around a bit. The only area we've seen so far is the Surry Hills.'

'I'm about to go over to the North Shore, would you care to accompany me and have a look over there? I'm just about to have my trap brought around.'

Her hesitation was fleeting. Her fear of him recognising her now had almost gone. 'Thank you, I would indeed. It is difficult trying to find your way around in a strange place.'

As she settled into the trap she realised this was the first time she had been alone with Rufe since the night of the ball. She was conscious of his closeness alongside her as they moved off. It was both pleasant and disturbing. He proved an entertaining companion as they drove through the city streets, pointing out places and people of interest as they passed. His comments on the local citizens were often amusing, if not always flattering.

Rufe pointed with his whip as they approached the quay. 'That's where we're going.' He indicated the other side of the harbour, across a wide expanse of water, deep blue now under the sun shining down from a clear sky above. Scattered houses showed between the green trees covering the sides of the slopes on the opposite shore.

'Across the water? How do we get there?'

'We'll cross on the ferry.'

'So, people live over on that side of the harbour too, and come to the city by ferry?'

'Yes, there are some very nice houses over there, particularly at Mossman's Bay and Neutral Bay.'

Rufe drove down and across a gangway onto the waiting ferry, joining the other wagons, carriages and horses waiting to cross, and in a few moments they were underway. Kitty looked around with interest. How different the harbour looked down at this level, so much closer to the water. She looked back at their wake streaming out behind them and at the small boats and yachts zigzagging nearby. A stiff breeze whipped up whitecaps on the water, causing Kitty to hold on to her hat with both hands. It was all so exciting.

They were nearly halfway across when the ferry started to roll and dip.

'Don't worry, we're quite safe,' Rufe said. 'It's often a bit rough on this stretch. It's caused by the swell from the ocean coming in as we pass the Heads.'

Kitty laughed with the exhilaration. 'I love it. It makes me feel so alive.' Her cheeks flushed with excitement.

For her, the trip was all too short. It seemed only minutes until they were waiting to cross the gangway onto the shore.

'What a fun way to travel.' Kitty's eyes sparkled, her cheeks were pink, her even white teeth showed as she laughed up at him, her face alive with the joy of the moment. Rufe caught his breath as he looked down at her. God, she was lovely. He was disconcerted to find he had to resist an impulse to scoop her into his arms and crush her against him. It was fortunate he had to pay attention at that moment to driving them across the gangway and up the incline on the other side, allowing him time to regain his composure.

'You enjoyed that, did you?' he asked, when they were on level ground again.

'Yes. I wish I could come to town like that every day.'

'If you live on the North Shore, it's what you'll do. Mind you, in a storm, it can be a bit wild.'

She still laughed. 'I guess you can't have it all ways, you learn to take the rough with the smooth.'

'Like life?'

'Indeed. Like life.'

Kitty loved the look of the north side of Sydney Harbour. Here, almost every house was set in its own plot with a front garden that was a riot of colour behind a picket fence. She noticed, too, that there seemed to be as many new houses being built here as on the other side of the harbour.

'Building is obviously big business in Sydney. It should be a good business to get into. And the timber industry, too.'

'Both very good with this building boom. Why, are you interested? Not still thinking of going into business, are you?'

'Oh, I'm thinking of it for my brother Robert, when he returns. And also, William Barron has gone to look at a timber logging business.'

Rufe turned and looked at her through narrowed eyes. 'Barron? I thought he was returning to England shortly?'

Kitty shrugged. 'It seems he's considering staying here.'

'I see. I imagine that decision would have something to do with you. Are you going to marry him?'

'I haven't decided. Not that it's anything to do with you.'

'I'd hate to see you make a mistake, that's all.' His voice hardened. 'You're too full of life to throw yourself away on a weakling like Barron. He could never make you happy.'

Kitty lifted her chin. 'And what qualifies you as an expert on what would make me happy?'

'I'm a good judge of people. Barron will never be a success out here. I've seen too many come out, like him, thinking life will be the same as it was in the old country. He should go back to his father's estates and his hunting, that's what he's cut out for. You've got more backbone than he'll ever have. You need...' he hesitated, 'you need someone stronger.'

Kitty tossed her head. 'I think I can judge for myself what I need, thank you.'

'Suit yourself. I'm only thinking of your happiness.'

But Rufe realised that wasn't true. He realised he was jealous of Barron. He knew he didn't want Kitty to marry him.

## CHAPTER SIX

'Kitty, you mean you went with Rufe Cavanagh alone, without anyone else? Just the two of you?'

'Oh, Mother, this is Australia, we're not in England now. I'm sure it's quite acceptable here. After all, we were out on the road all the time, in full public view. And if I hadn't gone, I wouldn't have found this wonderful little house.'

'And you've actually paid a month's rent on it? Without me seeing it?'

'Yes, I didn't want someone else to come along and take it. The North Shore is very pleasant. You'll love it. And Mrs. Walters will leave the furniture just the way it is for us. It'll suit us perfectly. We'll take a cab across tomorrow so you can have a look, and I told her we'll move in within the week.'

'Well, you certainly haven't wasted any time. How did you come to find it?'

'We were just driving along and there was a sign out the front saying it was for rent. I knew as soon as I went inside it would suit us perfectly. Now all we need is to find a servant to take with us. I asked Mrs. Walters if she knew of anyone but she didn't.'

Bella seemed to forget her annoyance. 'I wonder if Mary would know of someone.'

'What a good idea. We'll ask her. Actually, I passed her on my way in, and I thought she looked upset, as if she'd been crying. I wondered if she might've had bad news.'

'I hope not. At any rate, she'll soon be in. We'll ask her then.'

Mary knocked on the door shortly after, her usually bright face unsmiling.

Kitty came straight to the point. 'Mary, we're wondering if you might be able to help us. We've taken a house at Neutral Bay and we need a housekeeper. Do you know someone who might be interested in working for us? A friend or relative, perhaps?'

Mary's eyes widened. 'Why, miss, how strange you should ask me that today. It so happens I'd be happy to come with you. I'm looking to find another position myself, if you think I'd suit you.'

'I thought you seemed happy here. Has something happened to upset you?'

'Nothing in the hotel, but my young man and I have had a falling out, and I've a mind to go elsewhere.'

'Can you cook, Mary?' Bella asked.

'Yes. I'm used to running a house. I can do everything that needs to be done.'

'Very good. We'll pay you an extra ten shillings a month to compensate for leaving the main part of town. Will that suit you?' Kitty asked.

'Oh, yes, miss. That'll suit me fine.'

'We want to move as soon as possible.'

'I'll give my notice in straight away.'

'Very well. Come back and see us as soon as you've done that and we'll make the final arrangements.'

'That's a most generous offer,' Bella told Kitty when Mary had left the room.

'I haven't forgotten what it's like trying to make ends meet, have you?'

'Indeed not.'

The move took place a few days later. Rufe had taken on the responsibility of seeing them safely installed in the new house. He arranged the hire of a large carriage with two men, which duly arrived early on the appointed day. He supervised the loading of their belongings, and travelled with them to Neutral Bay to make sure all went smoothly for them.

Bella smiled as she saw him directing the men, for all the world as if it was his own move. 'A man can never resist taking over,' she whispered to Kitty. 'They all think we're helpless. But he's really been such a big help.' Seeing the men carrying the large trunk into the house, she left Kitty alone in the dining room and hurried into the hall to show them where to put it.

Kitty was lifting a basket onto a table ready for unpacking when a hand covered hers. Startled, she looked up to meet Rufe's gaze.

'Let me take that. It's too heavy for you.'

Kitty saw a flash of attentiveness in his eyes. Her heart thumped as she relinquished her hold.

His gaze held hers as he took the basket and placed it on the table. 'You've got a smut on your face. Let me get rid of it for you.' He took a snowy handkerchief from his pocket and wiped her cheek. 'That's better.' He replaced the handkerchief in his pocket then let his fingers slide gently down her cheek. 'It's too pretty a face to have a blemish on it.'

Kitty's cheek tingled beneath his touch. She drew in her breath as he took a step closer.

'Kitty…' he was interrupted by the door opening as one of the men carried another basket into the room.

'I'm told this belongs in here, mate.'

Rufe stepped back and turned towards the door. 'Yes. Just put it here, alongside this one.'

Kitty started to unpack the basket on the table, hoping the action covered her confusion. She felt sure he had been about to kiss her –she had seen it in his eyes. And she had wanted him to. Very much. And she was sure he knew.

At that moment Bella bustled in to report that the men had finished unloading, and the carriage was ready to leave.

'Then I must leave with them,' Rufe said. 'It would be a long trip back to town on foot. I'll call and let you know as soon as I hear anything from my agent up north.'

'Thank you so much, and for all your help today. I don't know how we'd have managed without you,' Bella told him.

'It's my pleasure. I'm sure you'll be very comfortable here.' He turned to Kitty with a warm smile. 'Kitty, we must resume that discussion some other time. Good day, ladies. I'll see you again soon.'

Two days later, Rufe knocked at their door again. His face was grave as Mary showed him into the morning room where they were both sitting.

He came straight to the point. 'Mrs. Morland, I'm afraid I have some bad news for you.'

Bella's hand flew to her mouth. 'Oh no. Not Robert?'

'Yes. It's about Robert.' His voice was heavy.

The colour drained from Bella's face. 'Is he…dead?'

'I'm afraid so.' His eyes were full of sympathy. 'I'm so sorry.'

Kitty stared at him, her eyes wide. She felt faint. She wanted to scream but she couldn't, no sound came.

Bella sat as if turned to stone.

Kitty forced herself to stand and crossed to kneel beside her mother, putting an arm around her. 'What happened?' she asked Rufe through stiff lips.

'I had a cable from my agent and it seems a claim was registered in Harry Mulligan's name. The three of them were working the claim, which was quite a long way upstream from where the main diggings were. They were quite isolated; there were no other miners anywhere near their site.' He paused and took a deep breath. 'They were attacked and killed by hostile natives.'

'No! Oh no. Robert, poor Robert.' Despair wrenched Kitty's heart as tears welled in her eyes. 'What a terrible way to die.'

'They wouldn't have suffered long.' Rufe spoke gently. 'Death would have been quick.'

'Where is Robert's grave?' Bella's voice was lifeless as she looked up at him with anguished eyes.

'I'm afraid there is no proper grave site.' He paused to take a deep breath. 'You see, it was a day or so before they were discovered, and it was necessary to bury them immediately, where they were found.'

Kitty felt a terrible pain stabbing her heart. She put her face in her mother's lap and sobbed, deep, heart wrenching sobs.

Bella stroked her hair, staring ahead with dry eyes. 'Thank you for coming to tell us, Mr. Cavanagh.' Her voice held no trace of emotion as she sat, unmoving except for the hand that stroked Kitty's hair.

'I can't tell you how sorry I am to be the bearer of such terrible news. My agent will cable me again when he's had another talk with the local police. I'll let you know as soon as I hear from him.'

'Thank you, Mr. Cavanagh.'

Kitty still sobbed.

Rufe's face was bleak and his voice full of compassion as he asked, 'What can I do for you, Mrs. Morland?'

'I don't think there's anything, thank you.' Bella spoke calmly. 'I'm so grateful for all you've done so far. I think…' she lowered her eyes as she stroked Kitty's hair again, 'I think we probably need to be alone for a while now.'

'Of course.' He moved to the door. 'I'll come back tomorrow, but if you need me, for anything at all, just send word.'

Bella inclined her head in acknowledgement.

Mary stood close by in the hall as Rufe left the room, closing the door gently behind him.

'Look after them, Mary. They're going to need it. They've had some bad news.'

'Oh, dear. The son, Robert, is it?'

'Yes.'

'Is he dead?'

'I'm afraid so.'

'Oh, the poor ladies. How terrible for them.'

'Yes. I'll be back again tomorrow, but if you think they need me before then, just send me word and I'll come straight away.'

'Right you are, Mr. Cavanagh. I'm glad they've got someone to rely on; all alone they'll be, now. He was their only family.'

'I know. Take care of them, Mary.'

Rufe was filled with sadness for them as he rode back to town.

Bella seemed numb. She sat in her room, dry-eyed and silent, staring into space. Mary brought her a cup of tea.

'Thank you, Mary,' she said tonelessly.

When Mary came back later, the tea was sitting where she had put it, cold and untouched.

Dinner was a silent affair. Bella looked at the plate but made no attempt to touch her food. Kitty pushed her food around and tried to swallow a mouthful but felt it would choke her. Finally, she pushed her plate away. After dinner they sat in the sitting room, still without talking, and retired early.

The next day they both remained in their rooms all day.

Rufe called, bearing a large bunch of flowers, but he refused to have them disturbed.

'I'll tell them you called,' Mary told him, as she took the flowers.

'Thank you. And I'll come again tomorrow.'

Breakfast next morning was no better, the food left untouched on their plates.

As they rose from the table, Kitty looked at her mother, pale and silent, and for a moment she put her grief aside. She took Bella by the arm. 'Shall we walk in the garden for a little while?' she asked.

Bella shook her head. 'No, I think I'll just sit for a while.'

Kitty's heart ached for her, but then she retreated into her own grief.

The next morning the two women were still sitting silently in their chairs when Mary entered the room. She paused inside the door, looking at them, her face showing concern.

Moving to a table she picked up a framed photo of a young man who stood holding the bridle of a horse, a smile lighting his face. She turned to Kitty with the photo in her hand.

'Is this your brother Robert, Miss Kitty?' she asked, looking at the photo.

'Yes, that's him,' Kitty replied. Standing, she came over and stood beside Mary, gazing sadly at her brother's likeness.

'He was handsome, wasn't he? He looks so nice; I bet he had a really nice way with him.'

'Yes, he did.' Kitty sighed. 'He was always so patient with me when we were children. He was my big brother and I thought he was wonderful. I used to follow him around. He never got cross with me, like a lot of boys would have. And, when we were older, we used to ride together.' She put out a finger and traced his figure through the glass, then stroked the horse's image. 'That was his horse, Major.'

Turning, Kitty spoke to Bella. 'Do you remember how we used to ride together on Hampstead Heath, Mother? Such good times we had, I'll never forget.'

Bella sat like a wax figurine.

Mary looked at Bella then back to Kitty. 'It's important to have good times to remember, Miss Kitty, makes him feel not so far away, somehow, doesn't it?'

Kitty swallowed before replying. 'Yes, it does.'

Bella's hands gripped the arms of the chair, her body stiffened. She threw back her head, her neck arched, and from her mouth came a long, thin wail, the scream of an animal in pain. 'Why? Why? Why Robert? First Charles, now Robert.'

Kitty flew across the room and put her arms around her.

Bella turned to her and gripped her arms. 'I can't bear it.'

The fierceness of her grip made Kitty wince.

'Both gone. I can't bear it.' She dropped her head against Kitty's breast and wept, great tearing sobs that came from deep within her.

Kitty cradled her mother, rocking her like a child, her own tears mingling with Bella's.

Mary looked at the two women sharing their grief. She drew a deep breath, then left the room, closing the door quietly behind her.

After their tears were all spent they sat, each busy with her own thoughts. Finally, Bella roused herself. 'We must let Mrs. Nash know what's happened, I'll write to her this afternoon. She needs to know; she will be so distressed. She obviously cared deeply for her brother.' She paused. 'It's so hard not even to have a body. I think I'd feel better if we could bury him, with a proper service.'

Steel bands tightened around Kitty's chest. 'I know. I feel the same. I wonder if it would be possible to find where they were buried?'

'I don't suppose so, when it's so far away, in such a wild place.' Bella sighed, and her fingers twisted her beads. 'And, Kitty, I suppose we must consider our position. What are we going to do now?'

Kitty shook her head. 'I really can't think what we should do for the best, at the moment. I just feel so sad, to think that whatever we decide to do, we won't be sharing it with Robert. We probably need to do what we'd planned, find some sort of business, something to support us.'

'But what? It won't be easy on our own.'

'No, I know. But we'll manage. Don't worry about it just now.'

'Our resources won't last forever.'

'I know.' Kitty's heart contracted. 'Leave it to me, Mother. I'll find us something.'

But she wasn't as confident as she sounded. Had she brought her mother all this way only to fall into hardship again? What could she do?

Kitty tried to force herself to think of their future but logical thought eluded her. Fragmented memories of their childhood chased themselves around in her head, leaves scurrying and spinning in an autumn wind. Robert whistling to the dogs as they walked across the heath, running with her along the beach on a visit to the seashore, racing their horses alongside each other, wind streaming past them, laughing with the sheer exhilaration of it. And Robert, comforting her after their father's death, trying so hard to be strong, trying not to show his own grief.

Kitty realised how much she had been looking forward to seeing him again, how all her thoughts of their bright new future in Australia had been bound up with his presence, with them all being together again. It seemed as if her chest must burst with the pain of it all.

Rufe called again that afternoon and this time they received him. Mary brought tea and while they sat over it, Rufe encouraged them to talk about Robert, about the life they had shared back in England. Their sadness was heavy in the room. When he rose to leave, he promised to let them know as soon as he heard again from his agent.

Kitty walked with him to the door. There he turned and took both her hands in his. 'You must let me know if there's any way at all in which I can help.'

'You've been most helpful already.'

He kissed her gently on the cheek, then left.

Sadly, she watched him ride away. It had been a brotherly kiss, a friendly gesture.

She had mistaken his intentions when they had been alone before. It would have been a comfort to think someone loved her.

## CHAPTER SEVEN

William had never seen so many trees. He tried to recall the names he'd been told, blackbutt was one, and some kind of box, but cedar was the important one. He couldn't remember the others, but it didn't matter, he would soon learn.

What was important was that the logging business was profitable. The three of them had examined the books together. All those figures didn't mean much to him, but his father and George both said it was profitable, and they would know. He felt a bit sorry now that he hadn't paid more attention to the running of the estate back in Buckinghamshire, but he'd never really understood much about figures and hadn't been interested to learn. Oh, well, he'd soon pick it up.

The countryside seemed a bit wild to him, but it had a certain beauty, he supposed. Not like England, of course, but some would find it attractive, he hoped Kitty would like it.

Certainly the nearby mountain was impressive, a great rocky mountain with steep sides covered with forest and a series of sheer, flat faces at the top that shone in the rays of the sunset and looked really splendid. He was sure she'd like that; he couldn't wait to tell her.

He'd been a bit surprised to find that Bulahdelah was only a miscellaneous collection of wooden cottages scattered about in twos and threes amongst the trees, hardly a proper street to the town. Well, it was hardly a town, hardly even a village, really. The inn they had stayed in, the Plough Inn, had been passable. There was a weekday school, but when he and Kitty had children would go back to England for a proper education, of course.

His father agreed with him that the house needed more rooms to make it liveable; after all, nobody could be expected to live in only four rooms. They would build on several more rooms before he brought Kitty here to live. His father would see it was all done in the best of taste.

William preened a little when he thought of how the colonials would look up to him with this property, with the biggest house around here. And a wife far more beautiful than any of the local women.

He wouldn't mind being isolated when he had Kitty to share his life with him. He could see himself riding every day, supervising his property, while Kitty did whatever it was women did in the house all day. And George had told him there were some jolly decent clubs in Sydney. He must make arrangements to join one or two.

Yes, he could see a happy future ahead for himself. It would be good to be away from the family. They had never really appreciated him; they had all looked down on him, thought he was no good for anything. Well, he'd show them. He'd make a fortune for himself here in Australia.

He let himself dream all the way back to Sydney.

On arriving, he hurried to his hotel to freshen up before going to see Kitty. Here he found a note awaiting him, telling him that she and her mother had taken a house at Neutral Bay. By the time he made enquiries as to the whereabouts of Neutral Bay, it was too late to cross the harbour to call today. Reluctantly, he put off his visit until tomorrow.

When William arrived at the house, it was to find the blinds drawn and a wreath on the door. Mary opened the door to his knock and told him Mrs. and Miss Morland were not receiving visitors, due to the recent death of Mr. Robert Morland. He left his card and told her to tell Kitty that he would call again tomorrow, and hoped she would be able to see him.

As he rode back to town, he turned over this new development in his mind. Now that her brother was dead, Kitty would be more concerned about her mother than ever. He must be prepared for the fact that she might want her to come and live with them in Bulahdelah. He wondered if they could consider leaving her here in Sydney; he would certainly prefer that, but he didn't think Kitty would agree.

When he thought about it, he decided that the situation put him in a better position than before with regard to Kitty's response to his proposal.

He'd been so carried away with his daydreams he'd almost forgotten that she had not given him a definite answer. In fact, she had not been over-enthusiastic, he recalled with a twinge of misgiving.

Her brother's death would work to his advantage. She would need someone to look after her, and if it meant taking her mother, too, then he would do so. He would have an extra room built on for her and he wouldn't need to see a great deal of her. Anything to have Kitty for his own.

He set out the next day determined to press his case and receive a firm commitment from Kitty, no matter what concessions he had to offer. He would appear sympathetic and caring. She would see him as her saviour. Yes, that was the line to take. It was probably a good thing she'd lost her brother, now there would never be anyone to interfere with them; she would have no one but him.

'Dearest Kitty, I can't tell you how sorry I am to hear of your sad bereavement.' William lifted her hand to his lips.

Kitty had been tempted to refuse to see him, but Bella urged her to talk to him, even if just for a moment or two.

She felt so low she decided he could make her feel no worse, and at least he was someone else to talk to. Realisation had hit her that they were here with no family and no real friends to share their burden or care about their loss.

'Thank you, William. It's been a terrible loss for both of us.'

'Ah, your poor mother, how I grieve for her, for you both.' He gazed earnestly into her eyes. 'It makes me long to take care of you, to keep you safe and sheltered from the world.' He leant forward and kissed her clumsily on the cheek. When there was no response he continued, 'I'm anxious to tell you of my trip to Bulahdelah, when you feel ready to hear about it.'

Kitty felt a flicker of interest. 'Sit down, William. I'll order some tea, and you can tell me about it now.'

'It's a wonderful business opportunity,' William enthused, when they were settled. 'My father and my brother-in-law both agree with me that it has wonderful potential. And the countryside is so beautiful, I'm sure you'd love it.'

He went on to describe it in glowing terms, emphasising the beauty of the mountain and the nearby river. He told her that, while Bulahdelah was a small village, the town of Stroud was only twenty miles distant, so they would not be really isolated but would be able to share the peace and tranquillity of the countryside.

'Tell me about the business. It sounds interesting.'

'Oh, yes indeed. You should see the wonderful trees on the property. The men are busy all day logging.'

'What happens to the trees once they're cut down?'

William seemed surprised that she would be interested in the business side of things.

'They're dragged down to the river where they're loaded onto a punt and floated down the river. Then they're taken to a sawmill where they're cut into timber, and then sold in timber yards here in Sydney.'

'There's so much building going on I can see how it would be profitable.'

'My dear Kitty, it surprises me that you notice such things. But, yes, it's wonderfully profitable. You need have no cause to worry about that.'

Of course, Kitty thought, he had no idea she was thinking how good it would have been for Robert. Well, Robert was gone. If she wanted to be involved in a business, here was an opportunity presenting itself.

And she had her mother to think of, too. Bella had lost her husband and now her son. Kitty was all she had left, and she felt the responsibility keenly. And over it all hung the shadow of what would happen if George Arnold should ever track her down. What would become of Bella then? If she decided to marry William their financial future would be secure. And in Bulahdelah they would be safer than here in Sydney.

'Did you decide to stay in Australia because of me?'

'Of course, I would do anything to make you happy. Oh, Kitty, please say you'll marry me. I'm dying a thousand deaths waiting for your answer.'

Kitty looked at him and tried to imagine being with him every day. It was not a prospect to fill her with joy. She sought to gain more time. 'But, William, I'm in mourning. It's not the right time to make such a decision.'

'I must know, Kitty. We needn't make an announcement just yet, if you don't wish.'

'I couldn't leave my mother alone. That would be impossible now.'

'I would never think of leaving her alone. She must come and live with us. I'll have an extra room built for her so she'll be comfortable.'

He was really very kind. If she became involved in the business, that would be her interest, and she could see no reason why not. Things were different in Australia. After all, Mary had told her that her mother ran a drapery business. At that moment she made a sudden choice, and decided to make it definite before she changed her mind.

'I would be honoured to be your wife, William.' There, the die was cast. 'I can see that we would be happy together. But we wouldn't be able to wed until I'm out of mourning.'

William's eyes gleamed and a pink flush coloured his cheeks. 'Whatever you say, Kitty. I am truly the happiest of men. I'll treasure you always.' He jumped up and pulled her to her feet. His lips found hers.

It took Kitty by surprise, and it was all she could do not to pull her head away. 'Why, William...' she backed away, 'your passion overwhelms me.'

He let go of her with obvious reluctance. 'Forgive me. Your answer affected me beyond belief.' He tugged at his collar. 'Are you ready to tell your mother the good news?'

Kitty pushed down a feeling of hopelessness. 'Yes.'

Bella seemed delighted at the news. She kissed William on the cheek. 'I'm sure you'll be very happy together. I'm pleased to have some good news to brighten us up at this sad time. When are you planning on being married?'

Kitty replied before William had a chance to speak. 'It can't be until we're out of mourning, Mother.'

'There's some work to be done on the house before it will be ready for us, but, perhaps, when that's done? My parents will be ready to return to their home then, and I'm sure they'd wish to see us married before they leave.'

'That could be too soon.'

'I'm sure they would wish to see William married before they leave, Kitty,' Bella prompted.

In the end, Kitty agreed with reluctance that when the house was ready, they would marry.

Rufe stared at her hand as Kitty passed him a cup of tea. There on her finger was a ring with a large, shiny, very new-looking diamond flashing. He grasped her wrist as she leant back.

'What's this?' he asked harshly. 'Does it mean what I think it means?'

'It means William Barron and I are engaged to be married.'

He glowered at her. 'You little fool. He's not the man for you. He'll never make you happy; he'll bore you silly within a month.'

Kitty wouldn't admit this was her secret fear. 'I don't know what right you think you have, to tell me what I should do.'

'Only the right that I can see you're making a terrible mistake. Why didn't you give yourself time to get over your brother's death? Time to settle in to life in Sydney and to meet a few people and get a feel for life here before rushing headlong into this disastrous relationship?'

'It's none of you business.' Kitty jerked her wrist. 'And let go of me, you're hurting me.'

He let her wrist go and sat back, breathing heavily. 'You fool, you little fool.' His tone was scathing. 'You'll shrivel up and waste away, married to a milk-sop like Barron. Are you going back to England with him?'

'No.' She spoke defiantly. 'He's bought a logging business in Bulahdelah. He's up there now overseeing the building of extra rooms on the house, and we'll be going there to live as soon as we're married.'

He glared at her, amazement on his face. 'You're going to bury yourself in Bulahdelah? That's even worse.' He raised his voice. 'He'll turn you into a meek little country mouse, with only his welfare to worry about and church on Sunday to brighten your days. A fine future to look forward to.'

Kitty swallowed, longing not to believe him. 'I believe Bulahdelah is a pleasant village, and Stroud is nearby. There'll be plenty of social life, you're just trying to alarm me.'

'You'll find out, but it'll be too late then.' Kitty heard the bitterness in his voice. 'I hope you love your future husband, because he's going to be almost your only company.'

'I don't believe you.'

'Are you going to be happy spending all your time with him? Can you tell me you love him?'

Kitty tightened her lips. 'It's none of your business.'

'Of course you don't love him. You don't need him, Kitty, you need a real man, one who'll make you feel alive. One you'll be able to have some fun with, who'll show you how good life can be.'

'How is it that you know what I need?'

'I can tell.' He jumped to his feet and pulled her from her seat. His arms went around her. 'You need someone to show you what love and passion are all about. Someone to make you feel alive. Someone who can kiss you like this.'

He bent his head and kissed her, hard, passionately, until she felt she had no breath left in her body. Her heart beat a wild tattoo, and she felt a fire rising inside her, setting her blood pounding.

When he raised his head he kept her pressed to him. 'I'll bet Barron has never kissed you like that. You're made for love, Kitty. You don't know it yet, and you'll never find out married to that clumsy oaf. You don't love him. Change your mind, before it's too late.'

'I can't.'

'Of course you can.'

She shook her head weakly. 'No, I can't. I have my reasons.'

Rufe dropped his arms and pushed her away. He glared at her, his mouth set in a straight line. 'Then on your own head be it. I can only offer my hopes for your future happiness. You need all the good wishes you can get. Please tell your mother I'm sorry I missed her. I won't wait.' He turned on his heel, anger in every line of his body.

As he stormed from the room Kitty stood motionless, her heart still beating madly. She moved to the window and watched him ride away, urging his horse to a gallop. Her insides suddenly turned to an empty hollow, making her feel as if she had lost something, something she had never even known she had. What hope had she of ever regaining it?

Rufe urged his horse on, impotent fury goading him to push it to its limits. Wildly they tore along the cliff top, the wind whistling past his head, stinging his face, causing his eyes to stream.

Finally commonsense prevailed and he slowed to a canter, then reined in his mount to give them both time to regain their equilibrium.

Patting his horse's neck he stared out across the ocean below. White fluffy clouds scudded across the blue sky and the seagulls wheeled and screeched as they pursued their endless search for food. A stiff breeze filled the sails of the yachts as they raced their way across the harbour, parting the whitecaps in front of them and trailing their wake behind. A ferry pushed its way through the waves, rolling as it reached the long breakers coming in from the ocean beyond the Heads.

How could Kitty be so stupid? That insensitive clod would stifle her vitality; he would never allow her to reach her potential as a woman. If she married him and went to Bulahdelah, she would be condemned to a life of boredom, producing children while he pursued his own selfish interests. What made her act so hastily? It was as if she couldn't wait to be married. And yet he remembered her telling him, on the day when the ship arrived, that she didn't intend to marry at all. And she had certainly been less than encouraging to Barron then. What made her change her mind? She said she had her reasons. Was there something in her past that was influencing her?

It was obvious she was not thinking clearly, grief stricken at her brother's death and concerned for her mother. If she married Barron in a hurry she would regret it in a short time, but by then it would be too late. Well, he could do no more, he' thought the attraction he felt for her was mutual, but perhaps he was wrong. Perhaps the passion he felt in her had simply been the arousal all young women would feel at being properly kissed.

He wheeled his horse about and headed slowly down to the ferry landing. It was time to head back to Sydney,

## CHAPTER EIGHT

Kitty felt trapped as William put the ring on her finger and the minister pronounced them husband and wife. She should have done as Rufe said, changed her mind while she still had time. Now it was too late. As she signed the register, Kitty realised it was the beginning of a new life. She was now Mrs. William Barron.

The reception was a quiet affair, a family dinner held in a small anteroom at Adams Hotel, where Alexander Barron insisted on them having the honeymoon suite for their wedding night and the week they would spend in Sydney before leaving for Bulahdelah. It had been a gift from him to the young couple.

'You make a charming bride, my dear.' Alexander smiled at Kitty, handing her a glass of champagne as she stood alone for a moment. 'William is a lucky man. I hope he appreciates his good fortune. To your happiness, my dear.' He raised his glass and toasted her.

Kitty smiled back. Alexander had charmed her with his old-world courtesy and unfailing kindness in the time leading up to the wedding. At least she liked one of her in-laws, she thought, as she thanked him for his good wishes.

Lady Barron crossed the room to join them, rather like a battleship in full sail, with William following. 'So, Kitty,' she boomed, 'have you finished the purchases for your new home? I doubt you will be able to purchase anything in the way of furniture or household goods in this Bulahdelah.'

'I've bought what I believe we'll need without having seen the house. If we need more, then it might mean I'll need to make a trip to Sydney.'

'I see. It is a pity you didn't bring furniture with you from England, the quality here must be inferior, I am sure.'

'Not really. From what I've seen, the quality here is quite good.'

William took over. 'If we can't find what we want here then we shall have to wait until we make a visit to England.'

Lady Barron frowned. 'William, I thought I made it quite clear that I do not expect to see you both in England. The reason I've allowed this marriage to take place is because you will both be living here. Permanently. The scandal surrounding your father's death would prevent me from ever receiving you in Buckinghamshire, Kitty. I do not expect to see you in England. I want that firmly understood.'

The words hit Kitty like a slap in the face. For seconds she stood, dumbstruck. Then her anger flared. 'My father did nothing to be ashamed of,' she retorted with vehemence. 'He was ruined by an unscrupulous scoundrel, and took the only way out that he could conceive of.'

Lady Barron lifted her chin. 'I do not wish to discuss the matter. As long as you remain here it's not a problem. I repeat, I do not expect to see you in England.'

Kitty felt her face flush. 'You can be assured that I will never come to visit you, Lady Barron,' she fumed.

'Good. Then we understand each other.' She nodded dismissively and walked across the room to join her daughter.

Her husband winced 'My wife sometimes presents her point of view in a forthright manner that seems discourteous. I'm sorry she offended you.'

Kitty controlled her anger. 'I'm not happy with her remarks, but she need have no worry that I will ever visit her.' She turned to William, narrowing her eyes. 'Did you know about her attitude?'

William squirmed. 'She had mentioned some reluctance to ask us to visit her, but I'm sure she'll forget it in time.'

'You can be sure I will not.' Kitty spat the words out. 'If I never see her again, I'll be very happy.'

'Kitty, please…' William put out his hand.

'I don't wish to discuss it further.' She swept away to talk to Bella, leaving William and his father alone.

Kitty lay in the big bed in the honeymoon suite waiting for her husband to join her. She knew she should be looking forward to this, her wedding night, but she was dreading the thought of William touching her. How different it would be if it were a man like Rufe who would be initiating her into the mysteries of love. One whose touch could excite her, whose kiss aroused feelings of passion in her.

William emerged from the bathroom and stood beside the bed. His eyes shone as he looked down at her, then he pulled the bedclothes back. He sucked in his breath. 'My God, you're beautiful. And now you belong to me.'

He stood looking down at her and she looked away, embarrassed, as his nakedness beneath his bathrobe revealed all too clearly his arousal. He climbed into bed alongside her, breathing heavily, and pulled her nightgown up over her head and removed it, raking her from top to toe with his eyes.

Kitty dropped her arms, trying to cover her bareness, but he pulled them away.

'No, let me see you,' he muttered as he pressed himself hard against her. Instinctively she moved back, away from him. He pulled her to him and his mouth was on hers, his tongue inside her mouth. She hated the feeling. His hands moved over her body, kneading her breasts.

'God, you're beautiful,' he said again, 'and you're all mine.' His hands moved down her body and forced her legs apart. He was half on top of her now. His fumbling fingers probed at her most private parts, exploring, touching, stroking. Kitty gave a little gasp as she began to feel a sensation down there, tingling, warm, and not unpleasant.

Then suddenly he was fully on top of her and forcing himself inside her. All pleasure left as she felt sudden pain. She cried out and tried to push him away but he took no notice, forcing harder, pushing, thrusting, it felt as if he was tearing her apart. On and on he went, faster, harder, oblivious to her cries, to the tears of pain that slid down her cheeks.

Then suddenly she felt him spasm, once, twice, a third time and then he shuddered and went slack on top of her. He lay there inert, panting, and then slowly lifted himself up.

'You'll get used to it, Kitty,' he said, rolling off her. 'I know well-bred ladies like you don't like it, but you'll get used to it.' With that, he turned on his side and in a few moments she heard him snoring.

Kitty climbed from the bed and made her way painfully to the bathroom. She ran a hot bath and soaked in it until the pain eased, then gently washed herself to remove all traces of William's onslaught.

Putting her nightdress on, she climbed back into bed, fully expecting to lay awake for hours but, exhausted by the stresses of the day, she quickly fell into a deep, dreamless sleep.

The next morning, as soon as he woke, William turned to her again and started to fondle her breasts.

'Oh, no, not again,' she said, pushing his hands away.

'It won't hurt so much this time, the first time is always the worst,' he told her. 'This is what marriage is all about, Kitty, and you'll soon find it won't hurt at all.'

His hands were insistent. Kitty knew she must submit, this was what women had to endure in marriage.

Within minutes he was on top of her again. The pain was less this time, and she endured it without a sound. Afterwards, he collapsed back on his pillow and lay there watching her, getting his breath back.

A self-satisfied smile appeared on his face. 'I can see we're going to be happy together, Kitty. Yes, our life together will be very satisfactory.'

'I see. I take it that means I please you.' The sarcasm in her voice was lost on him.

'Oh, yes, immensely so. I was sure you would, and I'm pleased to say you've exceeded my expectations.'

Her lips set tight. 'How nice for you.'

'Yes, it is. And now I find I'm hungry. Let's dress and go down to breakfast.'

Their last day in Sydney was taken up with arrangements for the transport of their purchases and with farewells to William's family. Kitty heaved a sigh of relief after the last farewells were said. It had been a strain trying to maintain polite relations with William's mother, and she had found she had nothing in common with Anne and George. The only one of the family she had a liking for was Alexander, William's father, and she was genuinely sorry to see him go.

The Hunter River steamer taking them north didn't leave until late at night, so William suggested dinner at the Paris House, a smart restaurant in Phillip Street.

As they entered the restaurant, Kitty was disconcerted to see Rufe walking towards them. She'd not seen him since the day he had called on her in Neutral Bay, and she felt her heartbeat increase as she remembered their last meeting.

Rufe greeted them cordially. 'Mr. and Mrs. Barron, I do believe. I must congratulate you on your marriage, I'm sure you're looking forward to happy years ahead.'

William beamed. 'Thank you, Cavanagh. We are indeed. We're already the happiest of couples.' He turned to Kitty. 'Isn't that so, my dear?'

Kitty forced a smile. 'Yes, of course.'

'I am pleased to hear you say so, Mrs. Barron. I'd hate to think it was otherwise. And will you be returning to England soon?'

'No, no, indeed.' William shook his head. 'We're staying here in Australia. I've bought a business here.'

Rufe raised his brows, polite interest on his face. 'Is that so? Here in Sydney, I presume?'

'No, in Bulahdelah. I've gone into the timber business.' William spoke with pride. 'I've just completed additions to the house on my property, and we leave tonight to take up residence there. How these colonials manage to live in the cramped quarters they do, I'll never understand, but I've added several rooms. Our home will be quite the largest in the area.'

'Of course, I'd expect nothing less. I have some interests myself near Stroud, which is nearby, so I travel up there occasionally. Perhaps I might have the opportunity to visit you one day.'

'My dear fellow,' William gushed, 'you will be most welcome. Any time at all.'

'Thank you.' Rufe turned to Kitty. 'And your mother, Mrs. Morland, will she be staying in Neutral Bay?'

Kitty met his gaze. 'No, she'll be coming with us. She and Mary are staying here for another week to complete the packing and then they'll join us.'

'I'm sure she'll enjoy the country too.' He turned again to William. 'Ah, the solitude of the bush, so quiet, so peaceful. Why, you can go for weeks on end without seeing anyone apart from your own workers. So different from Sydney with its hustle and bustle, its tiring social life. I'm sure you'll find it a congenial lifestyle.'

William stiffened. 'Er…yes. I'm sure we will. We're both used to country life in England, you know.'

'Of course.' Rufe smiled silkily. 'Well, it might be a little different to what you're used to, but I'm sure that won't worry you.'

'No, indeed. We're looking forward to it, are we not, my dear.'

'Of course. Immensely.'

Rufe flashed her a sardonic smile. 'I am pleased.' He paused. 'Please pass on my best wishes to Mrs. Morland. And now I must let you continue in to your dinner. Good evening to you both.' He bowed slightly and walked away.

The steamer left at midnight. Kitty was asleep before they left Sydney and didn't wake until they stopped to let passengers disembark at Newcastle early the next morning. She turned to look at William, relieved to see him still sleeping. Quietly, she slipped from the bed and dressed, anxious for her first sight of the countryside.

Dawn was breaking as she emerged on deck. The ocean was behind them now, for they had turned inland at Newcastle and were steaming up the Hunter River. Alone on deck, Kitty leant on the rail, watching the tree-lined banks glide by. An early morning mist rose from the water. The sky gleamed pale grey, seeming to melt into the mist, and the trees on the bank looked dark and sombre in the early light.

Kitty drank in the cool air as she turned over the events of the last few days in her mind. Had she made a terrible mistake in marrying William? She remembered how she had felt with Rufe's arms around her. Could she ever feel that way with William? No. Well, it had been her own choice; now it was up to her to make the best of it.

She knew Bella was happy, for she believed Kitty was safe, now she was Mrs. William Barron. And rightly so, for the Barrons were an important family, and anyone would hesitate to accuse her now, even if they could find her. Her future seemed secure; Bella had no need to worry. But at what cost?

The sky became slowly tinged with pink as the sun sent its first cautious rays into the air. Suddenly it rose abruptly, anxious to start the new day, revealing the landscape below. As Kitty watched, the mist turned into feeble wisps, then dissipated in the soft breeze. The sun glinted silver on the water. The green leaves of the trees were in full view now, and she could see vines trailing and dipping into the river. A flock of pink and grey parrots flew overhead, their raucous squawks breaking the silence.

It was a new day, the beginning of a new life in a new place. Could she make a success of her marriage?

## CHAPTER NINE

Rufe helped to unload the building materials from the bullock drays, ensuring they were all stacked neatly alongside the prepared building site. The last thing to come off was a large safe. It took four men, grunting and groaning, to lift it down. When the drays were empty he looked around at the sea of tents and makeshift humpies nearby that clustered along the riverbanks and beyond, and wiped his hands on a rag, glad to be finished by midafternoon.

'It's a pity someone hasn't set up a mill nearby, closer to these diggings,' he observed. 'So much timber's being cut hereabouts, but we still have to spend weeks carting it from the closest mill.'

'Yeah, they send it down river and we 'ave to cart it all the way back.' A grin spread over the teamster's weather beaten face. A small, reedy man who wore baggy trousers, flannel shirt, a dun coloured waistcoat, and a battered felt hat. 'Still, it's good for my business.' He reached into his waistcoat pocket and took out a small, black pipe and a wad of tobacco, and filled the bowl, tamping the tobacco well down, before lighting it and clamping it between his teeth.

He puffed out a cloud of evil smelling black smoke. 'Well, reckon we'll mosey along now, Rufe. You'll let me know when your next load o' supplies is ready, I s'pose, so I'll see ya next time.' He cracked his long whip over the bullocks' backs as Rufe waved him goodbye. 'Move along, ya bloody gutless wonders,' he bellowed, cracking the whip again. 'Too bloody lazy to get out o' yer own way, you lot. Get going' or ya'll end up as mincemeat. I ain't feedin' ya fer bloody nuthin'.' Yelling obscenities and continuously cracking his whip, he managed to coax his team to a plodding start.

Rufe turned to a large, sandy haired man in his mid-thirties, who was busy checking off items against entries in a book. 'Well, looks like everything's here, Harry, all ready to start building.'

'Yes, the men are starting in the morning. We should have everything ready and secure by the time the stock arrives next week.'

Rufe looked around at the sprawling mining encampment with satisfaction. 'It's a good field, this one, with more claims being pegged every day. All indications are that there's enough gold to last for years. The store should do well.'

'More miners are arriving every day, and they all want equipment and tucker. It can't go wrong. And most of them'll be pleased to take advantage of being able to sell their gold here, without the worry of getting it down to Sydney themselves.' Harry nodded. 'Yes, we'll do well, no doubt about that.'

'I couldn't have a better man than you to manage it, Harry. Now, I'm going to the inn to book a bed for a couple of nights. Are you sure you don't want to stay there until this is ready?' He nodded towards the building site. 'You'd be more comfortable than in your tent.'

'No, I want to be here where I can keep an eye on things. I don't want anyone helping themselves to any of this stuff overnight.'

'All right then. I'll see you later.' Rufe picked up his bag and walked over to where his horse stood tethered to a nearby tree. 'Come on, Banjo, old boy,' he said, patting the horse's neck before untying him. 'We'll get you settled first.'

Leading Banjo by the bridle he headed down the rough dirt track. A few minutes' walk brought him to the inn. It was a sold looking bark slab building, roofed with corrugated iron, with a heavy timber front door. He was surprised to see lace curtains showing in the glass windows each side of the door. It had to mean a woman's touch.

A youth came around the corner as he stopped outside. 'G'day, mate, you comin' to stay?' he asked.

'Yes, I am. You work here, do you?'

'Sure thing. I'll see to your horse for you, if you like. We got good stables here.'

'What's your name?'

'Tommy.'

'Okay, Tommy.' He reached into his pocket, took out a coin, and flicked it to the lad, who caught it, looked at it and grinned. 'I want Banjo looked after well. You make sure he's rubbed down properly and has a good feed of oats. I'll be out later to see that you've done it properly.'

'No worries. I'll treat 'im as if 'e's me own.'

'Good lad.'

'And what's your name?'

'Rufe.'

'I can see you an' me an' Banjo's goin' to get on real well, Rufe' He took the bridle. 'Come on, Banjo, let's go see your new 'ome.'

Rufe pushed open the door and stepped into a large room.

Placing his bag on the floor, he looked around. A long bar ran down one side and tables and chairs down the other. Two men stood at the bar, glasses in their hands, talking, but otherwise the place was deserted. The miners would still all be working their claims; most would not knock off until dark.

As he stood there a woman came through a door at the back. She wore a blue gown that matched the colour of her eyes, and was inset with a bib front of fine white lace reaching modestly to the base of her throat, where it was finished with a thin velvet ribbon. Her features were even and her dark hair swept up and caught at the back of her head to fall in clusters of curls over the nape of her neck. Her feet were shod in slim leather boots, and an amber necklace and earrings completed her dress.

Definitely not the sort of woman Rufe expected to find on a gold field. After standing for a few seconds appraising him, she came forward with her hand outstretched. He noticed she wore no rings. A further surprise.

'Good afternoon. I'm Irene Donovan, the innkeeper. What can I do for you?' she asked in a bright, pleasant voice.

Rufe took the outstretched hand. She had a light but firm handshake. 'Rufe Cavanagh,' he replied, as he released her hand, 'and I need a room for two nights, if you have one available.'

She nodded. 'Certainly. Just for yourself, is it?'

'Yes. And Tommy's already taking care of my horse for me.'

'He's a reliable lad, he'll take good care of him. If you follow me I'll show you to your room.' Turning, she walked back to the door she had come through.

Rufe picked up his bag and followed her down a long hallway. Halfway down the hall she stopped, opened a door, and stood aside for him to enter. 'This is a quiet room. I hope it'll suit you.'

Rufe took in the plain furnishings, brightened up with a cotton quilt on the bed and curtains at the window. It was spotlessly clean. He turned with a smile. 'This will do very nicely, thank you.'

'I hope you'll find it comfortable, Mr. Cavanagh. Will you want dinner tonight?'

'Yes. And please call me Rufe. You'll be seeing me from time to time. I'm about to open a store here.'

A wide smile showed her white teeth. 'Ah. So it's you who's been the cause of so much speculation recently. In that case, you must call me Irene.'

Rufe raised his brow. 'I didn't realise I was causing interest. I haven't been trying to keep it a secret.'

'There's been all sorts of conjecture as to what's happening with the land that's been cleared. How wonderful that it's to be a store. I hope you'll be able to supply me with some of the goods I now have to bring in from outside.'

'I plan on stocking a wide range of supplies, and if there's anything extra you want, just let my manager know and he'll order it in for you.'

'So you won't be managing it yourself?'

'No, Harry Jones is my manager. You'll find him excellent to deal with, I'm sure. He's managed other stores for me and he always offers good service.'

'But you'll be calling here from time to time, you said?'

'Yes. I like to keep an eye on things, and I have other interests in this part of the world.'

'Then perhaps you'd care to have dinner with me tonight, as my guest. I have a Chinese cook, Ah Lee, who usually manages to find me something a little different to what he cooks for the main dining tables.'

'Thank you, I'd be delighted.'

'Not that it's not good food in there,' she added, 'but it's not easy to make meals special, when you're serving so many, especially when fresh food is hard to come by.'

'Of course not.' He smiled down at her, wondering what an attractive woman like this was doing in such a place. 'I hope we'll be able to make it easier for you as far as supplies are concerned.'

'I hope so, too. I look forward to us doing business together.'

'So do I, and I look forward to dining tonight.'

'Good.' A touch of pink tinged her cheeks and she turned away. 'I'll go and tell Ah Lee I have company for dinner tonight.'

The dinner was good. Ah Lee was an excellent cook, and Rufe brought a bottle of good wine from his stores to go with the food.

Irene thanked him, but assured him that she had some wine that she felt was equal to the dinner, and that she would appreciate his opinion of it. In the end they drank both bottles, and it was late when he stood up to go to his own room.

As Rufe left she smiled up at him. 'I am sorry you won't be staying. There's not much congenial company around here.'

He returned her smile. 'Thank you for a pleasant evening. I'll see you tomorrow, I'm sure. Good night.'

## CHAPTER TEN

William and Kitty left the steamer at Raymond Terrace and breakfasted at the inn before commencing their journey.

'I've arranged a horse and carriage with a driver to take us as far as Stroud,' William told Kitty. 'It is a distance of some thirty miles or so and although there is seating on the mail coach for those who would wish it, I don't think it's suitable transport for us.'

Kitty appreciated his concern for their comfort.

'Unfortunately,' he continued, 'the rest of the trip tomorrow from Stroud to Bulahdelah will be by horseback, as the road is narrow in places.'

'Don't worry,' Kitty replied. 'I'll enjoy riding.'

'Good. I expected you would.'

After a good night's sleep at the inn in Stroud, Kitty rose the next morning eager to complete the journey to their new home. Emerging from the inn after breakfast, they found a man waiting outside for them. He was tall and rangy, his dark hair showed streaks of grey at the temples and his beard was neatly trimmed. He introduced himself to William as Jack Morgan, his manager, and told him he had brought horses for them.

'They're round the back. Do you want me to bring them round here?'

'Yes. I take it you've brought one for the luggage, as well?'

'Sure thing.' He turned to Kitty, his face splitting into a wide grin. 'And you must be Mrs. Barron. Pleased to meet you.'

'And you too, Mr. Morgan.' Kitty returned his smile.

'Jack will do, if you like. We're not too formal up this way.' He nodded and left to get the horses.

William watched him go with a scowl on his face. 'They're all so familiar, the workers here. I don't like their attitudes.'

Kitty laughed. 'Oh, William, don't be so stuffy. Things are different out here. I've noticed it everywhere. Staff are not subservient like they are in England, it seems to be a much more free and easy way of life.'

His lips set in a hard line. 'I don't like it. It shows a lack of respect.'

She shrugged, spreading her hands. 'I think you'll have to accept it. As long as they do their work well, you can't complain.'

Glowering, he narrowed his eyes. 'We shall see. And I do not expect you to encourage their familiarity.'

Kitty sought to divert his attention. 'How far is it now to the house?'

'About twenty miles.'

'Are there any towns on the way?'

'No. I've ordered Morgan to bring food with him; we'll have a meal on the way. We won't reach the house until afternoon.'

Morgan returned with a string of horses. 'Here you are, Mrs. Barron.' He helped her to mount before handing her the reins.

'Right-oh and this one's for you.' He handed the reins to William. 'And these two are pack horses.' He loaded their luggage.

A group of Stroudites turned out to watch their little procession wend its way through the town, which was not really more than a village. Kitty smiled at some of the children, but William kept his gaze fixed firmly ahead as they followed Jack Morgan.

He led them down the main street and a little way out of town before turning on to a narrow track.

'It's just a bush track from here to Bulahdelah, but we go through some nice countryside,' he called back over his shoulder. 'Just let me know if you need a spell, Mrs. Barron, just give us a yell and we'll stop for a while.'

As she followed him Kitty looked around. He was right about the countryside, it was beautiful. On one side of the track dense forest came almost on top of them. Some of the trees were giants. These must be the types of trees that were logged for the timber trade. It seemed a shame to cut them down, they were so wonderful, but, after all, sentiment must play no part in business. Each one would certainly yield an enormous amount of timber.

She turned around to William. 'Do we have trees like these on our property?'

'Yes. Hundreds of them. And each one worth a great deal of money.'

They were continuing along the track at a steady pace when a sudden screeching overhead caused Kitty to stop and look up. A flock of white and yellow birds swooped overhead, their raucous cries filling the air.

'My goodness, what are those?' she called out.

'They're sulphur-crested cockatoos,' Jack Morgan called back, slowing his horse and turning around.

'What noisy birds. And so many of them. There must have been about twenty.'

'Yes. There're plenty of birds up here. You want to look out for some of the brightly coloured ones, they're real nice.'

'I'll watch out for them.'

'I'm sure this is all very interesting, but could we move along?' William's peevish voice came from the rear.

They rode on in silence until they came abreast with a patch of smaller trees with spiky leaves. Kitty slowed her horse to watch as a pair of bright green and red parrots swooped across in front of them, chattering loudly. Fluttering their wings, they came to rest in one of the trees, their beaks pecking at its bright red flowers.

'What beautiful birds. What are they?'

'King parrots,' Morgan answered, slowing his horse and turning. 'And these little fellows...' he pointed as several smaller birds, decked out in red, green and yellow feathers, flew by, screeching as they went, 'they're lorikeets. If you like birds, there're hundreds of 'em up this way. Plenty of other wildlife, too.'

He reined in his horse. 'Look up there,' he pointed up into one of the tall trees at the edge of the forest. 'See that grey furry animal? That's a koala.'

Kitty looked up to see a small animal with a round head, a flat black nose, and large round ears. Its black button eyes stared down from where it clung high in a crook of the tree with its legs wrapped around the branch. 'Oh, I see it. It looks like a little bear.'

'Sort of a bear. They can come down and walk on the ground, but they spend most of their time up there, even sleep up there, clinging on to a branch. The only thing they eat is the leaves of gum trees, special kinds of gum trees. And if you keep your eyes peeled you'll see kangaroos around, too.'

Kitty laughed. 'Oh, kangaroos. They're such odd creatures. I saw one down near Sydney.'

'Plenty of 'em up here.'

Setting off again they continued their ride, up rocky ridges and down into grassy vales, crossing several creeks along the way, the horses splashing through the water with no hesitation. And everywhere there were trees.

About midday they came to a level, grassy bank by a creek, with plenty of shade. Jack Morgan called a halt and they dismounted. While he busied himself producing a meal from a saddlebag, Kitty and William took a short walk along the track ahead, glad of the chance to stretch their legs. When they returned Morgan had the food spread out on a cloth beneath a shady tree, and he had lit a small fire to make billy tea.

'Here you are,' he said when they returned, handing them each a pannikin. 'Best tea you'll ever taste.'

William nodded at Kitty as he took his mug. 'It is surprisingly good, my dear,' he told her. 'I tried it when I was here before. I think you'll be pleasantly surprised.'

Kitty sipped the hot tea. 'You're right. I must say I am surprised.' Sitting alongside William on a fallen tree trunk she ate with relish, enjoying the simple meal of cold beef, pickles, and bread.

Kitty looked around the clearing, fringed with tall, grey-green trees 'It's so quiet here, you can almost feel the silence, it's so still.'

'Not a lot 'round here to make a noise, apart from the birds,' Morgan replied. 'There's sheep back near Stroud, but not here.'

'This is mainly timber country,' William told her, indicating the forest around them.

'So I see. There's certainly plenty of that. Is it as thick on our place?'

'Yes, indeed, enough to make my fortune.'

Lunch finished, Morgan cleared up, then took a small spade from his saddlebag and scooped up some soil to throw over the fire, taking care to ensure it was completely extinguished before they set out again. The track became steeper as they climbed a range of hills. Around them were rocky peaks and deep gullies, with creeks gushing their way down to join the rivers below. At the summit they stopped to rest the horses and stood for a few moments, admiring the view.

'Our new home, my dear,' William told her, waving an arm expansively.

Thickly timbered plains spread out below them. A silver river snaked its way through the trees and, far ahead, a tall mountain rose to one side. Further still, the river emptied itself into a large body of water that seemed to spread for miles.

They followed the track down, moving at a slower pace, until they reached gentle rolling countryside below. It was late in the afternoon when they finally reached the bank of a river.

'The Myall River,' Morgan told them. 'We're nearly there.'

After crossing by punt, another ten minutes riding alongside the river brought them in sight of a house. Kitty reined in her horse and William urged his forward to stand beside her.

'There it is. Redwoods!' William pointed proudly.

'Oh, William, it looks beautiful.'

The house stood on a rise above the river. Behind it, the mountain loomed, a benign giant watching over its realm. Late afternoon sun slanted through the trees to dapple the shingle roof and highlight the posts on the wide verandah across the front.

'Redwoods is the finest house in the district,' William said with satisfaction.

As they came closer Kitty saw that the verandah at the front continued around both sides of the house. Vines twined up the verandah posts, dripping pendulous purple flowers. Roses bloomed in the garden at the front, their heady scent wafting out to meet them, while chrysanthemums and other flowers, for which she had no name as yet, formed a riot of colour. A low fence surrounded it all.

Kitty smiled at William, feeling pleased. 'It's really charming, quite the prettiest house I've seen in Australia, and larger than I expected.'

'Wait until you see inside.'

When they reached the gate they dismounted, and Morgan took charge of the horses and led them away. They walked up a path and mounted the front steps. On the verandah, Kitty turned and looked back down to the river.

'What a pleasant outlook. We must have chairs out here so we can sit and enjoy the view while we take tea. Now, let me see the rest.'

William preened. 'It was so small before we did the additions that we couldn't have lived here. The old house has been almost totally rebuilt and now you'll find we have all the room we need, including a room for your mother.'

Kitty turned impulsively, placing her hand on his arm, delighted with it all. 'That is important for me, William, and I want you to know I appreciate it.'

'I expect you to.'

Kitty felt her smile fade and she removed her hand. 'Well, now, let's see the rest,' she said briskly as they went inside.

'We've more than doubled the size. It was only four rooms before, now we have nine, as well as the kitchen at the back, and rooms for the servants.'

A long central hallway met another, leading at right angles to the new wing. Kitty walked through quickly, inspecting each room and expressing her pleasure as she went. Each had a fireplace and French windows opening onto the verandah, which continued right around the house. All the rooms were of generous proportions with high ceilings. Carved mantelpieces of polished cedar topped the fireplaces. After the first inspection, she retraced her steps at a more leisurely pace, standing in the middle of each room and turning around slowly, visualising how each one would look when furnished. She was well pleased. Yes, she had needed to choose furniture without seeing the house, but everything would suit very well.

'Well, my dear, are you happy with it all?' William asked a trifle impatiently.

'Oh, yes, it's very handsome. When our own furniture arrives it will look splendid. We might need to order some things from Sydney when we're settled; I would like to choose extra silk for curtains. I've bought some, but we will need more. And perhaps papers for the walls.'

'Whatever you want, my dear. I have done the building, now I rely on you to make the rest just as impressive.'

'Certainly, William, if that's what you want. And I must say you've done a good job with the building. It's beautiful. You must have had many men working here to finish it on time.'

'Yes, and of course I was on hand to supervise, so I made sure they did everything properly, how I wanted it, with no time wasted.'

'You did a wonderful job.'

'Yes, I know how these things should be.'

'Of course. And now I must inspect the kitchen.'

'I'll leave you to do that alone. I have things to attend to. I'll go to my study.' He left her and made his way to his study, which was at the end of the new hallway.

When she opened the kitchen door, Kitty found a woman already there, chopping vegetables at the sink. Stopping her work she turned as Kitty entered. She was a big woman with a round face, flushed now from the heat of the stove.

'Good afternoon, you must be Mrs. Barron. I'm Mrs. Porter. My husband's one of the punt men, and I help out in the house.'

Kitty smiled. 'I'm pleased to meet you. Will you be helping permanently?'

'Yes. I've always worked in the house and I'm happy to stay if you want me. I don't usually cook, but I agreed to do it until your own woman comes.'

'Thank you. My housekeeper, Mary, will be here next week, with my mother, but if you'll cook until then I'd be grateful. What about supplies? Are we able to get fresh meat and vegetables, things like that?'

'Oh yes, there's no trouble with that. We get beef or lamb from one of the settlers who kills every week or so, and we've got our own fowls and milking cows, and there's a vegetable patch. We've got beef stew for dinner, with vegetables, and fruit pudding to follow. I hope that's all right?'

'That sounds wonderful. I'm rather tired after our long trip, so we'll have dinner early tonight.'

It seemed a promising start to her life at Redwoods.

## CHAPTER ELEVEN

Kitty walked around the verandah the next morning, anxious to see the surrounds of her new home. The land around the house was cleared and she could see down the hill to the river at the front, to where a man stood loading timber onto a punt. On one side of the house the grass had been neatly cut and a few large, shady trees stood here and there. What a lovely spot to put a table and chairs for tea on a warm afternoon. However, when she crossed to the other side of the verandah, she saw garden beds on that side of the house had been laid out in an attempt to create a formal garden, but many of them were empty. Clearly this side needed work. Beyond the fences, two cows grazed in pastureland; these must be their milk cows.

The sun shone and a light breeze lifted the leaves on the trees and kept the day from becoming too hot, a perfect day for a walk. Kitty decided she would explore the surrounding countryside as she waited for Bella and Mary to arrive. Going through the front gate she headed down the hill to the river.

Tied up at the bank was a large, flat punt, and a big, brawny man in working clothes was in the process of loading logs onto it from a huge pile that stood alongside. As she approached him he stopped his labours, and wiped his perspiring face with a cloth from his pocket.

'G'day, Mrs. Barron. Out for a walk, I see. Enjoying the sunshine, are you?'

'Indeed I am. And you must be Mr. Porter, am I right?'

His round red face beamed. 'That's me. Horace Porter. Usually called Tiny by all and sundry.'

'Do all you Australians have nicknames?' Kitty laughed. 'Our young lad is called Bluey, though his name is Tom. Now why would that be?'

'Well, he's got red hair, hasn't he?'

Kitty laughed again, shaking her head. 'And you're called Tiny. I can see you like your little jokes.' She turned and indicated the pile of timber. 'That's a lot of logs you've got to load. One wonders it won't sink the boat.'

'No, she's built to take the load. Mind you, she don't move too fast when she's loaded, but she'll get this lot down the river, no worries. Reliable old girl, she is.'

'And there's another boat like this, I believe.'

'Yep, she's up the river, closer to where they're working now. Well, I better get on. Gotta finish loading these today. Nice to meet you, Mrs. Barron.'

'And you too, Mr. Porter.'

'Ho. Call me Tiny.'

How friendly everyone was.

Kitty made her way along the bank of the river, stopping often to gaze around. The land had been cleared on the banks, and she could see, by the size of some of the stumps, that many of the trees must have been giants. Rounding a bend she came upon a large stump left at seat height. She brushed its surface to remove a few leaves and twigs, sat down, and gazed out over the river. The stillness closed in around her. The only sound to be heard was the distant thud of axes as another forest giant was laid low, and the occasional call of a butcherbird. The peace and solitude engulfed her.

The smooth surface of the water in front reflected the sky, but across the other side, close to the opposite bank, the deep green of the trees lining the river was mirrored in the water. A fish leapt into the air, breaking the surface and causing a splash as it plopped back. Now, what would have caused it to do that? Was a larger fish chasing it, perhaps? Or was it simply the joy of living that caused its brief aerial display? Kitty watched as the eddies caused by the disturbance glinted silver in the sun. When the ever-widening rings faded away, she stood and resumed her walk.

Soon she reached the end of the cleared land. The forest came right down to the river, leaving no room to walk on the bank. The trees stood close together and vines and creepers twirled and twined around many of them. No sunlight penetrated the dense mass, and Kitty shivered a little as she imagined how easy it would be to become lost in its dark heart.

Turning, she followed a track alongside the forest, leading up and away from the river. Soon the trees began to thin out. Another track branched off and made its way into the forest, wending its way in amongst the trees. After hesitating a moment, she decided to see where it led.

It was cool in among the trees and she wandered along the track, stopping often to look up at the brightly coloured birds flitting about. A sudden screech above her head made her stop to peer up. High above her, perched on the limb of a large eucalypt, a pink and grey parrot regarded her with beady eyes. As she watched, it fluffed its wings and the comb on top of its head stood up as it screeched again, several times in succession. It seemed as if it was screeching at her, so intensely did those beady eyes seem to be regarding her, but an answering screech from another tree drew her eye, and she saw it had been calling to its mate. A few moments later the maniacal laughter of a kookaburra sounded nearby, drowning out the screeches of the parrots and the chatter of the lorikeets. She stopped again, listening, and heard a second bird join in the laughing chorus. But this time the noisemakers, high above her, were not to be seen. What strange birds lived in her new home!

Reaching a clearing Kitty stepped into the open and saw she had come to a settlement of some kind. Houses were dotted about in groups of twos and threes, dwarfed by the great trees growing near them. The track wound down and widened out into a dusty street. She followed it, passing a few cottages on the way, until she reached a large building with a horse trough and a hitching rail outside. Here she stopped. Three horses were tied to the rail but their riders were nowhere to be seen. Plough Inn, she read from the sign swinging in the breeze. A chatter of voices came through a window that was open to the street, and as she looked inside she realised it was a bar, with a small group of men standing at it with tankards of ale before them.

A rider cantered along the street and halted. Dismounting, he tied his horse to the rail. Kitty moved on past the window, embarrassed to be seen staring inside. Tipping his hat to her, the rider said 'G'day,' as he passed her on his way inside.

Kitty tilted her head in acknowledgement. 'Good day,' she replied as she resumed her walk.

Feeling thirsty, she decided to see if she could buy a drink and crossed the street to a shop with the sign 'General Store' above the door.

'Good morning, what a pretty spot you have here,' she said to the tall, gaunt woman who came to serve her.

'Pretty enough, I guess. And would you be Mrs. Barron, then?' She wiped her hands on her apron.

'Why, yes, how did you know?'

'Not many strangers here in Bulahdelah.'

'Oh,' Kitty lifted her brows in surprise. 'This is Bulahdelah, then?'

'Of course. What did you think it was?'

'I didn't know. I've just walked down from our house, and I didn't know where I was.'

'It's the only town hereabouts, so it wasn't likely to be anything else.'

'Of course not. How foolish of me. I wonder if you have something to drink? It's quite warm out walking.'

'There's some lemonade I just made this morning. Would that suit you?'

'Yes, please.'

'You're English, aren't you?' she asked, as she poured the drink and handed it to Kitty, then stood watching her drink, hands folded on the counter in front of her.

'Yes. My husband and I have decided to settle here and make this our home now.'

'The Palmers were from England, too. They've gone back now. She found it too isolated. And missed her family too much as well.'

'I see.' Kitty finished her drink and put the glass down. 'I'm fortunate my mother will be with us, otherwise I'm sure I'd miss her, too.' She placed a coin on the counter. 'Is that enough?'

'Yes. Thank you.' The woman put it in the till. 'You're just married, aren't you?'

'Yes, that's right.' Kitty realised she and William were probably objects of interest to the local community. 'Well, I must be getting back now. It's been nice talking to you, Mrs…?'

'White, Mabel White. What's your mother's name?'

'Arabella Morland.'

'And do you think she'll like it here?'

Kitty saw Mrs. White was reluctant to end the conversation. 'I'm sure she will. The countryside is beautiful.'

'Not a big place, Bulahdelah.'

'No. But I see you have an inn here.' Kitty gestured across the road. 'Do you have many travellers pass through?'

'Some. But there's always people in there. The bar's always busy.' She sniffed. 'The local workers are partial to their ale, you know. And what with the fishermen from the Myall Lakes coming in as well as the farm workers and the timber cutters, there's always a few men around. To say nothing of the land owners who come from round about for their business meetings.' She sniffed again. 'Least that's what they call them, closeted in that private parlour for hours.'

Small villages were obviously the same the world over, Kitty thought with amusement. Nothing remained unnoticed. She smiled as she moved away from the counter. 'Goodbye for now, Mrs. White. I must get along. Thank you for the drink, it was delicious.'

'Well, I hope you settle in all right. Time will tell.'

'Indeed it will.'

Looking around Bulahdelah as she went back the way she had come, she remembered Rufe's words about the solitude of the area. It was certainly a smaller community than she had imagined when William told her about it.

When Kitty told William of her walk at dinner that night he frowned. 'I really don't like you traipsing all over the place like that, Kitty. It's not seemly for the wife of the most important man in the area.'

'Oh, William, really. I was out walking and just stumbled over Bulahdelah. It's a very small village, isn't it? I had a drink at the general store and a chat with Mrs. White who served me. There's no harm in that.'

His mouth set in a stubborn line of disapproval. 'There's no one in the town that's suitable for you to associate with. There are only shopkeepers and workers living there, not our class at all.'

'But William, we can't bury ourselves away here without any other company.'

'That's why we'll have your mother living with us, my dear. She will keep you company. That should be enough for you.' He picked up his glass and drank some wine, obviously considering the matter closed.

Kitty took a deep breath. 'I appreciate you having her come to live with us, but I would like to make the acquaintance of some of the other ladies nearby.'

'I'll let you know when I find some landowners who are fit to associate with.' He picked up his glass again. 'This is really excellent wine, Kitty. By the way, I received a letter from Anne today. If you feel the need of further company we'll arrange for her and George to come for a visit.'

Kitty sighed and let the matter drop.

William was enjoying himself as he rode around with Morgan, inspecting the gangs at work. He liked being a boss. This was what he was good at!

The first gang was working in the forest upriver from the house. They stopped to watch the work for a while.

The cutters fascinated William as they swung their axes rhythmically. With each tree they felled he mentally envisioned it as money in the bank.

A rough timber scaffold stood above a shallow pit. Here, two men used a crosscut saw to cut each log into more manageable lengths. One stood atop the structure, holding the handle of the long steel blade, which he pushed down through the log. His partner on the ground below pulled down on the handle at the other end, then pushed up as the stroke was reversed. Their even strokes made the sawdust fly as the formerly majestic giant was reduced to lumber.

Another group split timber into logs, ready to be taken to the river's edge and loaded onto the waiting punt. All very busy, William observed happily.

'Everything looks to be satisfactory here,' he told Morgan when he grew tired of watching.

'Then perhaps you'd like to inspect the store now?'

'Yes. We'll do that next.'

A genial man with a shiny bald head, fringed by wispy hair, greeted them outside the hut that served as the store.

'G'day, Jack. Howdy, Mr. Barron. Come to see how we run things here, have yer?'

'I have.'

'This is Curly Jones,' Morgan introduced him.

William nodded before dismounting and following the storekeeper inside the hut. He looked around and saw the room was lined with shelves, each one filled with packages and boxes.

'What do we keep here?' he asked.

'Everything the men could want in the way of non-perishables. They get their fresh stuff locally but we've got everything from tea, sugar and flour right down to soap and kerosene for the lamps.'

'How are the goods paid for?'

'The men draw what they want against their wages, and I keep a tally of everything they take. Then I pass it on to Jack and he works out how much has to come out of their wages.'

'I see.' William narrowed his eyes. 'And how often do you pass on the records?'

'Every month.'

'I think that's too long. In future you will do it every week. And you can bring the records straight to me.'

Curly wrinkled his brow and ran his hand over his head. 'It's always worked fine this way. Once a month is when…'

William cut him off. 'In future we'll do it as I've said.'

'Okay, Mr. Barron.' He shrugged. 'Seems like extra work for nothin' though, to me.'

'Don't argue with Mr. Barron,' Morgan said. 'What he says goes, he's the boss.'

'Quite,' William turned and left the store. 'So, where to next?' he asked when they had remounted.

'Over to where the other gang is working.'

They rode along a narrow bush track, with Morgan leading the way.

William was turning over the details of his visit to the store in his mind. It annoyed him that his orders had been questioned. It would never happen in England, but out here the workers had no idea how to behave toward their masters. There was this 'Jack is as good as his master' attitude that he found irritating. Well, he would show them who was boss around here.

Then his mind wandered to thoughts of Kitty. He was very happy with his marriage. What a good choice he had made. She was beautiful. He had seen the admiration in other men's eyes when he had her on his arm, which pleased him immensely, for she belonged to him. Her only fault was certain wilfulness; she could be a little headstrong at times. He frowned. Well, he would have to make sure he subdued that. She must learn she had no choice but to do as he wished.

But what pleasure she brought to his bed. The very thought of her caused a stirring in his loins. Yes, he had chosen well.

He decided he would allow her to accompany him occasionally as he went about the property, once he knew his way around. She rode well, and she had asked to come with him. It would gratify him to please her and, besides, it would be pleasant to have her company at times.

The sound of axes brought him back to his surroundings. They seemed to have come a long way. He looked around him as they reached the second gang. Everything looked much the same as at the other site.

'How far are we here from the other gang?' he asked after he had ridden around and surveyed the work in progress.

'About a mile,' Morgan replied.

'So, we have to transport the timber all that way to the river, at my cost.' His tone was scathing. 'Madness. We should be cutting down close to the river, then we could work our way up here when all that timber is gone.'

'But…'

'No buts at all. Order the men to remove what they've cut here, and then to commence cutting next to the river.'

'But Mr. Barron…'

William cut him off. 'Not another word. Those are my orders.'

Morgan took a deep breath, leaning back in his saddle. 'Very well, if that's what you want.'

'It is. And now I'm going back. You remain here and pass on my orders.'

'Just as you say, boss.'

William turned his horse and rode back along the track, well satisfied that he had shown Morgan how astute he was.

That night he boasted to Kitty of how he had been too clever for his workers and had foiled their plan to take advantage of him.

'Perhaps you would care to accompany me on my rounds of the estate this morning, my dear?' William asked Kitty as they left the breakfast table a few days later.

'Yes, I'd love to, William.' Kitty was delighted, this would be the first step in her goal, which was to learn as much about the business as possible. Changing into her riding habit, she hurried to join him at the stables.

They rode down to the river where the punt had been moored. It was no longer there.

'It's gone down the river with its load,' William told her in reply to her query.

'How long till it returns?'

'Several days. It's rather an unwieldy vessel, heavy and cumbersome, and slow. But ideal for its job, it can carry exceedingly large amounts of timber.'

They headed in the opposite direction Kitty had taken for her walk, until they reached the first gang, and reined in their horses.

It was the first time Kitty had seen the men at work and she sat watching everything intently, while William circled the clearing. She could easily follow the sequence of operations that converted the trees into the timber ready for milling.

Dismounting, she walked over to some logs that had already been split by the sawyers and ran her fingers reverently over the rich, deep red wood, allowing them to trace the grain.

'How beautiful, and what a wonderful smell it has. I take it this is cedar?' she asked one of the splitters, who stopped work to answer her.

'Yep, red gold it is, I reckon. Prized all over the world,' he added with pride, 'and there's plenty of it gone into building your house, too.'

'Did you help to build it?'

'Yes, most of the boys here lent a hand, in one way or another.'

'Then I must thank you all.' She smiled. 'It's turned out beautifully. What's your name?'

'Joe Barnes.'

'I'm pleased to meet you, Joe. I hope to get to know you all before long.'

William had been watching the exchange with annoyance. He could see the men were all watching Kitty and while he didn't mind seeing the obvious admiration on their faces, he wanted her to remain aloof.

'Kitty,' he called impatiently. 'We must move on. There's much ground to cover yet.'

Kitty hated his patronising manner. 'Of course, William,' she said, before turning back to Joe Barnes. 'Thank you for your information, Joe.' Wordlessly she walked back to her horse and remounted.

'I really wish you wouldn't encourage their familiarity, Kitty,' he said as they moved away.

'So much depends on our workers. Surely it's a good thing to have their goodwill?'

'I don't need their goodwill. I'll be a rich man before long, with or without their goodwill.'

Kitty wished he would relax a little, try to see that things were different here in Australia. Red gold. She looked up at the trees. Would they bring William the wealth he expected?

# CHAPTER TWELVE

Kitty tossed aside the sewing that had been resting in her lap, rose from her chair in the sitting room and crossed to the fireplace, where she picked up the poker. She jabbed at the blazing fire, sending sparks shooting up the chimney.

Her words erupted into the quiet room. 'I don't think William is ever going to let me become involved in the business. He let me ride out with him just once to see how the work is done and since then he's refused to take me again, or to discuss any aspect of the business with me.'

Bella looked up from her needlework. 'Well, my dear, he's no different from most men. They believe a woman's place is in the home, not in business.'

Kitty turned and again attacked the fire, her frustration making her poke it viciously, sending more sparks flying up the chimney. 'I would so love to be involved. I'm not like you, content just to work in the garden or do your needlework. It was fun when we were arranging the new furniture and making the curtains, but it's months since we finished that. And you and Mary run the house so efficiently, there's nothing for me to do.'

'I'm sure there are things you could do, if you want to help. Why, you could…'

Kitty cut her words short. 'No, that's not what I want. I want to be part of the business. I'm sure I could help William, but he won't even talk to me about it. He tells me not to bother my head about it, and that I wouldn't understand. It makes me fume. He can't bear not to be in complete control, he wants me to think he's so clever.'

'Perhaps that wouldn't hurt, dear, at least occasionally. All men want their wives to look up to them.'

'Then he should give me cause to look up to him. I hate the way he treats the men, and how he despises the locals. He thinks he's so much better than anyone else around here. He refuses to let us meet any of the other landowners' wives. He says he hasn't met anyone else good enough for us to associate with yet.' She shook her head. 'He's become so arrogant since we've been here. He was rather diffident, when we first met him, but since his family left he's changed. I think he was afraid of his mother and now she's gone he can be himself. Which can be quite unpleasant, I'm afraid.'

Bella sighed. 'I must say he does speak very sharply at times, even to you, I've noticed.'

'Oh, yes. To everyone, including me.' Kitty shook her head, her lips twisting wryly. 'I knew when I married him that I would have to make the best I could of our marriage, that it might not be everything I want, but I didn't expect him to isolate us like this. And to treat me as if I have no brain. I'm sure I could be helpful to William with the bookwork if he would only let me, and I would so love to help.'

'I remember your father always said you were very good with figures. Perhaps you'll be able to persuade William in time. Perhaps you should try flattering him a little, Kitty. That sometimes works, you know. Discreetly, of course.'

'Perhaps.' Kitty sighed loudly as she took a book from the bookcase and sat down to read as Bella bent her head again to her needlework.

Interest in the book eluded Kitty. Her mind focused instead on her life with William. She glanced across at Bella, engrossed in embroidering a cushion cover. Her mother was happy here, she knew, content to have security and a comfortable lifestyle, but Kitty was finding the lack of stimulation and other companionship tedious. She had not realised that Bulahdelah would be quite so small and isolated, although Rufe tried to warn her, she remembered.

Because William considered the other landowners in the district, who were mostly colonials, inferior to himself he refused to invite them and their wives to the house. Consequently when he retired to his study, as he did most evenings after dinner, she had only Bella for company. Much as she loved her mother, she longed for the company of other women of similar age. But if William would only discuss the business with her, let her take some part in it, she believed she would be satisfied.

The only time he showed her much attention was in bed, and his interest in that aspect of their life never waned. Her almost nightly experiences with William were certainly far from her expectations of what a loving marriage would be. She received little pleasure from his attentions. There had been occasions when she had started to feel sensations that were quite enjoyable, but it had all been over so quickly that she was left feeling quite up in the air, angry with William but not really knowing why. At times she pleaded a headache to escape his attentions, but mostly she resigned herself to accepting her lot.

Sighing, she returned once again to the problem of gaining a foothold in the business. She made up her mind that tonight, after dinner, she would try once more.

'Yes, what is it?' William asked irritably, frowning as he looked up from the papers on his desk as Kitty entered his study.

'Why, William, I thought perhaps you'd care to come and sit in the drawing room with me for a while tonight instead of being in here alone. I could play the piano, if you like.'

'I don't have time for such frivolities. I have a business to run, you know, and it's not without problems.'

'Of course I know,' Kitty replied sweetly, remembering Bella's advice. 'I know you work very hard. That's why I would love to be able to help you in some way.'

He banged his fist on the desk. 'I do not want to have to remind you again that women do not discuss business. I have made that clear on more than one occasion.'

Kitty winced, but forced herself to continue calmly. 'It's just that I would dearly like to relieve you of a little of your load. My father trained me to understand figures; he said I was quite good at them. What particular problem do you have at the moment? Perhaps I could assist you.'

William sat back in his chair and regarded her through narrowed eyes, tapping on the desk with his pen. He chewed briefly on its end for a few seconds, and then waved it over the pile of papers. 'I have all this work to get through and I'm just looking at this advice that has come regarding the payment we received for our last lot of timber. It's much less than the first lot, and I need to discover why. Probably they're trying to cheat me, but I haven't had time yet to peruse it properly.'

'Perhaps I could check it against the first one and see if I can discover why. That would let you continue with all the other work you have to do.'

'Well…hrrmph…' He cleared his throat. 'I suppose it's a fairly simple task. It would let me get on with these other pressing matters…hrrmph…if you think you might be able to understand it.'

'I could try, William.' She put out her hand to take the papers, and he handed them over with only slight hesitation.

Sitting at a small side table she compared the two statements, which listed the amount of each type of timber sent and the value of each lot. Running her eye over the figures she soon saw that the most recent statement did not include any cedar, which had paid the largest amount by far in the first shipment.

Glancing at William she saw that he was watching her surreptitiously while riffling through the other papers on his desk. It wouldn't do to let him see she had picked up the reason so quickly, when he obviously had no idea, so she continued looking at the sheets for a few minutes.

'Why, it seems there's no cedar on this last statement, but there was a large amount on the first one. Cedar is the most expensive timber we own, according to these figures, so that accounts for the difference. Didn't we cut cedar this time?'

'I'm sure we would have. I'll speak to Morgan in the morning. The mill owner probably thinks he can cheat me. Well, I'll soon put him straight about that.'

'Would there be any reason why the men would not have cut cedar this time?'

'I can think of none, but I'll sort it out in the morning. Have no fear of that.'

'I'm sure you will.' Kitty paused, smiling at him as she wondered how to persuade him to let her attend to the remaining paperwork. It was obvious that he really had little idea of what to do with it. 'You have so much to do outside, and now you have this extra problem to sort out. Could I possibly help with some of this other paperwork you have on your desk? I might be able to understand it and leave you free for the important things you need to attend to. What is it about, William?'

William waved a hand over the papers. 'It's the store accounts that have to be sorted for each worker so that money can be taken out of their wages. They're brought to me each week, but I've been far too busy to attend to them. It's quite simple really, I suppose even you might be able to understand them.'

Kitty bit down an angry reply. Her mouth curved in a sweet smile. 'I'll look at them in the morning and see if I can understand them. And now perhaps we can go into the other room and I'll play the piano for a while. It might help to relax you after your busy day.'

As William snored alongside her later that night, Kitty reflected on how she had acted. Her mother had been right, and she had achieved what she wanted, through scheming. If that was how it had to be, so be it. Now, without letting William realise what she was doing, she would make sure she made herself invaluable to him by doing all the paperwork. And then perhaps she could slowly ease her way into becoming more involved in the running of the business.

The next morning William set out full of anger. Was the mill owner trying to cheat him or was Morgan deliberately leaving the cedar uncut hoping to have the chance to steal it for himself when his master went to Sydney?

'I shall damn well find out,' he muttered, turning his horse's head towards the site by the river where the gang was felling trees. Arriving there he dismounted and stamped across to confront Morgan.

Morgan straightened up from where he was stacking logs onto a dray for carting to the punt and nodded to him. 'Morning, Mr. Barron.'

Without returning the greeting, William snapped at his manager. 'Show me the cedar you have ready to send down to the mill.'

Morgan shook his head, his face impassive. 'There is none.'

A wave of fury swept through William. So, Morgan was the offender. Obviously planning to steal it behind his back. The blood rushed to his head, causing a drumming in his ears. He raised his voice. 'What do you mean, there is none? Why aren't you cutting my cedar? I suppose you're planning to steal it for yourself when I go down to Sydney.' He took a menacing step forward, raising his arm with the whip in his hand.

Morgan stood his ground. 'No. There's none down here to cut.'

William dropped his arm. Out of the corner of his eye he saw the men had stopped work and were watching the exchange. 'What do you mean none to cut? I have plenty of cedar on my property.'

'Yes. But not down here. There's none left close to the river.'

'Then why are you cutting here?'

'Because you ordered me to.'

William's stomach lurched as he had a sudden recollection of the day he told Morgan to cut close to the river.

'Why didn't you tell me there is no cedar down here?' The only sign he could see that Morgan was upset was a slight narrowing of his eyes.

'I tried to explain, but you wouldn't listen. You objected to having to haul it so far to the river. You made it quite plain that you're the boss and I'm to do as you say, so I did.'

William longed to slash at that smug face with his whip. Resisting the urge with difficulty he clamped his jaw shut. He had to swallow before any words would come out. 'You will stop cutting here. Leave this and take the men back to the other site. And I want you to cut as much cedar as you possibly can.'

'Whatever you say, Mr. Barron,' Morgan replied.

Turning on his heel William walked stiffly back to his horse. Without looking around he remounted and rode away. He headed along the riverbank and then turned onto a track that led up an incline. The further he rode, the steeper the track became as it passed granite outcrops. He rode until the horse could go no further up the side of Old Bulladilla, the mountain clothed in forest with steep vertical cliffs at its top, which towered over Bulahdelah.

Reining in his horse he dismounted and, after tying it to a nearby sapling, climbed further up the barely discernible track until he reached a small clearing. Here, he sat with his back against a large boulder. This was his favourite spot, a place where he came by himself to look out over his estate and dream of the time when he would be wealthy.

Spread out beneath him William could see over the treetops from one end of his property to the other, and beyond. The winding river that formed one of Redwoods' boundaries far below glinted silver in the sun. Dotted here and there he could see the workers' cottages, each surrounded by a small clearing. And his own home, up the hill from the river, the largest house in the area. This sight usually gave him a warm feeling.

But this morning that feeling was replaced by a sense of dread – dread that Kitty would learn of his blunder with the cedar.

He'd always known he was not terribly smart. Whatever he tried to do, he never achieved success. His clumsy efforts had always been met with scorn from his smarter siblings and impatience from his father. Worst of all had been the endless sarcastic comparison with his brothers that his mother heaped on him. Try as he might, William had never been able to please her. How happy he had been when he saw his parents sail away from Sydney, happy to be free at last from his mother's scathing remarks.

Free. Free to be in charge of his own life, free to be the master of his own world, to know that the men who worked his property must look up to him as their master. It gave him a heady sense of importance that he had never known before. And he loved the feeling. In his daydreams William always saw himself returning to England in glory, wealthy, successful, a timber baron home from Australia. And his mother would be smiling at him and telling him how proud she was of him.

And he would have his beautiful wife at his side.

Of course, Kitty said that she would never visit his mother, but she would change her mind, she would do as he said. She was his wife and she would obey him. But first he must make sure she never learned of his error with the timber. Or that he had made a mistake by ordering the workers' store slips to be passed on to him each week. They had piled up and he'd been unsure of what to do with them. If Kitty found out she would consider him incompetent.

His insides churned at the thought that she might discover his mistakes. Anything but that. She must always look up to him; see him as master of her life. It was the measure of his success. Nothing must change that. Well, he'd become good at covering mistakes, he would put the blame on Morgan. She would never know. Yes, that was how to handle it.

Calmer now, William retraced his steps back to his horse. Remounting, he made his way down the hillside, and when he reached the bottom he headed into Bulahdelah and dismounted outside the Plough Inn. Tying his horse to the rail, he made his way inside to the private parlour. He checked the clock hanging on the wall; he was in good time for his usual session with his newfound companions.

## CHAPTER THIRTEEN

Bella finished firming the soil around the roots of the small lavender bush she had planted, then stood up and pushed the hair back from her damp forehead. Picking up the watering can she carried it to the pump and began pumping water. Suddenly, a large hand covered hers on the pump handle. Startled, she looked up, straight into the blue eyes of Jack Morgan.

'Here, Mrs. Morland, let me do that. It's too hot today for a little lady like you to be working outside.'

Bella's eyes widened. 'Oh. Thank you, Mr. Morgan.' Stepping back she watched him fill the can with a few strong pumps of the handle. Picking it up, he looked down at her with a small smile crinkling the corners of his eyes.

'Now, where do you want it?'

She walked back towards the lavender bush. 'Over here. I want to water this plant I've just put in.'

He poured the water around the plant. 'There now, that's fixed it. Mrs. Morland, you shouldn't work out in the sun when it's so hot. You're not used to our summers yet, you could make yourself sick. In fact, you don't need to do this work at all. There're plenty of men here who can do the gardening. You just tell me what you want done, and I'll see it's done for you.'

Bella was touched by his concern. 'That's very kind of you, Mr. Morgan. But I really enjoy gardening. I like to do it.'

'That's all right then. But you should give it away when it gets so hot. You should be inside out of the sun.'

'I'm going to sit over there in the shade now...' she indicated a table with benches under a quince tree, 'and have a cool drink. Would you care to join me?'

A smile lit his face. 'I most certainly would.'

'I made some lemonade this morning. Take a seat and I'll bring it out.'

When Bella returned from the kitchen he rose from his seat and took the tray she carried, with a jug and two glasses, and placed it on the table, waiting for her to seat herself before sitting again.

They sat in silence for a moment as they drank, then Jack was the first to pick up their conversation. 'So, how are you liking it here in Bulahdelah?' he asked her.

'I like it very much. It's so peaceful.'

'I would have thought you might find it a bit too quiet. You must be used to a much livelier life than you lead here.'

'Not really. I've always preferred the country to the city.'

He tilted his head to one side and a half smile lifted the corner of his mouth. 'A pretty little lady like you, I'd have thought you'd be the belle of the ball, out and about in society back in England.'

Bella's face grew warm as she looked into his face that, while it could not be called handsome, looked strong and dependable, and she realised he was flirting with her.

She smiled. 'Oh, no. I haven't done that sort of thing since I was a girl. We led a quiet life in England.'

'Forgive me for saying it, but you don't look much more than a girl now. It's hard to believe you're Mrs. Barron's mother.'

'Oh, come now.'

'I mean it. You look like her older sister.'

'You don't need to flatter me, Mr. Morgan. I'm past needing that. I'm happy to be her mother, and to be here with her.'

'I'm sure you are.' His voice grew serious. 'It must be difficult for you having to get used to a new country, new ways. Especially without your husband. If you ever need a hand with anything, anything at all, I'd like you to know I'll always be happy to help. You only need to ask.' His eyes held a protective concern.

Bella's fingers touched her beads. 'That's very kind of you. I will remember it.'

'Good. And how is Mrs. Barron enjoying living here?'

Bella looked into those clear, steady eyes. Here was a friend, one she could trust. 'I must admit she finds it very quiet, but now that she's helping with the paperwork in the business for William, she's happier. She felt at a loose end before, but now she feels she's helping him, making his work easier, seeing that he needs to spend so much time out on the estate with the men.'

A flash of surprise crossed Jack Morgan's face, but was gone in a second.

'I'm sure it must be a big help to him,' he replied.

'If you come with me into my study for a moment I have something to show you.'

Kitty followed William in and he picked up a paper from his desk and handed it to her, a satisfied smile on his face. 'Here, my dear, have a look at this.'

Kitty saw it was the latest statement from the timber mill. Her eyes went straight to the figure at the bottom of the column and she smiled back at him.

'William, this is wonderful. Why, it's almost double what we received last time.'

'Yes. I've made sure that my orders have been followed, and this is the result. Good management, my dear. That's what it takes.'

'Of course. Now I understand why you need to spend so much time on the estate each day supervising.'

William's eyes flickered momentarily. 'Yes. Yes, of course.' He turned, busily straightening the papers on his desk. 'It takes a great deal of attention to detail.'

'I would really love to come with you tomorrow, William. It's many months now since I've been around the estate.'

He cleared his throat before he turned around. 'I'm afraid that will not be possible tomorrow, my dear. Perhaps some other time.'

Arching her brows, Kitty smiled warmly at him. 'Why not? Is there a special reason?'

'I have a meeting to attend tomorrow afternoon. A business meeting.'

'A meeting? I didn't know you have business with anyone hereabouts. I thought there was no one here that you felt was your equal.'

'Well, I...perhaps I was a little hasty in making my first judgements. There are a few landowners that I find I have something in common with, and we have been discussing various aspects of estate management, among other things that I have occupied myself with.'

Kitty raised her brows. 'Really, how interesting. What other things are you involved in?'

William drew himself up, his face clouding. 'Kitty, I've told you before that business does not concern you. Because I allow you to help me with some small matters does not mean that you have the right to question me about my business.'

'But I want to know. I'm sure I could be of help to you in many other ways. I…'

He held up his hand, cutting off her words. 'Stop,' he shouted, his face reddening. 'I want to hear no more of this nonsense. I've said I will not discuss business with you.'

'But William...'

He took a step towards her, his eyes glittering. 'I said no more,' he thundered. 'You're my wife, you'll do as I say. You will obey me.'

Kitty felt a wave of fury. 'I'm your wife, not your chattel.'

'That's where you're wrong. You belong to me as much as the timber on this property, and the cow in the paddock behind the house.'

'How dare you speak to me like that?'

In a stride he was in front of her, his arm raised. 'I'll speak to you however I wish.' His hand lashed out and slapped her cheek, hard.

Kitty reeled from the blow. It hurt, and caused the blood to hammer in her ears. Jumping back, her hand flew to her cheek. 'You beast,' she shouted at him.

'I'm your master. You'll do as I say. It seems I must teach you a lesson.' He struck her again, harder this time.

He had large hands, heavy, and Kitty staggered as tears of pain sprang to her eyes. 'Bastard!'

Up came his hand again. This time it caught her a stinging blow on the cheekbone. She couldn't prevent herself from crying out, but she stood her ground, her heart racing, as he raised his hand to hit her again

'Yes, go on.' She glared at him defiantly, her hand at her face. 'Show me what a big strong man you are.'

William's eyes bulged. Kitty thought he was about to have a fit, but he dropped his arm.

'I warn you. I expect obedience from you.' He was shaking. 'You needn't think you won't obey me, because I'll make you.'

'And just how will you do that?'

'You're totally dependent on me, Kitty. You and your mother. Don't forget that. And the law upholds my rights.' His tone was threatening. 'It's up to me how you spend your lives. Perhaps your mother is a bad influence on you. Perhaps it would be better if I send her back to Sydney.'

'You can't do that.'

He narrowed his eyes as he looked at her. 'I can do whatever I like. If I decide you'd be better separated from your mother then she'll go back to Sydney.'

'No, never.'

He spoke more calmly now, sensing victory. 'Perhaps it's your mother's influence that makes you want to disobey me. Yes, the more I think of it, that's probably the cause. I think it would be better if she goes back to Sydney.'

'If she goes then I go, too.'

'I think not, my dear.' His voice held a triumphant note. 'Because I'd have you returned to me. By force if necessary. I'm your husband. You belong with me. The law is on my side.'

The blood pounded in Kitty's head. She fought down her rage, knowing he held the upper hand. Breathing heavily she stared at him, hating him. He had won. She could not risk him sending her mother away.

'So, my dear,' he continued silkily, 'let us have no more of this nonsense. Shall we agree that you've made a mistake and you're sorry for it?'

'What do you mean by a mistake?'

'I'm sure you now that it was a mistake to try to pry into my business affairs. My business has nothing to do with you.' He paused and looked at her expectantly. 'Does it, my dear?'

Kitty spoke through clenched teeth. 'No.'

'I'll allow you to continue to take care of the paperwork for me, so I can devote myself to more important affairs, but that's all you'll do. Do I make myself clear?'

'Yes.'

'Good. Then you may leave now. I have some things to attend to, and then I shall have a quiet drink before dinner. And I think we will have an early night and...I do not expect you to have a headache.'

Without another word Kitty left the study.

William drew a deep, shuddering breath and retreated to his chair. He put out his hand and shakily picked up the whisky decanter sitting on his desk, poured a large measure into a glass, and tossed it down in a single gulp. He'd really gone too far, hitting Kitty. He'd not meant to hit her; he didn't know what had come over him. But she would despise him if she knew that his days were spent at cards with the small group of landowners who met in the private parlour at the Plough Inn, instead of working on the estate, as she believed. Just as his mother had despised him for gambling at his club back in England. He couldn't bear to see that same look in Kitty's eyes.

But she must learn not to pry into his affairs, she must obey him. It was in her wedding vows. And the law was on his side, it made sure that a husband's rights were overriding. If he decided to send Bella away, she could not stop him. Kitty must learn that he was to be obeyed in all matters.

Bella was standing by the window as Kitty entered the sitting room. 'Kitty, whatever is happening. I heard William shouting. I thought I heard you cry out. And what's happened to your face? Why are you covering it like that?'

Kitty dropped her hand, her pulses still hammering. Bella rushed over, but Kitty waved her to a chair. 'Sit down and I'll tell you.'

As Kitty recounted what happened, the blood drained from Bella's face.

'Oh, my God, to think he actually struck you. I never would have believed it of him.' Her fingers twisted the beads at her throat.

'He's been very moody and irritable at times of late, but I never expected him to behave like this. What worries me most is his threat to force you back to Sydney, by yourself. I'll never let that happen.' Kitty's voice was fierce.

'I don't see how you can stop him, if he decides to do it,' Bella answered. 'What can you do?'

Kitty was calmer now. 'At the moment, nothing. There's nothing we can do. As long as I do as he wants, everything will probably be all right. And if it's not…' She lowered her voice and looked around to make sure the door was securely shut. 'If it's not then we'll find a way to leave together. Thank God I never told William about the safety deposit box. If we go to Sydney we can empty that and go somewhere he won't find us.'

Bella's voice shook as she replied. 'You mean run away…again.'

Kitty set her lips in a determined line. 'If we have to. Whatever happens, we'll stay together. And you're not to worry. If I let William think I'm the docile wife he wants, he'll be happy.'

'You must be careful to give him no cause for complaint. He could hurt you badly.'

'Don't worry, I won't. But believe me,' determination lent an edge to her voice, 'we are not going to spend the rest of our lives cooped up here as we have been.'

Bella frowned. 'What are you planning to do?'

'For a start I'm going to learn to manage the horse and buggy, so we can both go out whenever we want. We'll start by going to church at Markwell on Sundays. It's only five miles away. William can't object to us doing that, even if he refuses to go himself.'

Bella brightened. 'I would like to do that. If you think we can manage it.'

'Leave it to me. Also, if the time comes that we have to leave, it would be easier if we can use the buggy.'

That night Kitty lay stiffly in the bed, waiting for William to climb in alongside her. When he did, he raised himself on his elbow and looked down at her. He lifted his hand and touched her cheek gently, running his fingers over the reddened, swollen area.

'Ah Kitty, my poor Kitty, did I hurt you? I'm sorry, but you must learn to obey me. I don't want to hurt you, but you must accept that you don't question my word. You must realise that you must obey my wishes.' He leant over and kissed her on her lips, tenderly at first and then more insistently. The next moment he was on top of her, panting.

# CHAPTER FOURTEEN

Kitty's cheek was red and swollen the next morning and a bruise was darkening her eye. When she entered the dining room for breakfast Bella clapped her hand over her mouth, but in response to Kitty's shake of the head, she said nothing.

After glancing at her, William continued with his breakfast and when he was finished he rose from his chair and left without a word.

'Oh, my God, Kitty, you need to see a doctor,' Bella told her as soon as he left the room. 'We'll have to go into Stroud.'

'No, definitely not. Do you think I want anyone to see me like this? Do you think I want anyone to know that my husband beat me? I'm ashamed enough that Mary has to see me like this. I'll stay inside the house until it's better. Now, if you want to help me, get me one of your poultices to help make it go away quicker.'

Bella's eyes filled with tears. 'Whatever you say, Kitty.' She rose from her chair and left the room, returning later with a poultice that she put on the offending eye.

When Mary came in with a fresh pot of tea, she stopped and drew in a sharp breath. 'Oh. Whatever's happened to you?'

'I left the wardrobe door open, and when I turned around in a hurry I bumped into it. So silly of me.'

Mary opened her mouth as if to speak, but then said nothing. She crossed the room and put the teapot on the sideboard. 'You'll have to learn to be more careful, Mrs. B,' she said as she turned around. 'You need to keep out of harm's way.'

During the following week Kitty behaved as if nothing had happened. The swelling and bruising faded daily with the help of Bella's potions and by the end of the week there was only a faint mark left. Kitty took care not to upset William.

On the eighth morning, as soon as William left, she asked for the buggy to be brought out. When it came, its smart paintwork gleaming, she saw Jack Morgan was leading it instead of young Bluey, and frowned. Would he cause them trouble?

Bella stepped towards him with a smile. 'Good morning, Mr. Morgan. Kitty and I have planned a surprise for William. We're going to learn to handle the horse and buggy ourselves. Today we'll have a little practice near the house.'

Jack nodded. 'A good idea. I think it's necessary for you both to be able to handle it. Out in the country like this, you never know when you might need it. Perhaps I can give you both some lessons.'

'That would be wonderful, wouldn't it Kitty?'

'It would indeed. But you must remember we don't want my husband to know until we've mastered it. I wouldn't want to worry him.'

'You can count on me. Not a word. Now, up you get.'

He held out his hand and helped Bella up while Kitty climbed in, then hopped up and took the reins, urging the horse forward.

'Now,' he told them, 'you both ride, so you know how to control a horse. I'll give you a few tips about the buggy.'

Two hours later he pronounced himself satisfied with his pupils' progress.

'You're both doing well,' he told them, jumping down. 'Just stay close to the house for a day or two and keep off rough ground as much as you can. You'll be fine.'

Kitty waited until they were at dinner on Saturday night before bringing up the subject of church the next day. After a couple of glasses of wine she judged William was in a good mood.

'Mother and I would like to go to Saint Mary's church in Markham tomorrow. Would you care to accompany us, William?' she asked.

'No, indeed not. I won't enter a church unless it's Anglican.'

'I wish you would come, William, but we'll just have to manage without you if that's how you feel. I wouldn't want to try to persuade you to compromise your faith.'

'But you're Anglican also.'

'Yes, but it doesn't bother me if I go to another church.'

Bella took a sip of her wine. 'I don't feel that my God will mind if I worship him in a church other than the one I'm used to. And I do feel the need to attend church sometimes.'

'Markham is a long way to ride on a hot day. Besides, it wouldn't be seemly for you to arrive at church on horseback.'

'We'll take the buggy,' Kitty told him.

'The buggy? But you've never driven the buggy.'

Kitty waved a hand airily. 'Oh, we're both accustomed to driving one in England, aren't we, Mother?'

Bella nodded. 'Of course.'

William frowned. 'But the roads here are so much rougher than in England. I don't know if you could manage.'

'Oh, we can manage perfectly well. We've practiced around the estate, it wasn't much different. We'll watch the road carefully, we'll be fine. And our buggy is so smart, I'm sure we'll be the envy of all who see it.'

William pursed his lips. 'I suppose it'll do no harm. Very well then. You may go.'

'Thank you, William,' Kitty said.

Kitty and Bella took their seats in the back pew of the church and remained there throughout the service. Making their way outside afterwards they were greeted at the door by the officiating priest. They thanked him for the service and passed a few cordial words before they left.

As they stepped outside they heard the wind sighing through the treetops. Suddenly, the wind increased and a strong gust made them both clutch at their hats. As they climbed into the buggy and Kitty picked up the reins, a clap of thunder made them both look up at the sky. Black clouds had rolled in and hung threateningly above them.

'I think we're in for some wet weather,' Kitty said as she flicked the reins on the horse's back. 'Come on, Rusty, head for home.'

Almost immediately another clap of thunder sounded, much closer this time and accompanied by a flash of lightning. They travelled only a quarter of a mile before the rain started to fall – large fat drops, spattering the hood of the buggy, but intermittently, as if in no hurry to wet the dusty ground below. Within minutes the tempo increased, and it soon became a downpour. Huge sheets of water fell from the sky, and the strong wind blew it into their faces. Thunder crashed overhead. Water ran across the road, turning the dust to mud.

In no time at all their clothes were soaked. Bella touched the brim of her hat. 'Oh dear. Our hats will be ruined.'

Kitty looked across at her mother. Her smart hat was waterlogged and its brim drooped soggily. Kitty knew her own was the same and her clothes clung wetly to her. She felt water trickling down her legs and running into her shoes.

'Yes, probably our clothes, too. But we have more to worry about than that. Let's hope the creek doesn't rise too quickly or we could be stranded.'

The heavy going caused the light carriage to swerve alarmingly, and Kitty slowed the horse to little more than walking pace. Bella sat silent as Kitty concentrated on peering ahead through the gloom.

They reached the creek and Kitty pulled up a short distance back and handed the reins to Bella. 'Just hold him steady. I'm going to have a closer look.'

She walked to the bank and stood regarding the water. Her stomach knotted with tension as she watched the water flowing swiftly across the stones that normally provided a safe crossing. If the horse slipped, they could be washed away by the force of the water. She stood biting her lip. What should they do?

It could be hours before the storm passed, and the creek would be rising steadily all the time. It could be tomorrow before the water subsided. That was if the rain stopped. What if it didn't?

Would William be concerned and come looking for them? Surely he would realise they could be in difficulties. Slowly she walked back and climbed up into the buggy, taking the reins from Bella. 'I think we'd better wait awhile. When we don't return, William will surely come looking for us.'

Slowly she drove the buggy to the side of the road, and pulled as close as she could to a large tree, its thick leafy branches offering at least some protection from the weather.

When Kitty heard a shout from the other side of the creek some time later, relief surged through her. William had arrived. But when the horseman splashed through the water and rode up to them she saw it was not William. It was Jack Morgan.

'Thank goodness you didn't try to cross the creek on your own,' he said, as he reined in beside them.

Bella leant towards him. 'Oh Jack, I can't tell you how pleased we are to see you.'

Even in the stress of the moment Kitty felt a stab of surprise. She glanced sharply at her mother. Since her father died she had never heard her address a man by his Christian name.

Jack Morgan brushed at the rain dripping from the brim of his hat. 'I knew the creek would be running high with all this rain. I just hoped I'd reach you in time.' He turned to Kitty. 'Now, I'll ride back to the other side, and wade back. Then I'll hold your horse's head and lead him across. You'll have to keep a firm hold on the reins, but we should be able to cross safely. Do you reckon you'll be okay to do that?'

'Yes.'

'Good.' He turned and splashed back to the other side and tied his horse to a tree. A moment later he was back, shaking himself as he emerged dripping from the creek.

He tied a piece of cloth over the horse's eyes then led him slowly to the bank and down the slope into the water, talking soothingly to the horse all the time.

Kitty felt the tug of the water as it rose almost to the floor, but she held the reins firmly to guide them across. When the horse reached the other side it slipped as it started to climb the slope. The buggy jerked and twisted in the surging water as it came to a stop. Kitty pulled hard on the reins. Morgan swore and urged the horse up again, looking anxiously back at them. Little by little they started to move again, and the buggy slowly straightened, inching its way through the swelling waters. Slowly, slowly up the incline they moved, and then lurched over the top with a rush as the wheels reached level ground.

Kitty relaxed her tensed muscles as she realised they were safe. Beside her, Bella let out her breath with an audible rush.

Morgan let go of the horse's head and walked back. 'I'll ride back with you,' he said, 'but you'll be all right now.'

'I don't know how to thank you enough,' Kitty told him.

'It's nothing. Forget it.' Striding across, he untied his horse and swung up into the saddle.

As they headed homewards Kitty wondered why it had been left to Jack Morgan to rescue them. Why had William not come?

They had almost reached Bulahdelah when the rain stopped as abruptly as it had started.

When they stopped in front of the house, Morgan quickly dismounted and came to help Bella down from the buggy. Holding her hand, he looked into her eyes as she stepped down, his face showing concern. 'You're soaked to the skin. I hope you don't catch cold from this. Make sure you have a hot bath and a tot of brandy to drive away the chill,' he said, still holding her hand.

A smile touched Bella's lips. 'I will. And thank you so much for coming to rescue us.' Her hand still rested in his.

He cleared his throat. 'It's nothing,' he said gruffly. Releasing her hand he took the reins from Kitty. 'I'll look after the horse,' he told her. 'You go in and get dry.'

Mary was waiting in the hall for them and bustled them into the sitting room, where she had a fire burning with towels warming in front of it.

'Just look at you both, you're like drowned rats,' she fussed. 'You'll both catch your death of cold if we don't get you warmed up. Now then, you take off those wet clothes and wrap yourself in towels and wait here by the fire,' she ordered Kitty. 'Just put your wet things on the end of the hearth and I'll collect them later. And you come with me, Mrs. M, I'm going to put you straight into a hot bath.' Taking Bella's arm she led her from the room, shaking her head and muttering dire warnings about the risk of pneumonia.

Kitty removed her wet clothes and rubbed herself down with the towels, standing in front of the fire until she felt the heat warming her bare body enough to stop shivering. Then she wrapped herself in one of the large, fluffy towels Mary had left and pulled a chair up to sit close to the heat. And as she sat there, staring into the flames, she thought about the way Bella and Jack Morgan had looked at each other.

Once she was warm and in dry clothes, Kitty went in search of William. She found him in his study, seated at his desk with a glass in front of him.

'Ah, there you are, my dear. Come in and sit down,' he waved at the chair opposite his desk, 'and tell me about your day. Did you enjoy it?' Leaning back in his chair he picked up his glass. Holding it up he twirled it around, watching the play of light through the amber liquid as Kitty seated herself. 'I hope you didn't get wet.' He took another mouthful and put his glass down.

Kitty glared. 'Of course we got wet. How could we help it in that storm? But it wasn't just that we got wet, the creek was up and without help we'd never have been able to cross it. Surely you realised that?'

William shrugged and spread his hands wide. 'How was I supposed to know?' he asked with a slight lift of his eyebrows.

Kitty's lips tightened. 'I thought you would at least be concerned for our safety. If it hadn't been for Jack Morgan coming to our rescue and helping us to cross the creek safely, we could have been washed away.'

William smiled thinly. 'Well, that was gallant of him.' Suddenly he sat forward, his palms flat on the desk in front of him, all traces of affability now gone as he regarded Kitty through narrowed, angry eyes. 'Really Kitty, if you and your mother choose to go haring about the countryside on your own, you cannot hold me responsible for your safety. If you had stayed at home you would have been warm and dry. Let it be a lesson to you. Perhaps you'll now stay at home where you belong.'

Kitty sucked in a breath. Surely he couldn't object to them going to church? But as she looked into his eyes and saw the vindictive look there, she knew he meant every word. Something sharp and painful twisted inside her as she saw this further evidence of the spiteful side of her husband's nature. How had he been able to conceal it from her before their marriage?

As Kitty watched silently, William rose from his chair and crossed the room to where the brandy decanter stood on a small table. Thoughts raced through his brain, a paperchase of grievances. Why was Kitty not content to stay at home where she belonged? Why must she refuse to obey him? Why must she flout his wishes? Pouring himself another drink, he turned and looked at her. She had risen from her chair and was staring at him with an accusing look on her face. Suddenly a white mist swam in front of his eyes. As he watched, Kitty's face changed into that of his mother, scolding, critical. The glass dropped from his fingers, unheeded as it shattered and spread brandy across the floor. In two strides he crossed the room, his hand ready to hit that hated face. He must be rid of it.

Kitty saw his raised hand, jumped up and raced towards the door. He landed a blow on the side of her head as she wrenched open the door and fled from the room.

As William's hand connected with Kitty's head, the mist lifted. He dropped his hand, but she had gone. He flopped into his chair, dropped his head onto his arms on the desk before him, and wept.

Outside the sitting room door Kitty stood for a moment, her hand against her racing heart, composing herself before she faced her mother. When her breathing returned to normal she made her way to the sitting room.

Bella was sitting near the fire as Kitty entered. Waiting until she had settled herself in a chair on the opposite side of the fire, Bella looked enquiringly at Kitty. 'Well, why didn't he come looking for us himself?'

Taking a deep breath, Kitty told her what had happened in the study. 'What I'm at a loss to understand,' she added as she finished, 'is how we didn't see this side to him before. Before we left Sydney.'

'Oh dear.' Bella sat staring into the fire, slowly twisting her beads. 'He reminds me of someone I knew as a girl. The Fosters lived near to us when I was growing up. The youngest son, Henry, was kept firmly in his place by the rest of the family. His mother was a domineering woman, and his father had no time for fools, and young Henry could never please either of them. He grew up seeming so meek and mild. When he married he changed completely. Away from his family's influence he showed his real character, and let out all the feelings he had obviously been suppressing all his life. He terrorised his wife.'

'That certainly sounds like William.'

Bella frowned. 'You'll have to be careful. Now that he has shown he can be violent…' She spread her hands wide in a gesture of despair.

Kitty bit her lip. 'You're right, I'll have to be careful of him. He has the upper hand. Who can I complain to? We have no family. All we could do is leave, and I think he would set the law to look for me. Could we find somewhere he wouldn't find us? I don't know...' She shook her head.

They sat silent for some time, until Kitty turned to her mother, hoping to ease her anxiety.

'Forget that for now.' She smiled. 'I have a question for you. I couldn't help noticing that there seems to be some feeling between you and Jack Morgan. Am I right?'

A faint pink flush coloured Bella's cheeks. 'I sometimes come across the men cutting timber when I'm out walking, and he's always very polite and friendly. He always explains to me what they're doing. That's how I first came to know him, and now he often comes to help me in the garden.'

'I have sometimes noticed you both together working in the garden, and occasionally sitting under the quince tree talking.'

'Well, the least I can do after he's helped me is to offer him a drink to quench his thirst.'

'Of course.' Kitty's eyes twinkled. 'Do you like him?'

Bella went even pinker. 'We have become friends.'

Kitty smiled at her mother's confusion. How wonderful if she could find new happiness here. 'It looked as if you're very good friends indeed, from the looks on your faces.'

'Oh, Kitty, he's a fine man, and we've found we have a great deal in common. Is it so wrong of me to take pleasure in his company? Do you mind?'

Kitty moved quickly to her mother and put her arms around her. 'I think it's just wonderful.' Returning to her own chair she posed a question. 'Do you think it might develop into more than just friendship?'

'You wouldn't mind?' Bella's voice was a mixture of surprise and hope.

'Of course not. Why would I mind?'

'Well, your father…' Her voice trailed away. 'It's not that I've forgotten him, but...'

'Mother, Father has been dead for over five years now, and he'd want you to find someone else if it could bring you happiness. He wouldn't want you to be alone for the rest of your life.'

Bella's eyes lit up. 'Do you really think so?'

'I'm sure. Now, tell me a bit about Jack.'

'He's a widower. His wife died six years ago. They lived in Sydney, and he had his own business as a timber merchant. When she died he decided to leave Sydney. He sold up everything and wandered around for a while, then he heard the previous owner here needed a manager, and decided to take the position.'

'Does he have any children?'

'No. His wife was sick for a long time, with consumption, and they never had children.'

'How sad for him.'

'It is indeed. He would have liked children of his own.'

'So, he knows all about timber from having his own business,' Kitty mused. 'But doesn't he miss Sydney?'

'No, he loves the quiet life here away from the bustle of the big city.'

'I see. And how about you? Do you enjoy this life we lead now, away from everything we're used to?'

'Oh yes. After what we've been through since your father died I'm content to live quietly. I enjoy the peace and the beautiful countryside here. I'm happy to have a home to run again and I enjoy walking in the bush and working in the garden. I'm quite content.'

'Who knows,' Kitty said, 'maybe you'll have a home of your own to run and a man of your own to look after again someday soon.'

Bella blushed. 'We certainly haven't discussed such a thing.'

Kitty laughed. 'Well, from the way I saw you looking at each other today, it wouldn't surprise me.'

'Enough of such imaginings,' Bella said firmly. 'We're just friends at the moment.'

'We'll see what develops. Time will tell.'

That night at dinner William made no reference to what happened in his study, but he was in a sullen mood. The atmosphere felt strained. Kitty made no attempt to converse with him. He consumed several glasses of wine with his meal and left the table immediately after the meal was over, returning to his study.

As Kitty watched him leave without even excusing himself, she wondered about his changeable behaviour of late. 'I've never really thought about the amount of brandy and wine William drinks, but I wonder if that can be what makes him so bad tempered at times. I must take more notice.'

Bella nodded. 'It can affect some men most unpleasantly, seeming to bring out the worst in their character.'

'He's been very moody and irritable lately. I've noticed that some days he comes in bright and cheerful, and other days he's in a really bad temper when he returns home.'

'I've certainly noticed that myself, but, after all, he wouldn't be drinking when he's going around the estate or supervising the timber cutting, would he?'

'No, I suppose not.' Kitty spoke thoughtfully. 'But he has spoken of having business meetings with some of the local landowners. I wonder how often these meetings take place.

## CHAPTER FIFTEEN

Rufe Cavanagh rode along Bucket's Way, heading for Bulahdelah. As he was not expected at his destination for several days, he planned to make a detour and visit the Barrons. As he rode, his mind was on Kitty. He couldn't forget her; she was often in his thoughts. How was she getting on with that oaf she'd married? Foolish girl – and that's all she was, just a girl – she should have waited, waited until she was over her grief at her brother's death.

He remembered the day they went to look at houses on the North Shore. How Kitty laughed as the swell and the wind gusts rocked the ferry. That was the day he realised she was special.

He'd felt a stab of jealousy when she refused to rule out marrying Barron. He'd wanted to change that, and he would have, if the death of her brother hadn't intervened.

On the day of the move into the house at Mossman's Bay he'd been about to take her in his arms when they were interrupted. And Kitty had wanted him to; he'd seen it plainly on her face.

Then he had to break the devastating news of Robert's death. There had been no alternative but to leave Kitty and Bella alone to their grief. But Barron had no such compunctions and took advantage of the situation to press Kitty into agreeing to marry him.

He had been so enraged when he saw the ring on her finger and realised what had happened, that he stormed out and returned to Sydney, where he proceeded to get very drunk.

Now, he wanted to see how the marriage had turned out. He'd be surprised if Kitty was happy.

After staying overnight at Stroud Rufe arrived at Bulahdelah in the afternoon and dismounted outside the Plough Inn. Looking around, he wondered how Kitty and her mother enjoyed living in this tiny village. And Barron, too, for that matter. As he tied his horse to the rail two men emerged from inside the building. One of them was Barron.

Barron stopped at the sight of him, and then stepped forward with his hand outstretched.

'Cavanagh, my dear fellow,' he said, wringing his hand. 'How wonderful to see you. I know you said you'd come to visit us, but it is a pleasant surprise.' He turned to the other man. 'Sampson, come and meet my friend Cavanagh.'

Surprised at the effusive welcome, Rufe returned the greetings. 'I'm on my way to Copeland and decided to pay you a visit on the way. I plan to stay here tonight,' he nodded at the inn, 'and come to visit you in the morning.'

'No, no, you must come home with me now. Sampson and I have finished our business, have we not?' he asked, turning to his companion.

'Yes, we have. It's time to head home. Our ladies will be waiting for us.'

Rufe nodded. 'In that case, I'll be happy to come with you.'

Barron turned to Rufe. 'Now, let's away. I'm anxious to show you my estate.' He puffed out his chest.

Still the same pompous ass, Rufe thought as they followed the rough road out of town and made their way into the bush along a narrow track. 'Great timber country you have around here, Barron.'

'Yes, indeed. And I own a large piece of it. Tomorrow we'll ride around the estate.'

The narrow track meant they rode in single file so Rufe felt no obligation to keep up a conversation as they made their way to the house.

'A nice place you have here,' he observed as he mounted the steps to the front door, which stood open to catch the breeze from the river.

'Yes, quite the best house around here, of course.'

'Of course.'

As they entered the hallway Barron stopped and called out, 'Kitty. Kitty.'

Kitty emerged from a room down the hall and started walking towards them. Rufe's heart raced at the sight of her.

Her eyes widened as she saw him and her hand flew to her throat. Her step faltered, and she stood still. Rufe heard her sharp intake of breath.

'Come here, my dear. See who I've brought home with me.' Barron moved down the hall towards her.

Reaching Kitty he put his arm around her waist, pulling her to his side. She stiffened at his touch.

'Isn't this a surprise?' Barron asked her.

Kitty looked pale but now colour suffused her cheeks. 'Indeed it is. Welcome, Mr. Cavanagh.' Moving away from Barron's side she held out her hand.

Rufe took her hand in his. 'It's a pleasure to be here, Mrs. Barron. I'm on my way to Copeland and decided to make a detour to see how you've all settled in to life in Bulahdelah.'

Barron's voice was hearty. 'We've settled in very well. We're remarkably happy here, is that not so, Kitty?'

'Yes, of course,' Kitty replied in a flat voice.

Rufe sensed tension in the air. They were not as happy as Barron would have him believe. He felt a prickle of satisfaction, followed quickly by concern for Kitty.

'Is Mrs. Morland with you?' he asked.

Kitty smiled, her face coming alive. 'Yes, of course. Come down to our sitting room, she'll be so happy...'

Barron cut across her words. 'Bring your mother into the drawing room. Cavanagh and I will go there and have a drink before dinner. Tell the housekeeper we have one extra for dinner and have her make a room ready for our guest. Come and join us for a drink when it's all ready.'

Taking Rufe by the arm Barron led him back along the hall and into a room pleasantly furnished, and looking out onto a shady verandah with a garden beyond.

Barron crossed the room and picked up a decanter that stood on a silver tray. He looked expectantly at Rufe. 'Brandy?'

'Please.' Rufe nodded.

Barron poured brandy into two glasses and handed him one. Rufe seated himself as Barron raised his glass in salute.

'Your health, Cavanagh,' he said, before tossing down his drink.

He turned as the door opened and Bella and Kitty entered. 'Ah, Mother, come and say hello to our guest.'

Rufe rose from his chair as Bella cam towards him with a smile.

'How pleasant to see you, Mr. Cavanagh. I hadn't expected you in our part of the world.'

Again, Rufe explained that he had business nearby. 'I couldn't be this close without coming to see you all,' he told her.

'I'm so happy that you have. You know, I've never thanked you for what you did for us when we lost Robert. I'm so pleased to have the chance to tell you how much I appreciated what you did.'

'I was sorry to be the bearer of such terrible news.' Rufe's heart filled with compassion for Bella as he led her to a seat on the sofa. Then he looked across at Kitty and caught his breath.

She stood framed in the doorway. A slant of sunlight fell across her face and highlighted her deep green eyes and a ringlet of honey gold hair that curled on her brow. Her beauty struck him afresh, and he felt as if he he'd been kicked in the stomach. How had he ever let her get away from him?

The spell was broken as she walked into the room and Barron's voice brought him back to reality.

'Ah, there you are, my dear. Come in and have a glass of sherry.'

Kitty sat next to Bella, and Barron brought them both a glass of sherry as Rufe sat down again.

'As you can see, Cavanagh, we lead a very civilised life here. My two ladies have every comfort they could want, isn't that so, Kitty, Mother?'

Kitty nodded as she sipped her sherry, while Bella replied. 'Indeed, every comfort. And it is a beautiful area to live in.'

Barron nodded complacently.

But Rufe felt tension in the room. Something was not right here. Kitty was certainly not happy.

Barron looked expectantly at Kitty. 'Now, Kitty, perhaps you will take your seat at the piano and play something for us.'

Kitty moved obediently to the piano. Her fingers trailed across the keys for a moment before she seated herself. Then she started to play, a soft haunting melody.

Rufe watched her as she played, detecting a sadness about her. She looked thinner than she'd been in Sydney, but it seemed to enhance her beauty rather than diminish it. Her cheekbones were more prominent and her eyes seemed even larger in her face, which had been kissed to a light golden colour by the sun.

When she reached the end of the piece she folded her hands in her lap and sat still.

'That was pretty, my dear,' came Barron's voice, 'but now play something a little brighter for us.'

'Very well. See if you like this better.' Her fingers moved swiftly as a lively Chopin polonaise filled the room.

'That's better.' Barron smiled as he filled his glass again and topped up his guest's. 'Didn't I make a wise choice of wife, Cavanagh?' he asked Rufe as he handed him his glass. 'Not only is she beautiful, but talented as well.' He nodded with satisfaction. 'Yes, she's truly a wife to be proud of.'

Rufe longed to smash his fist into the smug face. Too good for you, you bloody oaf, he thought. But there was nothing he could do about it.

The next morning Kitty woke early and left the bed quietly so as not to disturb William. Dressing in the silence she made her way out of the house, through the gate and down to the river, trying to sort out her feelings as she walked. The sight of Rufe standing with William in the hallway had been like a bolt of lightning. She had stood there, paralysed, her legs weak, while her heart raced and the blood hammered in her ears. With a supreme effort she managed to pull herself together enough to greet him coherently when he stood before her. The touch of his hand sent a tremor through her, but was somehow reassuring, helping her to face reality. Reality was that she was married to William. She must not show her agitation; no one must suspect how she felt.

She had tried to fathom Rufe's mood, but his pleasant manner betrayed no hint of his feelings towards her. Had he forgotten that day at Mossman's Bay when he had stormed out of the house and left her? Or had it been of so little importance to him that he had put it from his mind?

Sitting on a stump near the bank, Kitty stared out over the water, watching the play of light and dark on the surface. The sun slanted its early morning rays across the river, lacing the air with sunshine, causing the water on this side to sparkle while the other side remained dark. The sun kissed the tops of the melaleucas on the edge of the opposite bank, throwing them into light green relief against the sombre darkness of the taller casuarinas behind, still in shadow.

This was one of her favourite spots; she often came here, secluded from all except those who might come along the riverbank. All was still and quiet at this early hour except for the gentle lapping of the water and the sound of the birds as they chirped their early morning chorus.

Hearing a twig snap, she looked around and was surprised to see Rufe come around the trees and walking towards her.

'Good morning,' he called as he approached. 'I see you're an early morning riser, too.'

'Yes, I often take an early morning walk.'

'This is a lovely spot. Do you mind if I join you?'

Despite a quickening of her pulses Kitty replied calmly. 'Of course not.'

Rufe sat on a nearby stump.

'So, Kitty, here you are, an old married lady. I hope life here in Bulahdelah is turning out as you wanted. I hope you're happy.'

Taking a deep breath she turned to look at him. 'William told you yesterday that we're remarkably happy here, didn't he? I wouldn't argue with my husband.'

'Quite the dutiful little wife, aren't you?' Rufe asked with a twist to his lips. 'But I asked for your opinion, not his.'

Kitty turned back to look out over the water, sweeping her hand to encompass the scene before her. 'Look at all this, it's so beautiful, how could anyone not like it? You don't get this down in the city. And we lead a good life here.'

'That's not what I asked you, Kitty.' His voice took on a harsher note. 'Are you happy?'

'How happy is anyone, ever? I'm happier here than when I was back in England. Does that satisfy you?'

Jumping to his feet he came to stand in front of her. His hands reached out for her shoulders and he pulled her to her feet, shaking her lightly, angrily.

'No, it doesn't satisfy me at all. Blind Freddy could see you're not happy. And how could you be, married to that oaf?'

Kitty's heart thumped. 'You mustn't talk about him like that. He's my husband and I married him for whatever he is.'

'Why, Kitty, why? Why in God's name did you marry him?'

'Does it matter? I married him, I'm William's wife.'

'Why did you have to rush into it like that? Why couldn't you have waited, given yourself some time?'

Kitty swallowed the lump in her throat. 'What does it matter whether I'm happy or not? This is what I chose to do.'

'It matters to me.'

Savagely he pulled her to him, bending his head, and the next second his lips found hers. He kissed her passionately, demandingly, a kiss that seemed to fuse her to him. Heat flooded Kitty's body. Her heart raced and every nerve in her body tingled. Her body melted against him as her arms encircled his neck. The heat inside her made her throb with desire. So this was how passion felt.

The kiss seemed to last forever, until Rufe pushed her from him roughly, breathing heavily. She gasped and almost fell as he took his arms from around her. Her limbs had gone weak and her pulses pounded.

'You little fool.' His eyes glittered. 'This is what we could've had. But no, you couldn't wait. You had to marry that…that nincompoop.'

Kitty trembled as she stared at him, shaking her head. 'I didn't know…I had no idea…' her voice trailed away.

'You didn't know the first thing about love, did you? You had no idea how it could be. But why couldn't you have waited to find out?' His anger flailed her like a whip. 'That day when I came to see you and saw his ring on your finger I could have killed him. And you too.' He winced and shook his head as if to clear it. When he spoke again his voice was quieter. 'Tell me, Kitty, what made you rush into it so quickly?'

Kitty tried to match his calmer tone but a shuddering hitch caught in her throat. 'I had a reason, believe me. I can't tell you, but I had a reason.'

He looked at her for a long moment then asked her, 'Was it because of something in your past?'

The blood drained from Kitty's face as she felt herself go cold. 'What makes you think that?'

'I accidentally overheard a conversation between you and your mother, when we were staying at Petty's Hotel. I didn't mean to listen, but I was in a position where I couldn't help overhearing.

Not that either of you mentioned what you'd done. But I knew there was something.'

Kitty's hands were clammy and she felt faint. 'I see. Why didn't you ask me about it, then?'

Rufe shook his head. 'It wasn't any of my business. I didn't want to know what you did and I still don't. I don't care. It wouldn't make any difference to how I feel about you.'

Kitty's tongue flicked her lips. 'And how do you feel about me?'

He looked at her steadily. 'I love you.'

Kitty swallowed, her head reeling. 'Why didn't you tell me?' Her voice was a whisper.

'I would have if it hadn't been for your brother's death. That day when you first moved into Mossman, I realised it, but we were interrupted. You probably don't remember...'

Kitty interrupted him, her voice a mere breath. 'I remember.'

'And then, next time I came to see you it was after Robert's death. I wanted to say something then, but you were so full of grief, it didn't seem right, so I decided I should wait.' His lips twisted. 'Barron had no such scruples. And the next time I saw you, you were wearing his ring.'

'I thought you didn't care.'

'Oh, I cared,' he told her, his voice thick with emotion.

'I see. Well, it seems as if we made a mess of things, doesn't it? And now it's too late.'

'It doesn't have to be.' His voice pleaded. 'Come away with me. You can get a divorce.'

Kitty shook her head. 'It would cause a scandal. You wouldn't want to be with a scarlet woman, and that's what I'd be. We'd both be outcasts.'

'I don't give a damn for people's opinions. If it worried you, we could go away where no one knows us. Australia's a big country.'

Kitty shook her head. 'It's too late.'

'If you're worried about your mother, I'll look after her. She can come with us.'

'If only I could say yes.' Sorrow filled her, misting her eyes. 'It's not my mother. It really is too late. You see, I'm carrying William's child.'

## CHAPTER SIXTEEN

The next morning, Rufe cursed himself for coming here. As he sat on the stump Kitty had occupied the previous morning, he went over their conversation yet again. After she delivered her bombshell, he'd stood dumbstruck. She was carrying Barron's child. That altered the complexion of things altogether. Barron would never let her go now. And even if they managed to elude him, did he want another man's child? Did he even want Kitty, pregnant with Barron's child? He wasn't honestly sure that he did. How would he feel, seeing her growing larger week by week, knowing it was not his child inside her? How could he even make love to her?

But how could he give her up? He had felt her passion, her love for him flowing from the very pores of her being as he held her in his arms, savouring her kisses, feeling her body pressed against his, wanting him.

His mind writhed with anger, futile with thoughts that chased themselves through his brain. What was he to do? He was tormented by his longing for her. And to know that she returned his love drove him to frenzy. But she was pregnant. He drew a deep shuddering breath as he tried to consider all angles, but his mind jumped first this way then that, like a grasshopper in a jar.

He had endured Barron's self aggrandisement the previous day as they covered his estate from one end to the other. The pompous bastard. How he'd longed to smash his fist into that self-satisfied face.

Then to have to maintain a façade of normality through dinner last night had been almost more than he could endure. He'd drunk copious quantities of claret, which had helped him survive the dinner, but now he had an aching head as well as his problems. He knew that he should really ride away now, this minute, but he also knew he could not resist seeing Kitty again.

But to what avail? He relived once again the feeling of Kitty in his arms, how she had surrendered herself to him in all but physical consummation.

And then had come the revelation – she carried Barron's child. She told him he was the first to know, Barron himself didn't know yet, nor even her mother.

Rufe dropped his head into his hands. He loved her, God how he loved her. He'd not been without women in his life, there had been many. But never had he felt for any of them the way he felt about Kitty. Even the knowledge that she carried Barron's child could not diminish that. No, God help him, he still wanted her.

He lifted his head and stared up at the tall trees, hardly noticing as a kookaburra swooped from its perch high in a tree to snatch up a snake that had the foolishness to slither across an open patch of ground. As it flew off with its prey, he rose wearily.

Raising his arms above his head, Rufe stretched his muscles, closed his eyes, and breathed deeply for a minute or two. He shook his head to clear it and retraced his steps with a determined stride. He would leave after breakfast as arranged. That way he would see Kitty again but not alone, giving him no chance to compromise her.

It was a quiet group that assembled for breakfast. As he looked around, Rufe felt tension permeating the room, and it seemed to affect everyone except William. He was eating heartily as usual, but Bella was nibbling on a piece of toast, her mind seeming far away, while Kitty pushed her food around her plate, and drank several cups of tea. Rufe had no appetite, but forced himself to lift the silver covers from the dishes of hot food on the sideboard and select a small serve of egg and bacon.

He glanced sharply at William as he sat down, but the man seemed oblivious to the atmosphere, pontificating about the profitability of his cedar and how clever he had been to seize the opportunity to buy this property. Rufe replied shortly to William's discourse when necessary, but he excused himself from the table as soon as decently possible, pleading a hard day's travel ahead.

When Rufe said his goodbyes a short time later, Bella reached up to kiss him lightly on the cheek as he took her hand. 'I shall never forget your kindness to us when we were in Sydney, Mr. Cavanagh. I am greatly in your debt.'

Rufe forced a smile to his lips. 'I'll always be happy to be of service to you in any way possible, Mrs. Morland,' he replied, then added, 'And to all of you, of course. Any time at all.'

'Well, thank you, Cavanagh, most kind, I'm sure,' William responded. 'However, I doubt we shall ever need to call on you, indeed not.'

But Rufe's eyes were on Kitty, and he saw the look of pain on her face as she bid him goodbye.

Kitty left them and hurried down to the edge of the forest by the river. Secure from prying eyes she let the tears flow, great sobs that racked her body. Despair filled her, and she beat her clenched fists against a tree. If only Rufe had made his feelings known earlier. If only she hadn't rushed into marriage with William. But she had, and now she must take the consequences.

Finally her sobs subsided, leaving an occasional hiccup in their wake, and she sat on the stump by the water. Heedless of time, she stared out over the river, watching the play of light and shade on the water without seeing it.

Eventually, she rose wearily and smoothed her skirts. Walking slowly to the edge of the water she bent and wet her hands and pressed them to her eyes and to her cheeks. She stood there, racked with misery, until the breeze dried her face. Then with a deep sigh she returned to her seat, composing herself, before finally rising and making her way back to the house.

Avoiding the sitting room, Kitty went instead to the drawing room and seated herself at the piano. This time she played for herself alone. Music had always been her solace in times of stress and as the strains of 'Traumerie' filled the room she felt her resolve firm. No one must ever know what had passed between her and Rufe. Her life was here with her husband and their coming child.

Sometime later she joined Bella in the sitting room.

'Ah, Kitty, there you are at last.' Her mother looked up from her sewing as she entered the room and frowned. 'You look a little pale, do you feel all right?' A shadow crossed her face. 'Or is there something else the matter?'

Kitty closed the door behind her before crossing to stand by the window, her back to the light. 'As a matter of fact, Mother, I am feeling a little poorly this morning, that's why I went out early for some fresh air.'

Bella's frown deepened and she put her work on the small table beside her. 'Do you have a fever?' she asked, starting to rise from her chair.

'No, no,' Kitty stopped her with a gesture of her hand, giving a slight laugh. 'I believe I have some news for you. I think you're going to be a grandmother.'

Bella flopped back in her chair, clasping her hands together, her eyes shining. '

'Kitty, how wonderful. Are you sure?'

'Yes, as sure as I can be at this stage.' She forced a smile at her mother's delight.

'When will it be?'

'In seven months.'

Bella sprang from her chair and crossed the room quickly to put her arms about her daughter. 'My little girl. And now you're going to be a mother yourself.'

Kitty returned her hug. 'I'm glad you're so happy about it.'

Bella stepped back. 'Of course I'm happy.'

A flicker of a smile curved Kitty's lips. 'I hope I can be as good a mother as you've always been.'

Bella patted her cheek. 'Thank you for that.'

Kitty crossed to pick up a leaf that had fallen from a vase of flowers onto the mantelpiece. Twisting it in her fingers, she mused, 'I wonder how William will take the news?'

'You haven't told him yet?'

'No, not yet.'

'I'm sure he'll be delighted. Perhaps he'll change when he knows,' she said hopefully. 'When are you going to tell him?'

'Soon. I'll pick a time when he's in a good mood.'

'He seemed in a very good mood this morning. I think he enjoyed having company. He was certainly on his best behaviour while we had a guest.'

'Yes, wasn't he? Quite a transformation. Well, if it lasts, I might tell him tonight. I want to go down to Sydney to do some shopping. I need to get the few items we want for the house and now of course some baby things. I don't want to leave it much longer.'

'No, indeed. Travelling is very tiring. Don't you think you could order what you need by mail?'

'Yes, I probably could. But I would like to go to the city for a visit. If I don't go now, who knows when I'll be able to go? It will be too difficult to travel with a baby, and I won't be able to go and leave it for a good while.'

'Yes, that's true.'

As it happened, William's good mood was still evident when he returned late that afternoon.

'Ah, Kitty, my dear.' He pecked her on the cheek as he met her in the hallway. 'Come into the drawing room and have a glass of sherry with me.' Taking her arm he guided her through the door and seated her on the lounge. He rubbed his hands together, smiling. 'I've had a most satisfactory business meeting today. Most satisfactory.'

'I'm glad to hear that, but I don't know if I should have any alcohol.'

William paused with his hand on the decanter. 'Why ever not? You usually enjoy a glass of sherry.'

'I know, but perhaps not just now. However, you go ahead and have one. I want to talk to you.'

William shrugged and poured himself a glass of brandy, then came to stand in front of her. 'What is it you wish to talk about?' he asked warily.

'Do sit down, William.' Kitty forced a smile. 'I have something to tell you.'

Taking a seat opposite her, he drank some of the brandy then placed his glass on the table beside him. He crossed his legs and leant back in his chair. Narrowing his eyes, he asked, 'Well, what is it?'

'I hope it's something that will please you. Have you ever considered that one day you would be a father?'

'Indeed I have. It is one of the things you expect when you marry. I have been waiting for you to produce me an heir.'

'Well, you won't have to wait much longer.'

His eyes lit up. 'Do you mean that you're with child now?'

'Yes, I am.'

'Well now, this is wonderful news.' He sprang from his chair and began pacing the room. 'A son, at last. It'll be a boy, of course.'

Kitty's eyebrows lifted. 'We can't know that, William. Nature will decide.'

He puffed out his chest. 'Oh, I'm sure this child will be a boy. We'll name him after me, of course. Yes. And my father. William Alexander. Yes. William Alexander Barron. It has a nice ring to it, don't you think?'

'Perhaps we could leave names until a little later, William. Do sit down. There are many other things to think of.'

'Of course, of course.' He sat down and, picking up his glass, tossed down the rest of the brandy. 'I must write to the family immediately. They'll be most impressed.' Rising, he poured himself another brandy before returning to his chair. 'Now, my dear. You must take good care of your health from now on. You were quite right not to drink the sherry. It might not be good for the baby. We wouldn't want anything untoward to happen now. You must take care for the baby.'

'Yes, William, I will.' She drew a deep breath. 'We need to think of a nursery now. We probably need to make a trip to Sydney to do some shopping for the things we're going to need. There will be quite a lot to buy.'

'To Sydney?' He blinked, obviously considering the idea. 'Yes. Of course. You must buy whatever you need. But are you sure you're well enough to travel?'

'I'm quite well. I'm not ill, I'm having a baby.'

'Then it must be before your condition becomes apparent. It would not do to be seen in public then.'

'I'm quite agreeable to that. I'll leave you to make the arrangements. When do you think we can go?'

'As soon as I can arrange the accommodation. We'll stay at Adams Hotel again. You may begin to prepare immediately.' He finished his drink and stood up. 'Yes. A visit to Sydney will be excellent. I'll go to my study now and write some letters. I'll make arrangements to do some business while I'm down there, whilst you are doing your shopping.' He stood for a moment. 'Yes, come to think of it, I might have to spend considerable time on business down in Sydney. Perhaps it would be as well if your mother accompanies us. She'll be company for you, whilst I'm busy. You'd like that, would you not?'

Kitty forbore asking him what business in Sydney would take up so much of his time. Instead she smiled as she replied. 'Indeed, that would be very welcome.'

William spent the rest of the evening in his study, and when they retired to bed he turned to her. 'Kitty,' he said, his voice slightly slurred as he ran his hands over her, 'you are everything I expected of you.' He fumbled as he removed her nightdress and kissed her clumsily.

Kitty could scarcely bear the touch of his hands on her skin. She squirmed under his clumsy fingers but he didn't notice. She closed her eyes, and the memory of how she had felt when Rufe kissed her came to her. How would she feel if it was his hands on her, his lips insistently at hers? A sob caught in her throat as she tried to pretend it was Rufe. Rufe's hands caressing her as he whispered words of love – Rufe on top of her – inside her – as one with her.

## CHAPTER SEVENTEEN

Rufe reined in his horse as he reached the top of the hill, glad to have reached his destination. The goldfield at Copeland was set in rough, steep country and the ride had been hard for both horse and rider. He spent a moment viewing the scene below him. Night had closed in quickly, as happened in the bush, and the lights from hundreds of camp fires below made a pretty sight, twinkling in the darkness. Noise rose up to meet him, the hum of a thousand voices, joined by the notes of a mouth organ and a voice raised in song with it.

He picked out his destination, the inn, by the fact that it was a solid building with lights spilling out from its open doors and windows from numerous oil lamps within. No matter that its walls were of timber slabs, it had a solid iron roof, and the bed that would be prepared for him would be comfortable. A hot meal would be waiting, with ale to wash it down. And tomorrow he would immerse himself in business with Harry, his store manager. He must keep himself busy and engrossed in work. It was his only hope of easing the pain of the last few days.

He patted his horse's neck. 'Nearly there, Banjo, just down the hill and we'll be there.' The horse whinnied and tossed his head, then sure-footedly picked his way down the rutted track. As they reached the valley below, Rufe heard the noise of tumbling water. He knew this was from the river that dissected the shantytown into two – the river all the diggers here hoped would yield up its riches to give them wealth beyond their wildest dreams.

He guided his horse over the sludge of the tracks between the makeshift dwellings until they reached the inn. A youth raced forward as he dismounted. 'G'day Rufe. I heard you was comin'. I been waitin' for you.'

Rufe tossed him the reins. 'Hi, Tommy. Look after him for me, will you? Make sure he has some oats tonight as well.' He reached in his pocket and took out a coin. He flipped it to the boy, who caught it neatly with his free hand. 'You know what to do.' He stretched and flexed his shoulders. 'Aah, I'm knackered. Can't wait for a hot bath and a decent meal.'

The boy grinned cheekily at him. 'Yeah, looks like a quiet night for you tonight. Come a long way t'day, 'ave you?'

'Too bloody far. Take good care of him, Tommy, he's tired.' Rufe made his way to the open door as Tommy led Banjo away.

He paused inside and his gaze swept the room in front of him. The long bar that ran down one side of the room was full of men of all ages, sizes and skin tones, talking loudly and gesticulating as they drank or waited for their pints to be refilled. They were a rough looking lot, many of them dusty and looking in need of a good scrub. Most of them wore what seemed almost like a uniform, a dark blue or red shirt with a colourful, if somewhat grubby, kerchief at the neck and moleskin trousers and boots. Three barmaids behind the counter were busy filling glasses. The other side of the room was occupied by tables and chairs, many of them filled by miners eating great plates of stew and potatoes, with damper and a glass of ale beside, to wash it down.

The only clean-shaven face to be seen amongst all this lot was that of a young police trooper, now standing talking to Irene, the only woman in the place who was not behind the bar. As Rufe watched, the trooper nodded and walked towards the door. Rufe stood aside to let him past. The rest of the clientele ignored him.

Irene watched him go and saw Rufe standing there. Immediately, a smile lit up her face and she hurried across to him, her hands outstretched.

'Rufe. Here you are at last. I was beginning to think you weren't coming.'

Rufe took her hands in his and leant to give her a quick kiss on the cheek. 'Well, Irene, I'm here now.' He dropped her hands and stood back to look at her. She wore a green velvet gown, cut low, but not immodestly so. As usual, her dark hair was swept up and caught at the back of her head to fall in clusters of curls over the nape of her neck. A jade necklace hung at her throat and jade earrings swung daintily from her ears. 'And you're a treat for tired eyes, as usual.'

A faint flush coloured her cheeks. 'Your room's all ready for you. I expect you'd like to go straight away to clean up, or would you rather have a drink first?'

'No, I need a hot bath, if that's possible.'

'Of course. There's a tub in the room and I'll have Tommy bring some hot water for you.'

'Let him finish attending to my horse first, we've had a hard day's riding. I'll sit here until he's ready.'

She motioned him to a table away from the others. 'Sit here. I'll just let Ah Lee know to have plenty of hot water ready, and I'll be back. We can talk while you're waiting.'

Rufe looked around as he sat down, and had his interest taken by a large group at the bar, more boisterous than the rest, laughing and clapping the backs of three men who seemed to be buying the drinks.

He nodded towards them as Irene came back and sat opposite him. 'Seems like they're shouting the bar. Struck it rich, have they?'

Irene nodded. 'Yes. Dropped on a jeweller's shop today. According to them it's a beauty. Gustaf, that's the tall one doing most of the talking,' she inclined her head in his direction, 'he's been showing everyone a nugget the size of an emu's egg.'

Rufe frowned. 'That's not a smart thing to do in this company. I hope he's still got it in the morning.'

'I know. I tried to tell him, but he was too excited to keep quiet.'

'Where's their claim, is it near the river?'

'Yes. They're down amongst the furthest lot of tents, a bit off on their own.'

Rufe shook his head, his frown deepening. 'Pity they didn't keep quiet. I know a few large nuggets have already been prised from the banks. They should've given themselves more time to search before they started a rush to that end.'

Irene shrugged. 'You know what miners are like. You can't tell them if they don't want to hear. Now, there's Tommy taking the hot water to your room. You'd better follow him.' She looked up expectantly as he stood. 'Will you join me for dinner when you're ready? Ah Lee's brother is growing vegetables for us, so I can promise you a good meal. Not just stew and damper.'

'Thank you. I'll be delighted.'

'Good. Come directly to my private rooms, whenever you're ready.'

Rufe looked around with surprise as he entered Irene's rooms. It looked very different to last time he had been here. The table in her private dining room was set with snowy linen and polished silver cutlery. Crystal wine glasses sparkled in the light cast by two silver candelabra. A bottle of claret stood opened ready on the table. Irene indicated it as they took their seats.

'This is from my own special store. I chose it to go with our meal.'

'I see you've redecorated your rooms since I was here last,' Rufe said, looking at the gold-embossed wallpaper, the heavy drapes, and the silk cushions on the chairs.

A satisfied smile hovered around Irene's mouth. 'I'm glad you noticed. Do you like it?'

'Indeed, it's very elegant. Not at all like one usually sees on the diggings. You must be doing very well.'

'I'm very pleased with the way the business is going.'

At that moment the door opened and Ah Lee entered, carrying a silver tray. He placed the tray on the sideboard before bowing to them.

'Welcome, Mista Rufe. It a pleasure to see you again.' His lined face creased into a smile.

'It's good to see you too, Ah Lee. It's been a long time.'

'Too long, Mista Rufe. I have cooked you special meal, not miner's meal.' With a flourish he placed a plate each in front of them. 'Yabbies, fresh from water today.'

Rufe looked at the crustaceans in front of him. 'I haven't had yabbies since I was a boy at home. Where on earth did you find them out here?'

Ah Lee bobbed his head in delight. 'From cattle man. I trade him vegetables for them, they fresh today from dam.' After checking they had all they needed, he left them alone.

Irene seemed anxious to hear all that had been happening in Sydney and so throughout the meal Rufe kept the conversation light, with amusing anecdotes of the latest doings of well-known figures.

The yabbies were followed by succulent roast lamb with potatoes and tender baby green beans. The finale to the meal was rhubarb pie, with pastry light as air, served with thick clotted cream.

When Ah Lee came to collect the dishes after they finished Rufe sat back in his chair. 'You really are a marvel, Ah Lee. That meal would have done justice to any establishment in Sydney. I certainly didn't expect anything like it here.'

Ah Lee's eyes shone as he bowed his way out of the room. 'Thank you, Mista Rufe. You too kind.'

Irene rose from her chair. 'We'll have coffee and liqueurs in the sitting room,' she said, heading to a closed door that she opened to reveal a sitting room beyond, decorated in similar style to the dining room. She sat on a sofa and patted the seat beside her as Rufe followed her in.

'Come and sit beside me, then Ah Lee can put the drinks on the coffee table in front of us. Now, what would you like with your coffee? Brandy? I have some Courvoisier.'

Rufe's brows lifted in surprise as he sat down. 'Coffee? Courvoisier? You are doing yourself well. I hope they're from my store.'

'Of course. Since your store has been supplying me with such a good variety of foods and drinks my business has more than trebled. You'd be surprised. When a man strikes gold, even if it's not a big strike, one of the first things he wants is a slap-up meal with all the trimmings, prepared by someone else, in decent surroundings. I even have a private dining room for those who want it. It's well used.' She smiled up at him. 'I have you to thank for much of my success.'

'I'm pleased to hear the store has helped, and that business is doing so well.'

'Oh yes, I have all the comforts of Sydney here now.'

Rufe sat back as Ah Lee brought in the coffee and placed it on the table, along with a bottle of Courvoisier and two balloon glasses.

Irene nodded to him. 'Thank you, Ah Lee. We'll look after ourselves now. That will be all tonight.'

Ah Lee bowed and left the room.

Irene leant back, sighing gently. 'You know, Rufe, I really have most things I ever wanted here now. I should be completely happy.' She turned to look directly into his eyes. 'The business has grown amazingly and my bank balance with it. I live in relatively luxurious surroundings, as you can see.' She swept her arm around to take in the room. 'And my bedroom is even more comfortable,' she added, moving close against him as she sat forward to take her glass from the table.

Rufe was amused by her transparency. There was no doubt what she was offering. She had hinted she could be available when he had spent time here before. But the hints had been more subtle, and he had ignored them. Obviously, the trappings of success had increased her confidence and encouraged her to be more forward.

He swirled the brandy around in his glass, then raised it in salute to her. He smiled as he looked into her eyes over the rim. 'I guess you're happy with life here then.'

She sighed again, more dramatically this time. 'I know I should be but, well, the truth is, I do get lonely here on my own.'

He raised an eyebrow. 'Lonely? With all these hundreds of men around, any one of whom would be more than happy to keep you company.'

She pouted. 'But I don't want just anyone. I'm most particular about who I share my time with.'

He laughed then, a rich laugh full of good humour. 'Irene, my dear, you're a most delightful companion, and a very beautiful one at that. And I must thank you for a delightful evening. But it's probably time for me to go to my own room.'

'Wait, Rufe.' She put her hand on his thigh. 'You don't have to go to your room. You could stay here with me tonight, if you want.'

He looked at her, her lips parted invitingly and her wide blue eyes shining, and felt a flicker of interest. A picture of Kitty flashed into his mind. Honey gold hair and deep green eyes, soft body melting into his arms. Pain knifed his heart. Kitty was lost to him. Barron would never let her go now. He needed to forget about her, and perhaps Irene could help with that.

He tossed down his brandy and put the glass back on the table, then turned to face her. 'Irene, it's possible I might not be back here for another year, maybe even more.' His voice was serious now. 'Is that what you want?'

'No strings attached, Rufe,' she whispered.

He studied her, liking what he saw – an oval face with a generous mouth, long dark lashes that fringed glowing eyes, and creamy white skin marred only by a tiny mole next to her mouth. He lifted his hands and slowly removed the pins from her hair so that it tumbled down, falling in soft waves on her shoulders, then he ran a finger gently down the side of her face. He leant towards her and felt her breath warm on his face as she let out a quivering sigh. Taking her in his arms, his lips came down hard on hers.

Rufe woke at daylight next morning to what sounded like a chicken house full of roosters crowing. He looked across at Irene. She was still sound asleep, her hair tousled on the pillow, and one arm flung out. Yawning, he stretched, slipped out of bed, and padded across to the window, pulling aside the curtain. The scene below him brought a smile to his lips. 'Only on the diggings,' he muttered as he watched the ludicrous spectacle of fully-grown men strutting around outside their tents or humpies, flapping their arms like wings and crowing loudly. 'Morning wake-up call.'

Daylight revealed the diggings clearly. On both sides of the river, but set uphill from it to avoid danger from flash floods, stood a jumble of tents and shanties, the latter made mostly from slabs of bark hastily nailed together, some even of hessian or calico, roofed with sheets of iron. The ground in between these dwellings was churned to mud and slush by the daily tramping of a legion of boots taking the shortest route from home to claim and back.

The sight was nothing new to Rufe, and he gave it only a cursory glance from the window before heading back towards the bed. On the way he changed his mind and turned to the washstand instead where he used the water in the pitcher and quietly washed and dressed. He closed the door gently as he left the room.

A few men were already being served breakfasts of chops or steak and, for those who could afford the extra, bacon or ham. He ordered chops, bacon and eggs from one of the girls who had been behind the bar last night, and who was acting as waitress this morning. Ah, eggs from Ah Lee's brother. Another investment that had paid dividends for Irene. Tommy brought him a cup of tea as he sat reflecting with mixed feelings on the previous night.

Irene had not been what he expected, her inexperience had surprised him. He had taken her for the usual good time girl, but he now doubted this was so. He had no complaints about the night itself, but he wondered if Irene really accepted her own words of 'no strings attached'. He doubted that she gave her favours as freely as he had surmised. Was she really happy to accept what he had to offer? As he sat pondering this, and waiting for his breakfast to arrive, he became aware of someone standing beside his table.

Rufe looked up to see Gustaf, the finder of the gold strike yesterday.

'Excuse me, Mister Cavanagh, may I please have word with you?' he asked in an accented voice that Rufe judged to be Swedish or Danish.

'Of course. What can I do for you?'

'You are owner of store?'

'Yes, that's right.'

'I hear you are honest man.'

'I won't rob you, if that's what you mean.'

'You buy gold?'

'Yes.'

'I have gold I find yesterday. My partner, Joe...' he nodded towards a table where another miner sat watching them, 'he come here this morning to tell me last night our tent was ripped. Someone look for this gold.'

'But they didn't find it?'

'No. Last night I drink bit much vodka. I no go to tent, I sleep here. Gold with me.'

'You were lucky.'

'Yes. Now I no want to keep gold here. I think perhaps you buy it.'

Rufe nodded. 'I can do that. Are you eating here now?'

Gustaf nodded. 'Yah, we have good breakfast before we start digging again.'

'Good. Then after we've all eaten we'll go across to my store and weigh what you have.'

'Right. We go together. Is good. Now we eat.' With another nod, he went back to his table, sat down and commenced talking to his partner.

Rufe knew that theft was not uncommon on the gold fields. Those who found little sometimes took the easy way by helping themselves to another's find. Even some of the storekeepers on the fields, many of whom acted as gold buyers, were known to cheat those with little education when they purchased their gold.

It was one of the reasons Rufe had formed a group of honest men, who'd been lucky enough to strike it rich, into a consortium. They purchased and arranged safe escort for gold from the diggings. His thoughts were interrupted by the arrival of Ah Lee with a large plate of eggs, bacon and chops, that he placed in front of him.

'Good morning, Mista Rufe.' He bobbed his head. 'I hope you slept well.'

Rufe studied his face, knowing that Ah Lee knew full well where he had slept, but his countenance was bland.

'Very well, thank you, Ah Lee.' He sniffed appreciatively at the aroma coming from his plate. 'And I'll do justice to this, I can assure you.'

Ah Lee smiled and bobbed again. 'Good. You tell girl if you want anything more. I look after you myself.'

'Thank you.' He looked at the large helping in front of him. 'I think this will probably see me out.' As Ah Lee left Rufe applied himself to his meal, spearing a piece of bacon and dipping it into an egg yolk, cooked to perfection. Ah Lee was certainly an asset to Irene's business.

When he finished he crossed the room to where Gustaf and Joe waited for him. They pushed back their chairs as he approached and met him on the way.

'Ready?' he asked. When they both nodded, Rufe led the way through the door. Outside, the sounds of the diggings greeted them. Men's voices called out to each other, accompanied by the sound of picks and shovels breaking the earth, and the creak of windlasses being turned to lift the buckets up the shafts from the depths below.

Rufe led them to a building made of heavy timber logs with a corrugated iron roof, over which a flag flew. The solid door, now open, had a heavy lock and the windows, also open, had shutters, which were always closed at dark. All in all, the most secure building at the diggings.

As Rufe led the way inside they saw the shelves piled high with all manner of goods. Picks and shovels stood side by side with pudding pans and dishes, boots, clothing and bedding, tobacco, tea, sugar, flour, and fresh and salted meat. A side of bacon hung from the roof alongside a ham. Large bins on the floor holding food for horses stood next to rolled up tents and tarpaulins.

Harry emerged from a door at the back of the store and came forward with his hand outstretched and a smile on his face.

'Hello, Rufe. Good to see you.'

Rufe shook his hand, then clapped him on the shoulder. 'And good to see you, too, Harry. How's it all going?'

'Fine, Rufe, just fine. I've got everything ready for you.'

'Good man. But we've a couple of customers here first.'

'Ah, Gustaf, and Joe. Sure. What can we do for you?'

'Gustaf has gold to sell,' Rufe explained.

'I heard he had a good strike yesterday,' Harry said.

Rufe's eyebrows lifted slightly. 'Doesn't take long to get around, does it?'

'Not round here it doesn't. 'Specially news like that.'

'Come on then.' Rufe ushered them through the door at the back to the large room beyond. In one corner stood a heavy safe, with a set of scales on top.

Gustaf took the gold nugget from his pocket and hefted it in his hand, looking at it reverently. 'Ah, my beauty.' He rubbed it with his fingers. 'I hate to part with you. But is not safe to keep.' He looked at Joe. 'You still sure?'

'Yeah. Those thievin' bastards might find it next time.'

Gustaf nodded and handed it over to Rufe. Harry moved the scales onto a desk and they all watched as Rufe placed it in the pan on one side of the scales and added weights to the other side until the two were balanced.

He whistled softly. 'Ninety ounces. Very nice. Enter it up, Harry.'

Harry went to the safe and took out a ledger. Opening it, he wrote Gustaf's name in the first column, then the date and weight of the nugget. Finally he entered an amount and took a roll of notes from the safe. When he counted them out and handed them over, Gustaf nodded and smiled with satisfaction as he pocketed them.

'Thank you. What they tell me is true. You are honest men.'

After they left Harry placed the nugget into an already bulging pouch he took from the safe then returned both ledger and pouch to the safe.

'What time are you expecting the escort, Rufe?' he asked when he had closed and locked the safe.

'They'll be here early afternoon. I wanted to be here before them to let you know that one of them is a new man. Hank Masters. He's an American. According to his references he's had experience with armed escort over there. I hope he's as tough as he seems, I fear we could be in for some trouble in the future.'

Harry frowned. 'What kind of trouble? Something special? I thought things seem to have quietened down a bit lately.'

'There're still plenty of bushrangers interested in preying on the gold escorts, but I have reason to believe there might be someone new taking an interest, in both gold and diamonds. That's why I want to take them to all the diggings myself this time. From here we'll move on to Wangat and Gully before we take a bit of a break at Dungog.'

Rufe moved over to the books waiting in readiness for him on the desk. 'Anyway, let's forget about that for now. It might never happen. I just wanted to let you know my thinking. Let's get on with our work now.'

For the next few hours they were occupied with the general business of the store. They worked methodically through what had to be done.

Frank Purdie and Hank Masters, the two escorts, arrived shortly after they finished. Following the introductions, Harry produced a bottle of rum and they all sat around the table, relaxing with a drink.

'Do you want to get on today, Boss?' Frank asked Rufe. 'We could get a few miles up before dark.'

Rufe pursed his lips, thinking. They could indeed make several miles before dark. But he thought of Irene's warm bed and soft lips, which had been able to push thoughts of Kitty from his mind, at least for a while.

'No,' he said, 'I think we'll stay here tonight. I'll arrange a room for you. We'll make an early start in the morning.'

## CHAPTER EIGHTEEN

Over the next few weeks Kitty tried to rid her mind of thoughts of Rufe and focused instead on the baby growing inside her. A new life dependent on her for its wellbeing, a tiny creature to love and nurture and consider above all else. She took long walks daily and immersed herself in the peace and beauty that surrounded her on every side, drawing it around her like a protective cloak.

William became solicitous of her welfare and he no longer flew into rages. When the time came for them to leave for Sydney she had achieved a state of, if not happiness, at least of calmness and acceptance.

'Well now, my dear, this is most pleasing, isn't it?' William smiled appreciatively as he looked around the suite of rooms he had reserved in Adams Hotel. 'We'll be quite comfortable here.'

Kitty nodded. 'Yes, we will, and it's not far from the shops I'll need to visit to buy what we need.'

'Quite so. And when you're going out the doorman will summon a cab for you. And now my dear, I think you should rest until teatime. The trip must have tired you.'

'I could do with a short spell before I go shopping.'

'No, no, you mustn't start shopping until tomorrow. That will be soon enough. You must rest for today. You need to take care of yourself. And my son.'

Kitty was touched by his solicitude. 'Very well. I'll take your advice. Tomorrow will be soon enough to start.'

'Good.' He patted her shoulder as she sank into a chair. 'I'm going out for a while. I'll walk around to my club. If I'm not back by teatime you have your mother to keep you company.'

Kitty nodded again, amused by his stratagem to make sure she could not complain of being left alone while he spent the days at his club. But it suited them all.

The next morning Kitty and Bella visited Farmers store and made their way to the baby's department.

They were met at the entrance to the department by a dapper little man with a luxuriant moustache, and a gold watch chain draped across his waistcoat.

'Good morning, ladies, in what way may I help you?' he asked.

'I am looking for a complete baby's layette,' Kitty responded.

'Certainly.' He beamed. 'Please come this way.'

He led the way across the wide timber floorboards to a long counter, its cedar top polished to a gleaming brilliance, where he indicated two bentwood chairs placed conveniently alongside the counter.

'Please be seated and I'll have Miss Simpson attend to you.' He raised his hand to a rather prim looking woman at the other end of the counter who was engaged in unpacking tiny garments and placing them in the drawers of polished timber that lined the wall behind.

'Yes, Mr. Roberts?' she enquired, coming towards them.

'This lady, Mrs.…?' he turned to Kitty.

'Barron,' she supplied.

'Mrs. Barron wishes to see a complete baby layette. You will see that she has everything she requires.'

'Certainly, Mr. Roberts.' He moved away and she turned to her customers, the smile lighting up her face, totally banishing her stern look. 'We have some lovely things for baby. Shall we start with the basics first?'

'I think that would be best, don't you, Mother?'

Bella nodded. 'Yes, after that we can see the more interesting things.'

They spent the next few hours happily examining the vast array of baby goods available, with Miss Simpson tirelessly displaying all the different choices for them.

'It's a shame we don't know if it's going to be a boy or a girl, we don't know whether to choose pink or blue trimming,' Kitty lamented.

'Best stick to plain white,' Bella advised, 'it's safest.'

'Yes, I suppose so.'

By lunchtime they had chosen several dresses of finest lawn, half a dozen flannelette nightgowns, ribbed cotton singlets, and napkins, knitted matinee jackets, bonnets, and bootees.

Kitty picked up a shawl made from soft, lacy wool, so fine it seemed almost like cobwebs.

'It is nice to have something so fine and lovely,' Miss Simpson put the shawl with the growing pile of items. 'Now, for a change, perhaps you'd like to see a perambulator? We've just received a shipment of the very latest design from England.'

'Yes, let's do that.'

Miss Simpson came out pushing a perambulator. 'Isn't this stylish?' she asked, turning it around in circles for them to study it fully.

Kitty admired the elegant grey coachwork, the gold lines traced to follow the outline of its shape, and its high wheels with radiating spokes.

'I must say it's very handsome, but could I use it in Bulahdelah? We don't have smooth roads like here in Sydney, you know.'

'It's very well sprung, just like a carriage,' and the sales lady pointed out the sturdy leather straps as she bounced it up and down. 'I'm sure your husband would be proud to push the little one around in this.'

Kitty giggled at the picture of William pushing the elegant perambulator around the tracks of Redwoods, striving to maintain his dignity as he manoeuvred over the ruts. 'I'll take it,' she said. 'We still have to choose a christening robe, and some nursery furniture, but this is enough for today. We'll come back, probably tomorrow. If I give you our details can you arrange to have it all delivered to our home in Bulahdelah?' Kitty asked.

'Yes.'

Kitty gave the address to the sales lady, who carefully wrote it down. 'Thank you, Miss Simpson. We'll see you again soon.' Turning, she slipped her arm through her mother's with a smile. 'Come on then, we'll go and have lunch.' As they left the department, Kitty's heartfelt lighter than it had for some time.

Turning to their right as they reached the footpath, she released Bella's arm to walk in single file as they passed a group of lads clustered around a street seller with hot pies. Her attention taken by avoiding the noisy bunch, she took no notice of a man approaching in the opposite direction until he stopped, barring her way as he stared at her, his lips twisted in a smirk.

'Well, well, now. If it isn't Charlotte Morland. What a surprise. So this is where you've been hiding. Across the other side of the world. No wonder we couldn't find you.'

Kitty stopped dead, her heart hammering. Only at the Arnolds had she ever been called Charlotte, Kitty being deemed too frivolous for a governess.

The man's hand reached out to grasp her arm in a steely grip. 'But I've found you now, haven't I?'

Kitty stared, barely able to breathe, into the face of Craddock, George Arnold's manservant. Her blood turned cold as she stared into a face she had never thought to see again. How could it be? Craddock was twelve thousand miles away, back in Knightsbridge. How could he be here, here in Sydney? This must be some kind of apparition. But the hand that gripped her arm was squeezing her flesh. It was real.

Her blood went cold. William was here in Sydney. What if he came upon Craddock, what if he learned of her past? All this flashed through her mind in the seconds that she gazed spellbound at the man grasping her arm. She blinked. She must bluff her way out of this.

Haughtily she drew herself up and shook her arm, with Craddock's hand clamped firmly to it. 'Let me go, you ruffian, or I'll call the police.' Her voice dripped ice as she glared into his eyes. 'How dare you accost me in this manner? I have no idea what you are talking about. I am Mrs. William Barron, daughter-in-law of Sir Alexander Barron.' She pushed at his hand with her free hand. 'Get away from me before I have you arrested, you hooligan.'

A flash of indecision crossed the man's face and he removed his hand from Kitty's arm, but he made no move to stand aside and let her pass. His eyes narrowed as looked at her.

'So. Mrs. William Barron, are you?' Slowly he savoured the words. 'You might be now, but you were Charlotte Morland before you married, weren't you? Late of London, England.' He looked her up and down, taking in her fashionable clothes. 'Looks like you've done all right for yourself, too, by the look of you. Come up in the world since you were a governess, hey?'

Kitty's stomach turned nervous somersaults but she forced herself to appear calm. 'I have no idea what you're talking about. If you do not stand aside and let me pass, I shall call for the police.'

She tried to push past him but he barred her way and once again grasped her arm.

'I don't think you'll call the police.' His mouth twisted in a contemptuous sneer. 'You'd be too frightened of what I could tell them. About certain items that went missing, after I saw you leaving the master's study, and just before you left the house and disappeared. Oh yes, I think they'd be mighty interested in that.'

Kitty swallowed at the lump that seemed to be constricting her throat. 'You have obviously mistaken me for someone else,' she said coldly. 'Sir Alexander is a very influential man. I don't believe he'd take kindly to having his daughter-in-law falsely accused of, whatever it is, that you believe this Charlotte person has done.'

'So, part of the aristocracy now, are you? Well, I'll say this for you, you've got guts, trying to bluff your way out of this, but you don't fool me. I'd know you anywhere. However...' he looked at her speculatively, 'you might come in handy to me. So I'll let you go for now. Could be that I'll need a favour done one day, and you might be able to help me. Both me and Mr. Arnold. Yes, could be. You'd like to help him, wouldn't you? Make up to him for what you stole from him that night. Yes.' He nodded. 'Where do you live?' he suddenly barked.

Kitty recoiled. 'I have no intention of telling you where I live. Now, let me pass.'

'You won't be hard to find. You can expect a visit from me one day. I won't bother to let you know when I'm coming, I'll just turn up.' Craddock released her arm and stood aside, smiling unpleasantly. 'That'll give you something to look forward to.'

Kitty turned to Bella, who had been standing as if turned to stone behind her. 'Come, Mother,' she said imperiously. 'Let us leave this madman and go about our business.' And she swept past him, Bella trailing behind, white faced and wordless.

As Kitty held her head high and strode along the street she did not look back. The blood thundered in her ears, and she felt as if her legs must give way but she marched on until she reached the next corner, where she turned. Then she stopped and waited for Bella, who looked as if she was about to faint. Kitty took her arm without a word and led her along the footpath to where a sign announced 'Tearooms'. They went inside and Kitty found them a table for two in a corner, sat Bella down, and collapsed into the seat opposite her.

Bella slumped forward in her chair, her trembling hand pressed to her mouth, her eyes wide and staring in a face drained of blood. A low moan, scarcely louder than a sigh, came through her fingers.

Kitty leant over and gently took her hand from her face and placed it on the table in front of them, then covered it with her own and spoke softly. 'It's all right, it'll be all right, I promise you. Even if he didn't believe me, he won't be able to find us. How would he ever think of us being in Bulahdelah?' She shook Bella's hand gently. 'Come on now, Mother. Calm down. Take some deep breaths and listen to me.' Kitty breathed deeply, finding the effort of trying to soothe Bella had a calming effect on herself. 'As you always said, nobody is going to accuse one of Sir Alexander Barron's family of any wrongdoing without being certain of their facts. And it would only be Craddock's word against mine.'

If only she could be as sure of that as she was telling her mother she was. But the words penetrated Bella's consciousness and her face relaxed a little. She gave a shuddering gasp and her chest rose and fell as she started to breathe more evenly.

At that moment a waitress appeared by the table, ready to take their order. Kitty let go of Bella's hand and looked up.

'A large pot of strong tea, please, and yes, I think some sandwiches, a plate of mixed sandwiches. Is that all right with you, Mother?' When Bella nodded she continued, surprised to hear her voice sounding normal. 'Thank you, that will be all we need for now.'

When they were alone again Bella took a deep breath. 'Who was that man?' she asked.

'It was Craddock, George Arnold's manservant. He worked in the house at the same time I was there.'

'He said he saw you, that night. Did he?'

Kitty remembered her fancy that she saw the downstairs door closing as she paused by the stairs. Could Craddock have been there, or was he bluffing?

'I suppose it is possible he saw me leave the study. But that would be all. Nothing else.' She shook her head with certainty. 'No. Absolutely not.'

'But if he says that…'

'It would be his word against mine.'

'But, then, William would know…' her voice trailed off.

Kitty swallowed, imagining how he would react. She spoke sharply. 'Mother, that's enough. I'm William's wife. The mother of his child. You know William. Do you really think he would take the word of a servant above mine?'

'No, I suppose not…'

'Of course he wouldn't.'

'Perhaps not. But he wouldn't be happy. He'd make it hard for you.'

'Now you're looking at things that might never happen, and probably never will. Remember, Craddock has to find us first, and then go all the way up there. For what? What could he gain by it?'

'He said you might be able to help him.'

'Help him do what? Come on now; let's not worry about some nebulous threat that's probably without any foundation. Let's try and forget about the unpleasant incident.' Kitty had the satisfaction of seeing a tinge of colour creep back into Bella's face.

At that moment, their tea and sandwiches arrived and Kitty filled their cups. Only a slight tremor of her hand betrayed that she spoke with a certainty she wasn't feeling. She couldn't forget Craddock's vindictiveness to her when she worked in the Arnold household.

Craddock waited patiently, seemingly engrossed in the newspaper he was reading as he lounged outside the newsagent's shop where he could watch the door to the tearooms where Kitty and Bella were having lunch. She might well be useful to him in the future and he meant to find out more about her present circumstances and where she lived. She was a gutsy bitch all right, thinking she could bluff him into thinking he was mistaken in knowing her, but he'd recognised her straight away. His hand went to his cheek and he touched where she had scratched him on the night of the ball. He had good reason to remember her.

He'd seen her coming out of the study on the night the diamonds were stolen. But by the time he learned of the theft, she was well and truly gone, and unable to be found. And now George Arnold had sent him to Sydney to help his cousin Thomas develop the Australian side of the business, the same business that had been so lucrative in South Africa. His own experience in working with George would be invaluable to his cousin, who was somewhat a novice in the game.

He peered out from behind his paper as Kitty and Bella emerged from the tearooms and set off down the street, and then tucked it under his arm and followed behind at a discreet distance. He came closer as they approached a cab waiting at a kerb, then stopped and turned to gaze into a shop window.

'Adams Hotel, please,' he heard Kitty say to the driver.

He waited until they had gone before turning around and hailing a passing cab. Alighting at Adams Hotel, Craddock made his way inside. Kitty and her mother were not to be seen. He would have to take a chance and hope they were staying here. He removed his hat and approached the reception desk. He cleared his throat softly and twisted his hat in his hands, giving a small apologetic smile to the young woman standing behind it.

'Can I help you?' she asked.

'I hope you might be able to. I fear I've just missed Mrs. Barron and her mother, have I?'

'Yes, they've just gone to their rooms.'

'Oh, dear. I feel such a fool.' He made a wry face. 'The ladies have been shopping and they ordered some goods to be delivered to their home address. Like a fool, I only took this address, and I don't know where to send their parcel. I wonder if you could possibly give it to me so I don't have to let them know how stupid I am.'

She hesitated a moment. 'Well, I'm not really supposed to give out information about guests, but as it's only an address for a delivery, I suppose it couldn't do any harm.'

Craddock gave her an engaging smile. 'It would really help me. My boss won't be happy if he knows I made such a stupid mistake.'

She smiled back. 'Well, don't tell anyone I told you, will you?'

'Of course not.'

'It's Redwoods, at Bulahdelah. On the Myall River, so you'll be able to send your parcel by steamer.'

'Bulahdelah. That's up north, isn't it?'

'Yes, that's right. It's about fifty miles north of Newcastle.'

'Thank you so much.'

Once outside he rubbed his hands together with satisfaction. What a stroke of luck. In that district he would certainly be able to make use of Kitty. With gold strikes at Copeland and Gully, a safe bolthole for the gang, not too far from the diggings, would be very useful. He would lose no time in finding out her circumstances in Bulahdelah.

Kitty tried to cut short their stay by telling William that the shopping was completed, but it seemed William was enjoying himself, spending all his days at his club, and didn't want to leave early.

She knew it was no use trying to change his mind. Twice more, she and Bella visited Farmers store to complete their shopping, going both ways by cab, but they felt afraid to wander around Sydney in case they ran into Craddock again, so spent the rest of the time in the hotel.

The trip back to Bulahdelah seemed interminable. Although Kitty's back ached as the carriage jolted its way towards Stroud, she was grateful for every extra mile it put between her and Sydney. She breathed a deep sigh of relief as she finally stepped through the doorway at Redwoods, but she still feared that somehow Craddock might find her. However, as the days grew into weeks and nothing happened, her fear gradually grew less.

# CHAPTER NINETEEN

Mary looked around, startled, as Patrick Reilly fell into step beside her on her way back from the hen house to collect the eggs before breakfast. She'd noticed him amongst the other workers, with his tall frame and strong physique, and had been taken by his dark good looks, his black, curly hair, and deep blue eyes that held a twinkle. But they had never spoken before.

'You start work early,' he told her, in a voice holding a hint of Irish brogue. 'Have to collect those eggs before breakfast, I suppose.'

'That's right. My ladies are partial to a fresh boiled egg in the mornings. I'd have thought you'd be at work by now, too. Slacking off today, are we?'

'Not at all. I have to collect some things from the store for Jack, and I decided to take a detour when I saw you.'

'Oh, really now. And why would you do that?'

'Because I want to talk to you, of course. I've noticed you around the house, but I've never had a chance to talk to you alone before.'

'Why would you want to talk to me alone?'

'Because I think I'd like to get to know you, Mary Treloar, and the best way to do that is to talk, preferably alone.'

'How do you know my name?'

'I asked around.'

'Well, now you're talking to me. What do you want to talk about?'

'You.' Just the one word, spoken softly.

Startled, she stopped walking. 'Now, what's that supposed to mean? I work here, looking after the house. That's about all there is about me.'

He shook his head. 'Oh no, there's much more. What do you like, what don't you like, what do you do in your time off? I want to know everything. Particularly if you have a boyfriend. Though with your looks, I can't imagine you wouldn't.'

'Well, before breakfast is hardly time to discuss all that, is it now?'

'No. Which brings me back to what do you do in your time off?'

'Oh, I usually mend socks, or darn the sheets, interesting sort of stuff like that.'

'Then how about coming for a walk with me on Sunday instead?'

'All right then. You can call for me at two o'clock. I'll be free by then.'

'Righto.' He hesitated. 'What about the last thing, is there a boyfriend?'

'No. Now I must go, or breakfast will be late.'

'Okay, see you Sunday.'

As she turned he walked off, whistling jauntily. Mary felt a smile play about her lips as she continued on her way to the house. Life had suddenly become a lot more interesting.

When the goods from their shopping expedition arrived Kitty busied herself arranging the nursery, with Bella's help. She tried to involve William in the preparations for the baby, showing him the things she had bought, but he made it clear he was not interested; he regarded such things as entirely her province. When she wheeled the perambulator out for his inspection, he glanced at it briefly, but derided the idea that he might wish to wheel the baby around the estate.

His initial excitement at the news of the baby faded. He expected her to deliver him a son; apart from that he took no interest in the process. However, he treated her better than he had and as the baby grew and she began to show her pregnancy, he turned to her less at night. She suggested that she move into a room on her own until after the baby was born and reluctantly he agreed.

Bella was watering the roses one evening when Jack Morgan appeared by her side, taking the watering can from her hand.

'Let me do that, it's heavy for you.'

Bella laughed. 'Really Jack, anyone would think I'm a frail old lady.'

He looked at her with admiration in his eyes. 'Far from it, Bella. You're an incredibly attractive woman, in the prime of her life.'

Bella felt her cheeks warm. 'Thank you for the compliment, but I think you must be looking through rose coloured glasses.'

'Let's finish watering these roses, and then I'd like you to take a stroll with me, if you will.'

Something in his voice made a little tingle of excitement run through her. 'I'd be happy to, it's such a warm evening, and it is very pleasant outside.'

Jack slipped her arm through his when they finished watering, and led her down towards the river, onto a path winding in amongst the trees. It opened into a small clearing where a timber seat was set under a melaleuca tree. He led her towards it.

'It might be a bit hard, but would you like to sit for a while?' Jack asked.

'Yes, let's do that. It's a very peaceful spot. I didn't know it was here, tucked away like it is.'

'I brought you here because I didn't want us to be disturbed.'

Jack turned to her and took her hands in his. 'You must realise by now how I feel about you.' He lifted her hand and pressed it to his lips. 'You're the most perfect woman I've ever known.'

'You'll make me puff up with vanity if you say things like that to me.'

'I mean it, Bella. I love you.' His eyes searched her face. 'Can I dare hope you could feel something for me?'

'Yes, Jack. Oh yes.' She gave a tremulous little laugh. 'I feel the same about you.'

He pulled her to him and kissed her on the lips, gently at first then more urgently, and Bella responded to his passion.

When he finally let her go she leant back, her face alive with happiness. 'You've got me all in a tizzy, Jack. My heart's racing like a sixteen year-olds. I never thought to experience such feelings again, or that coming to Australia would lead me to find love again. I thought that was all finished in my life.'

'It's just starting.' He took her hand in his again, his eyes intent on her face. 'Will you marry me?' he asked.

'Yes, I will. I can think of nothing better, but it can't be for a little while yet.'

He frowned. 'Why not? I don't want to waste a minute of the time we have left. I want you to be my wife as soon as possible.'

'I can't leave Kitty until after the baby is born. She needs me. I can't leave her to William's mercy while she's so vulnerable.'

Jack narrowed his eyes. 'Is he cruel to her?'

'He can be, used to be. Although, since he's known about the baby he's changed. Perhaps, when they have the baby, he'll be all right.' She sighed. 'But I must be sure before I can leave her here with him.'

'She could come away with us. I'd look after her as well as you. We could go somewhere right away from here.'

Bella's hands fluttered and she swallowed as she shook her head. 'Thank you for that offer. I want to be your wife more than anything, but I must stay here for now. She wouldn't leave him before the baby is born. He's been better since he knew she was with child, but...I hope you understand.'

Jack took her in his arms. 'Whatever you say. It'll be agony, wanting you as much as I do, but we'll wait.'

They kissed lingeringly, then Bella drew back. 'We must keep it quiet for the time, my darling. William won't take it well, I fear. I'll tell Kitty, but that's all.'

A frown crinkled his forehead. 'And how will she feel about us?'

'She'll be delighted. You need have no fear on that account.'

His face cleared. 'Very well, my love. Hard though it'll be, I'll wait.'

Kitty fanned her face with a handkerchief as she leant on the verandah rail and scanned the leaden sky. Summer was drawing to a close. The promise of rain tantalised her, it was six weeks since the last downpour. The atmosphere was heavy; heat and humidity hung in the air like a wet sheet. She turned to look back at the top of the mountain. There had been a slow build-up of clouds over the last few days. The first, high white and streaky, had given way to round, rolling masses spilling over the mountain and billowing down above the tree tops, growing darker day by day. Now she heard the distant rumble of thunder and caught a sudden flash of lightning above the timbered slope. Looking down towards the river, Kitty observed everything was still and silent, even the birds were nowhere to be seen or heard. The surface of the water quivered as she watched, stirred by the faintest of breezes, then reverted to its brooding stillness.

Kitty dabbed her face with the handkerchief, then went down the steps from the verandah and walked along the path towards the water, hoping for a breath of cool air. Another rumble of thunder sounded, louder than before, and another flash of lightning came, closer now. Then all was quiet again. Reaching the riverbank, she sat on a tree stump and gazed across the water. Usually sunlight played on the surface and dappled the ground below the trees, while birds swooped about in their incessant search for food, but today all was motionless. The only sign of life was a pelican perched unmoving atop a stack of cedar aboard the punt. It seemed as if every living thing waited for relief from the oppressive heat.

Then, suddenly, a tiny drop of water broke the still surface, and then another and another. Kitty spread her hands out in front of her and felt a gentle touch of moisture on her palms. Was it really raining? She looked around her and saw a faint misty rain filling the air. Jumping up, she hurried back up the path, cautious optimism lending lightness to her steps. By the time she reached the house the faint mistiness had turned to rain, gentle but steady, and Kitty felt a gentle sigh in the air that hinted at a cooling breeze.

The rain continued for the rest of the day. By night time it increased its tempo, falling heavily now, and rivulets ran down the sloping track on the far side of the garden and flowed down the drain alongside it.

The next morning, Kitty sat on the window seat, looking out at the steady, drumming rain. How the garden would love it. She imagined the plants lifting their heads to catch the precious water as it fell from the sky. Bella would be happy, she loved the garden so. Her mind drifted languidly, picturing the new life ahead for Bella as Jack's wife. She hoped they would live nearby. William would be angry. Would he allow Jack to remain as manager? She doubted it.

Her attention returned to the present with a jolt as a strong gust of wind blew a spray of rain heavily against the window at the same moment as a loud peal of thunder sounded overhead. The next moment, a tree on the far side of the garden exploded as a flash of lightning speared into its leafy centre. Kitty's heart jumped and she cried out. She jumped up and ran to the front door. As she opened it a fierce gust of cold wind snatched the door from her grasp and slammed it back against the wall. Desperately she pulled at it as the wind howled past her down the hallway, blowing a vase of flowers from the hall table and smashing it on the floor. Finally, she managed to wriggle in behind the door and, pushing with all her strength, slowly forced it closed. She panted from fear as well as the exertion of pushing the heavy door against the force of the wind.

Leaning her back against the door, Kitty surveyed the damage in the hall. As well as smashing the vase and sending the flowers scattering, with a pool of water spreading over the floor, the force of the wind had blown rain inside along with leaves and twigs, which now littered the wet floor.

A sob rose in her throat as thunder sounded overhead again. What if lightning struck the house? Would it be blown apart like the tree? And could the house withstand the fierce winds?

The door at the bottom of the hall opened. Bella and Mary hurried in.

'Oh, Kitty, are you all right?' Bella rushed to her daughter. 'What happened? How did all that water come in? And who knocked the vase over?'

Kitty took a deep breath to steady herself. 'I opened the door after the lightning struck the tree and the wind was so strong...'

'Lightning struck a tree?' Bella reached for the door handle. 'Let me see.'

Mary grabbed her arm. 'Oh, no, Mrs. M, don't you open that door. Not in a storm like this, the wind's too strong. We can see through the window.' She led the way to the window where Kitty had been sitting.

The scene outside had changed amazingly. The rain bucketed down; the ground was now a sodden mass. On the other side of the garden the drain was a furious torrent as it raced down to the river below.

Bella's hand flew to her mouth. 'Oh my God.' She turned to Mary. 'Does this happen often?'

Mary nodded. 'Yes, we often have storms. It's nothing to worry about. It'll pass over.'

'I hope you're right. It seems very violent.'

'Don't worry. Why don't you and Mrs. B go down to your sitting room and draw the curtains to shut it out. I'll just clean up this mess here.'

A loud knock sounded on the back door, and Mary hurried to open it. Jack stood outside under the sheltering verandah, rain dripping from the brim of his hat and trickling down his coat. The storm raged behind him.

'Jack. Whatever are you doing out in this rain? Come on in.'

'Thanks.' He removed his hat and coat and shook them before stepping inside. 'I've just come to see if you're all okay.'

Mary closed the door behind him, took his wet garments, and hung them on pegs inside the door. 'Yes, we're okay. The ladies had a bit of a fright what with the lightning and all.'

'I thought that might be the case. They're not used to our wild weather.'

Bella appeared in the hall. 'Jack. I thought I heard your voice. Come into the sitting room.'

He shook his head. 'I've just come to see if everything's all right here. Seems as if it is, so I won't stay.'

She put her hand on his arm. He covered it with his own as their eyes met.

'You must at least stay for a cup of tea after braving this weather. There's only Kitty and me here, and it's time for our morning tea.'

Jack looked unsure and stepped back. 'I don't know. I wouldn't want to cause trouble.'

Bella tilted her head. 'Listen to that rain. You can't go out again yet. Besides, it's coming in cool now, and you could light a fire for us.'

'Well, if you put it that way, how can I refuse?'

He followed her into the sitting room, where Kitty stood by the window, watching the lightning flash across the sky. She shivered and turned as they entered.

'Hello, Jack. What wild weather. The lightning is so frightening, after seeing what it did to that tree. And all that water pouring down the hill – I hope it doesn't cause any damage.'

'It depends how long it lasts.'

'Is it likely to last long?'

He shrugged. 'It's hard to say. After a dry spell like we've had it could go on for a day or so, maybe even more.'

'With all that water going into the river, could it overflow?'

'It's been known to break its banks. It's not just this water, but what enters the river upstream. But you don't have to worry; you're well above the flood level.'

'But what about that terrible wind? Can the house stand up to that?' Bella asked.

'Easily. This house is solid. I should know; I helped to rebuild it.'

'Are you sure?'

'Quite sure. You'll be safe here. Now let's see about this fire.' As he busied himself with lighting the fire, Bella pulled the curtains to shut out the storm.

'I wonder where William is,' Kitty said as she pulled chairs up to the round table in the middle of the room and seated herself. 'The men won't be working in this weather. I wonder where he can have gone?'

'I suppose he must have gone into Bulahdelah,' Bella answered as she sat down alongside her.

At that moment Mary entered with the tea tray and placed it on the table. 'Let me know if you need anything more, Mrs. M,' she said as she set out the teapot, cups, saucers, plates and biscuits, ready for Bella to serve.

'Thank you, Mary. I'm sure this will be all we need.' She turned and spoke to Jack as Mary left the room. 'Come on, Jack, that fire has caught now. Come and have some tea.'

Jack seated himself opposite her and Bella poured tea.

'I noticed we have a good pile of cedar on the punt ready to go, so I suppose the men have been working hard and won't mind a day or so off. What do they do with themselves when they can't work?' Kitty asked.

'Most of them catch up on jobs around the house, the married ones, that is. The single blokes usually go to the pub, play cards, darts, whatever.'

'There's not a lot for young people to do here, is there? Do the younger men usually stay, or is there a big turnover in cutters?'

'Oh, they come and go. Young Billy Ryan left just before you went to Sydney, but not long after we had another man, Patrick Reilly, come in looking for work, so we put him on. He's not really a cutter but he's young and strong and he's willing to learn. He's coming along quite well.'

At that moment the door opened and William strode into the room. At the sight of the three people at the table he stopped abruptly, his face flushing and his jaw tightening.

'Well, what have we here? A tea party?' His voice was hostile. 'So this is what you get up to when I'm not at home.'

Kitty put her cup down carefully in its saucer. 'We're having morning tea, William. Won't you join us?'

'What's Morgan doing here?' he asked.

Jack put his hands down flat on the table on either side of his cup and plate and spoke calmly. 'I came to see if everything was all right, because of the storm, and Mrs. Morland kindly invited me to have a cup of tea before I went back.'

William glowered. 'Oh, did she now? Well, you can just get out. I do not entertain workers at my table.'

Bella paled and she put a hand on Jack's arm as he pushed back his chair. 'Wait, Jack.' She addressed herself to William. 'I think you overstep the mark, William. Mr. Morgan is my guest at this moment. I expect you to be civil to him.'

'Oh, do you now? This is my house, and I'll say what I like in it. I repeat – I do not fraternise with workers.' His eyes narrowed as he glared at Bella. 'I recently heard a rumour that you're becoming friendly with Morgan but I ignored it. I didn't believe you would lower yourself to consort with someone so inferior to you, but it seems as if I was wrong.' He raised his voice. 'I warn you, if I see you so much as talking to Morgan from now on, I'll fire him immediately.'

Jack shook off Bella's arm and stood up, pushing his chair back and taking a step towards William. 'I'm sorry if you feel I've overstepped the mark.' A pulse beat at his temple, but he spoke calmly. 'However, perhaps I should remind you, Mr. Barron, that you'd find it difficult to run this place and oversee the men without me.' His expression was grim. 'You need me more than I need you.'

William's face distorted with rage. 'How dare you speak to me like that? You colonials are all the same. You have no respect for your masters. Get out. Get out of here this minute, or it will be the worse for you – for all of you.' His face was brick red, his eyes bulged, and his lips were flecked with spittle.

Jack took a step towards him. 'Look here, Barron…'

Bella cut him off. 'Jack, I'm sorry, please go. Please leave now. I'll see you later.' Jack threw her an imploring look. 'Please, Jack, for all our sakes.'

Without another word he strode past William, throwing him a disdainful look as he passed.

When the door had closed behind him, William turned his fury on the two women. 'How dare you invite riff-raff into my home behind my back?'

Kitty trembled with rage. 'Jack Morgan is a decent man. He came here to make sure we were all right. There was no harm in offering him a cup of tea.'

'Shut your mouth. You connived with your mother to get this man into my house. I'll deal with you later. And as for you, madam,' he directed his spleen at Bella, 'is this the way you repay me for all I have done for you? I brought you here to live in my home out of the goodness of my heart and this is what you do in return? Bring scum in here behind my back?' He narrowed his eyes. 'Don't think that you are going to get away with this. Or you either, Kitty. You have to be punished. Both of you.' His mouth twisted. 'Oh yes, you'll be punished.' He turned to the door. 'I'm going to my study now to decide what I'll do. Don't disturb me.' He went out, slamming the door behind him.

# CHAPTER TWENTY

The room was silent except for the drumming of rain on the roof.

When Kitty finally spoke, her words were weary. 'So, it all starts again. Once more we're to be browbeaten and subdued to his wishes.'

Bella answered with a sob in her voice. 'It's all my fault. I should never have asked Jack to stay.' She buried her head in her hands.

Kitty shook her head. 'No, Mother, if it hadn't been today, it would have happened again sooner or later. Don't blame yourself. We must get away from him somehow.' She rose from the table and crossed to the window. Drawing the curtains aside, she was unable to hold back a scream at what she saw, and pressed a hand to her mouth.

The rain was falling in torrents and brown, seething water rushed angrily past the verandah, ripping shrubs and plants from the ground and spinning them away on its surface. Only the larger trees withstood its fury as it washed away everything in its path in its headlong charge to join the river.

The sound of her scream galvanised Bella into action. Jumping up, she tipped her chair over backwards in her haste. 'Whatever is it?' She gasped, rushing to Kitty's side. She let out a scream of her own as she saw the scene of destruction before her. 'We'll be washed away. The house will be washed down into the river.'

Kitty bit her lip as she considered the sight before them, forcing herself not to panic. The water was covering the bottom step to the verandah but had not reached the verandah itself. Was it rushing underneath the house? She clutched Bella's arm.

'I'm going to look out the back.' She turned and hurried from the room to the back door and opened it, peering out into the murky atmosphere. Water rushed down from the mountain and overflowed the deep drain at the side of the garden, spreading out over the grass, over the garden. Brown water flowed wherever she looked, causing chaos at the side of the house, but the drains at the back were coping with it. At the moment the house was safe.

What was happening down at the river? Would it be able to cope with this amount of water flowing into it? Kitty closed the door and quickly retraced her steps, passing the sitting room, where Bella still stood looking out, and went to the front window. From here she could see down to the river. It had risen but still remained contained within its banks.

Returning to the sitting room she saw that Bella still seemed dazed, staring from the window. She crossed the room and put her arm around her shoulders, giving her a gentle squeeze.

'It's all right, Mother,' she said quietly. 'We're safe. The water is bypassing the house.'

Bella turned away from the view outside, fingering the beads around her throat. 'Well, that's a mercy. But, Kitty...' she paused, and her eyes filled with tears, 'what are we going to do? About William, I mean.'

Kitty felt another rush of anger at William. She strode over to the fire and poked it viciously with the poker.

'I don't know. I have to think, make a plan, but we have to get away from him.'

'We can't do anything in this storm.'

'No, we must wait until it clears. But William can't do much, either. I it gives us time to plan what to do for the best.'

William paced around his study. Really, Kitty had gone too far this time. She knew how he felt about encouraging the workers to familiarity. To have one of them at his table was unforgivable. His fists curled. At this moment, he felt he could kill her. He would like to wrap his hands around her throat and squeeze it until she went limp in his hands and he could toss her aside like a piece of rag. Just as he had killed Rupert's puppy when his two brothers made him look a fool in front of his parents by revealing his gambling habits. But he couldn't do that to Kitty, the law did not allow it.

Picking up a paperweight from his desk he hurled it across the room. The crash as it landed made him feel a little better. He must devise a severe punishment this time, something that would really hurt her, something that would make her realise she must obey him. He had thought often of sending her mother away, making her live down in Sydney where she wouldn't be around him all the time. Her presence annoyed him. Without her, he could more easily bend Kitty to his will. He was sure Bella encouraged her daughter to disobey him. Yes, this time he would send her away, but, to make the punishment complete, he would not provide her with any support. She could starve for all he cared.

He turned his mind to his other worry. The cards had not run in his favour lately, and he had lost large sums of money. Thank God he had a load of cedar ready to sell. He must make sure Morgan sent the timber immediately. He must take more care in future – if Kitty should ever learn of his losses she would despise him, just as his mother had done.

He picked up the brandy decanter and poured himself a large measure, tossing it down before refilling it and sitting in his chair.

The rain continued unabated, and by lunch time the river had risen alarmingly. Sticks and debris floated on its surface, bobbing and twisting as they were caught in the strong currents as the river churned its way down to the sea. The punt with its load of timber bucked and dipped with the movement of the water, but remained securely at its mooring.

William didn't appear for lunch, he'd not left his study since he stormed off after ordering Jack from the house.

By midafternoon the river had broken its banks and the water started to rise up the hill towards the house. Kitty sat with Bella on the window seat, watching and waiting, hoping Jack was right when he said they were above the flood level. There was no letup in the rain.

Kitty gnawed at her lip. 'I hope the rain stops soon.'

'I hope so too, and the wind is still strong. Look how fast the clouds are moving.'

'There's nothing we can do. We just have to wait.'

Kitty stood up, stretching her arms above her head, and then shivered. 'It's becoming colder, shall we go back in by the fire?'

The fire had burned down to coals, but the sitting room was warm and cosy. Mary came in with more wood, put it in the wood box, and added a log to the fire. 'This'll keep it going,' she said cheerfully. 'Do you want me to light a fire in the dining room before dinner?'

'Leave it until closer to dinner time, I think,' Bella said. 'Have you seen Mr. Barron leave his study?'

Mary shook her head. 'No. He didn't have any lunch, so I expect he'll be ready for his dinner. Same time as usual? Or do you think he'll want it earlier?'

'I'll let you know if it's to be earlier, but I think it'll be as usual.'

Mary nodded and went to draw the curtains. 'The rain's stopped but, goodness, look at those black clouds,' she exclaimed.

As she spoke thunder rumbled overhead and a flash of lightning lit the sky. Wind buffeted the house, making it shudder. Kitty ran back to the front window and knelt on the window seat, looking down to the river. The wind was lashing it, whipping it up, and the surface seemed to boil, carrying branches and other wreckage swiftly along with it. As she watched, a dead animal, she thought it was a goat, floated by and then disappeared as the strong current sucked it under. The punt was gyrating at the end of its chain, tossing and pitching, its load still securely in place.

Suddenly the study door crashed open and William charged into the hall. 'My timber,' he shouted, waving his arms wildly. 'My cedar.'

He lurched towards Kitty and stumbled, almost falling. 'My cedar, it'll be lost. All my lovely cedar. All that money.'

Again he stumbled and as Kitty went to his side she smelled brandy. He had been drinking, and heavily. His clothes were in disarray, his coat undone and his shirt hanging out. His flushed face was agitated, and his hair stuck out in every direction.

'My cedar,' he shouted again. 'I have to save my cedar.' He staggered to the door.

'No, William,' Kitty yelled frantically. 'You can't go out there. It's dangerous in this storm. The timber's safe. The punt's tied up.'

He ignored her and reached for the doorknob. Kitty tried to push his hand away, but he shoved her violently and she fell back against the wall. Again he grabbed the knob and wrenched the door open, swaying from the force of the wind. The wind outside pushed William off balance. He straightened up and put out his hand and clutched a verandah post, and stood there, steadying himself.

At that moment Bella and Mary came rushing up the hall.

'No, William,' Kitty shouted. 'You can't go out in this. It's too dangerous.' She turned to Mary. 'Go and find some of the men, any of them. We have to stop him.'

Mary ran back through the house.

William walked down the steps one at a time and started to splash through the water, heading for the river. The shock of the water around his legs seemed to steady him somewhat, and he moved quickly. The wind howled around him.

Kitty followed him, panting a little as she caught up to him, wind tearing at her skirts, and her shoes deep in the water. 'Come back.' She grabbed his arm and shook it. 'Come back. You can't do anything. The punt is safe, it's tied up.'

He shook her hand off. 'I have to save the cedar. It's all I've got. It's red gold. I mustn't lose it, I need the money.'

'You don't know what you're talking about. There's plenty more cedar, and you have plenty of money.'

'No, no. You don't know. You don't know anything.' He slipped and almost lost his balance, but saved himself and continued.

They were almost at the river now and the wind kept up its banshee howl. Kitty looked around to see if help was coming. Bella was struggling through the water behind them, but there was no sign of anyone else. The rain started again.

William drew level with the punt and grabbed hold of the chain. He tugged with all his might, trying to pull the punt closer to him, but it stayed put. He shook the chain hard, up and down. At that moment a large wave surged down the river and hit the punt. It tilted, and then turned slowly over on its side. The saturated logs broke their ropes and tumbled off, down into the water.

'My cedar. My cedar,' William screamed. He plunged forward through the water.

'Stop. Stop. You'll drown yourself.' Kitty grabbed at his coat, but he pushed further ahead. Bella joined her and they both held on to his coat, but he put his arms back and it fell off him. All the time he was moving steadily forward. Kitty dropped the coat and tried to catch up to him.

Bella screamed at her and grabbed her arm. 'No. Don't go any further.'

At that moment William lost his footing, and shrieked as he disappeared below the water, his arms thrashing.

Kitty screamed. Then she was pushed back as Jack raced into the water beside her.

He dived down where William had disappeared. As he came up, gasping for air, another man appeared and dived into the water alongside him.

Bella hung on to Kitty and Mary suddenly joined them, taking Kitty's other arm. They stood together watching, Kitty shivering.

The two men dived again and again, taking a different direction each time. Finally, they came slowly back to the women, both breathing heavily.

Jack shook his head. 'It's no use. We can't find him.' He put out his hand and touched Kitty on the shoulder. 'I'm sorry.'

'We can't do anything more, missus,' the other man said, wiping his arm wearily across his eyes. 'He's gone.'

'Gone?' Kitty shook her head and stared at him blankly, unable to believe what had happened. From the moment William had stepped outside the door she had acted on instinct, aware only of the danger of going to the flooded river, intent simply on stopping him. And now…surely he couldn't survive in that turbulent water. Could he swim? She didn't know. 'But we can't just go and leave him. He'll need help to get out.'

Bella put her arms around her. 'Kitty, no one can help him. He's been washed away. He's gone.' Dropping her arms she took Kitty firmly by the elbow. 'Come on now, we must go back to the house. You need to get out of those wet clothes. We all do,' she said firmly.

Obediently Kitty turned and started to walk, dazed. It had all happened so quickly.

With Bella and Mary on each side of her and the two men following, they splashed through the water and trudged back up the hill. Bella hurried Kitty up the steps and into the sitting room, and stood her in front of the fire that still burned brightly, and started to remove her sodden clothes. Kitty stared into the fire, numb, trying to comprehend what had happened.

Mary came into the room with a bundle of towels and dry clothes. 'Here, Mrs. M, you let me do that. You get out of those wet clothes and rub yourself down.'

'But you're still wet yourself,' Bella protested.

'Don't worry about me. Dry yourself off and get into these dry things.' She pushed Bella gently aside and took over removing Kitty's clothes. As she stepped out of the last of them Kitty took the towel from Mary.

'Thank you, Mary,' she said, her voice little more than a whisper. 'I can manage now. You go and take off those wet things.'

'Are you sure you can manage?'

'Positive. Go on.' She gave her a little push, and commenced to rub herself all over. When she was dry she put on the dry clothes and stood warming herself.

Bella finished dressing and pushed Kitty gently into one of the two chairs by the fire. They both sat silently staring into the flames.

After a few moments Bella leant across and covered one of Kitty's hands with her own. 'You feel warmer now. Are you feeling all right?'

Kitty nodded. 'I'm just stunned. I can't seem to take it in. I can't believe he won't come marching in that door. Furious because we all left him.'

Bella shook her head. 'It would take a miracle for that to happen. I think you must face it, Kitty; he couldn't survive in that flood. If Jack and that other man couldn't find him, he's been washed away.'

Kitty tried to pull herself together, to concentrate. 'Perhaps he came up further down, while we were all watching the place where he disappeared, and managed to struggle to the bank.'

'That's a very small chance, Kitty.'

Kitty bit her lip. 'I know I wanted to get away from him…for both of us to get away. But I would never have wished this on him. Not for him to drown.'

Bella drew a deep breath. 'I can't understand why he went down to the river in that storm. Whatever made him do it?'

Kitty frowned as she remembered how he had come rushing out of his study. 'He'd been drinking,' she said slowly, 'and he seemed almost out of his mind, he was raving about saving the timber, the cedar. Red gold, he called it. He said he needed the money.'

Bella lifted her hand to the beads at her throat and she twisted them slowly. 'But he has plenty of money, hasn't he?'

'Of course.' Kitty hesitated and frowned again, looking across at Bella. 'He must have.' She pulled her mind away from the events of the day to think back to the last payments she had entered into the ledger. 'The cedar has been bringing good prices.'

'Then what can he have meant?'

Kitty shook her head. 'I have no idea.'

The door opened and Mary came into the room carrying two steaming cups. 'Here, I've brought some hot drinks for you; they'll help to warm you up. And Jack told me to let you know he's organised the men to search the river banks downstream.'

Kitty took the hot drink gratefully, and as she sipped it, she felt the baby move, and wondered if her baby would be born without ever knowing its father.

The three women sat together until the men returned from their search, weary and dispirited, to report there had been no sign of William.

When Kitty finally went to bed, exhausted, she tossed and turned for most of the night, but fell into a troubled sleep two or three hours before dawn.

## CHAPTER TWENTY ONE

As Kitty woke the next morning, the previous day's events rushed back into her mind. She rose from her bed and put on a wrapper, then went out on to the verandah and leant against the rail.

The morning was fine and clear. The rain had stopped, the early morning sun shone over the watery world and a few white clouds hung like flossy cotton in a blue sky. She looked down towards the river. The water still reached up the hill towards the house and, on the other side of the river, it had spilled over and stretched away in a great sheet. The river itself still rushed along, fed by the waters upstream, but on both sides it laid flat now, the turbulence of last night eased, looking more like a lake than a river. The smooth surface reflected the sky above. Everything was still and silent. As Kitty looked out she saw two birds circling high above the water. Large birds, eagles, searching for vulnerable victims forced from the shelter of their homes by the flood.

Unwilling to face conversation at the moment, she sat on one of the seagrass chairs dotted along the verandah and stared out over the scene before her.

All at once she heard a bird calling, and first one, then another, flew out from the trees, inspecting their changed habitat from a safe perch. A magpie called to its mate, not its usual melodious warble but more of a plaintive quaver. Then the swallows came, darting and swooping.

Raindrops clung to a spider's web that stretched between the slats of the balustrade beside Kitty's chair and, still intact after the storm, sparkled in the sunlight.

Slowly Kitty forced her unwilling mind back to her situation. Probably the men were out even now searching again in the light of day, but she acknowledged she must accept the fact that William had perished in the wild waters of the normally placid river. What difference would it make to her life now? A widow with a child on the way. And what would become of Redwoods?

She placed her hand on her stomach; in there was a new life, a life that must be provided for. That she must provide for.

Redwoods was this child's heritage and she must make sure it was kept safe for him, or her. William had been sure the child would be a boy, but would it?

Perhaps it would be a girl. Her lips curved at the thought. A little girl to cosset and love. And she would never have to endure William's tyranny. Kitty bit her lip as the thought sprang to her mind, and she looked around guiltily, as if anyone nearby would be able to read her thoughts. She took a deep breath. Probably it was wrong of her, but, being honest, she could feel no grief at William's loss. She would not have wished it on him, she would have saved him if she could, but now he was gone she could feel only relief. She would bring up their child as she wished. She would provide for it, her – and Redwoods.

Yes, she knew enough about the business side of timber cutting, and she had Jack to manage the men. She would take over and run it efficiently. As a widow with her own business she would be in charge of her own destiny. Never again would a man force his will on her. Her heart beat a little faster at the realisation, and, rising, she went inside to wash and dress.

When Kitty entered the sitting room, it was to find Bella and Mary sitting together, drinking tea and talking. Mary rose hurriedly as she came in, but Kitty lifted her hand to stop her. 'No, don't get up, Mary. Stay where you are and drink your tea. You're pretty much part of the family now and seeing that William's not here, we no longer have to bother with the formalities.'

Both women looked surprised, but Mary sat down again as Kitty crossed the room to pour herself a cup of tea from the pot keeping warm under its woollen tea cosy on a table by the window.

Bella spoke first as Kitty seated herself next to them. 'How did you sleep, Kitty?'

Kitty shrugged. 'Not too well, I'm afraid. Have the men gone out looking again this morning?'

'Yes, they're out there now.'

'They told me they won't come back until they find something,' Mary added.

Kitty nodded, sipping her tea. 'I realise it's extremely unlikely that William has survived. We must face that fact, and decide what must be done now. If he has perished, there'll be formalities to be taken care of, people to be advised and arrangements to be made.'

'Jack will be able to help with all that,' Bella said. 'You must think of yourself and the baby now.'

'Yes, she's my first concern now.'

'She?' Bella put down her cup. 'Have you decided it's a girl?'

'Yes.' Kitty smiled. 'Perhaps it's just fancy, but this morning when I was sitting, just thinking, I had this strong premonition that my child is a girl. How I hope it is.' She rested her hand on her stomach again and rubbed it gently. 'This little one is my main concern in life now; she must grow up in a happy environment, secure in the knowledge that she's loved. As I did.' She stretched across and patted Bella's hand. 'I was fortunate to have two loving parents, but this one might well have to manage with just one.'

'Maybe better one, with love, than two, when the second one's uncaring,' Mary said as she collected the cups and left the room.

Jack came to the house later in the morning. Mary showed him into the sitting room where Kitty and Bella waited. They looked at him expectantly.

'I'm sorry to have to tell you that we've found Mr. Barron's body. He'd been washed downstream quite some distance with the force of the water. We found his body wedged against the bank by some tree roots. We've brought him back, and Mary and Mrs. Porter are attending to him now.'

Kitty bit her lip. So he really was gone. Sadness and relief warred inside her. She took a deep breath, and when she spoke it was calmly. 'I see. Thank you, Jack, and please thank the men for me. I can't tell you how much I appreciate what you've all done. And now I must go and help.' She made to rise from her chair, but Jack shook his head.

'No, don't you worry about it. Mrs. Porter's used to doing this; she and Mary will take care of everything. Mary's getting some dry clothes for him now. Don't you worry about it,' he repeated concern on his face. 'You just look after yourself. If you'd like me to, I'll contact the authorities for you.'

'That would be a big relief to me, Jack.'

'Right-o.' He hesitated. 'I don't want to presume, Mrs. Barron, but perhaps Mrs. Morland and I could arrange the funeral for you, seeing as how you have no male relatives to look after it for you.'

'Thank you again.' She smiled briefly. 'And seeing as how we are soon to be related, I think you should start calling me Kitty.'

Relief showed on Jack's face. 'Your mother's told you?'

'Yes. And I want you to know I'm very happy for you both.'

His face lightened and he smiled, his eyes crinkling at the corners. 'Thank you. I'll look after her well, you know.'

'I'm sure you will, and that you'll be happy together. And I see no reason, now, to put off the wedding. When all this is over, we can talk about it. And I need to talk to you about the business, too.'

'I'll help in any way I can.'

'I'll rely on you to continue managing the work, but we'll talk later. For now, we must arrange to pay our respects to William.'

The funeral took place two days later. A small group of mourners gathered at the graveside, the workers from the estate and a few locals, mostly unknown to Kitty. Anne and George sent word they were unable to attend as Anne was expecting their first child within weeks. The mourners then returned to Redwoods for refreshments. Kitty could not exhibit a grief she did not feel; she received the formal condolences with dignity and thanked those who attended.

She went to her room and undressed as soon as everyone left, putting on her comfortable wrapper. The days were cooler now and Mary had lit a fire for her. It burned cheerily in the grate and Kitty sat in front of it in the armchair. Staring into the flames, she turned her mind to the future. As a mark of respect to William, she had ordered no work to be done on the estate until after the funeral.

Tomorrow, work would begin on salvaging the timber from the bottom of the river. Jack would see to that, and it would be sent away for sale. She would take over the reins of running the business, with Jack remaining as her manager, while she waited for the birth of her baby. It seemed that her life stretched before her, calm and uneventful, into the future.

Before she went to bed Kitty went to the sitting room, where she found Bella sitting over a cup of tea.

'I thought you'd be asleep by now,' Bella said in surprise.

'There's something I want to talk to you about first. When you and Jack are married, I hope you won't want to move away from here, I'd miss you so much. Of course, I'd understand if you want to manage your own home again, and you could live in the manager's house, where Jack lives now, or we could build a new house on the property. But Jack could always move in here with us, if you're both happy to stay on here.'

'I'd rather stay here, Kitty. I'm happy here and I know Jack would be, too. He's very fond of you, you know.'

Kitty put her arms around her mother. 'That's wonderful. I was dreading that he'd want you to move somewhere else. Then we'll consider it all arranged. There's no need to wait any longer for you to marry.'

'It can't be too soon after William's death.'

'No, but I think it should be within the next few weeks. Would that suit you both?'

Bella smiled. 'If you don't think that will be too soon, it will be perfect.'

The next day Kitty sat at her desk in what used to be William's study and was now her office. She finished adding up the figures, put down the pen, and closed the book in front of her. She knew exactly how much she needed to draw from the bank for the coming month's expenses. Tomorrow she would take Bella with her in the buggy and they would drive to the bank. Jack would ride with them. She needed to make herself known to the bank manager and she would make arrangements for Jack to be able to collect money on her behalf if necessary.

'Good afternoon, Mrs. Barron.' The bank manager welcomed her warmly, even though he seemed surprised to see her. 'Please take a seat.'

After offering his condolences, he spoke in a business-like manner. 'And now, how might I help you?'

'I need to draw some money from the account and make arrangements for the manager, Jack Morgan, to collect on my behalf in future, if necessary.'

He eyed her intently. 'Forgive me for asking, Mrs. Barron, but what are your plans for the future. I understand you come from England, will you be returning there?'

'No, Mr. Hyde. I'm staying at Redwoods,' Kitty told him firmly.

He raised his eyebrows. 'Indeed. And who will be running the business, may I ask?'

'Jack Morgan will stay on as manager, he will attend to the timber as he has always done, and I will manage the business myself.'

Mr. Hyde leant back in his chair, astonishment all over his face. 'My dear lady, surely you do not realise what you are saying. A lady, such as yourself, is not equipped to run a timber cutting business.'

'May I ask why not?'

'Because you would be attempting to deal with matters completely outside your experience, matters of which you could have no conception.'

'Really, Mr. Hyde, and what matters would they be?'

'Matters pertaining to the financial aspects of the business.'

'I'm already conversant with the financial aspects of the business. I've always kept the financial records for my husband. I'm fully aware of the details of the sales of the timber, the prices we receive, and the costs involved. Figures hold no mysteries for me, Mr. Hyde.'

The bank manager regarded her incredulously. 'You mean Mr. Barron involved you in his business?'

'Certainly. And as long as I have a manager to oversee the timber cutting, I can't foresee any difficulty in the business continuing exactly as it's been doing.'

He drew a deep breath and inclined his head. 'Very well, Mrs. Barron. Then let us proceed. You wish to draw some funds today?'

Kitty nodded. 'Yes, this is the amount I need.' She handed him the slip of paper with the amount written down.

Taking the paper, he nodded. 'Certainly, you have the funds for this amount.' He glanced at her keenly. 'However, are you aware that this will almost deplete the account?'

Kitty gasped, his words hitting her like a blow to the midriff. 'Surely not,' she exclaimed, 'our last cheque we received was for a substantial amount. I entered it in the ledger myself.'

He nodded again. 'Yes, that is so. However, Mr. Barron made several large withdrawals since then.'

Kitty shook her head in confusion. 'But, surely, we had a substantial balance before the last cheque? The business has been operating profitably for some time.'

'I'm afraid that everything that came in went out again.' He pushed back his chair. 'And now, if you'll come with me, I'll arrange a statement for you, so you can see the amounts, and you can withdraw your funds.' He walked around his desk and opened the door, standing back to allow her to precede him.

Kitty rose and walked out ahead of him, her mind in turmoil. Why had William made large withdrawals and what had he done with the money?

All the way home Kitty pondered the question, but no answer presented itself, so she turned her mind to her problem, what was she to do when this money was gone?

'How is the salvage of the timber coming along?' she asked Jack as she handed him the reins as they reached home. 'How long do you think it will be before it's all out of the water?'

'Now that the water's receding we should be able to finish in another two to three days. I've arranged the use of extra bullocks, which will make things easier.'

'What sort of condition is the timber in? Will it be all right for sale?'

'Yes.'

'Good.' Kitty breathed a sigh of relief. 'Will you make sure it goes as soon as possible? We're going to need the money.'

'Of course, Kitty. I'll let you know when it's ready.'

He moved off with the horses, Bella walking with him for a little way, and then they stopped to talk. Kitty felt a surge of happiness for them, seeing them with their heads close together, but as she went inside her mind returned to the business. If the timber left within the next few days she could expect payment within the month. It was going to be tight, she had only a few pounds left in the account at the bank, and she knew there were outstanding accounts to be paid. Could she manage? She set her lips. Yes, she would manage.

Kitty was sitting at her desk working on financial projections for the coming months when Mary appeared at the door.

'There're two gentlemen here to see you, Mrs. B,' she said, 'a Mr. Sampson and Mr. Trenoweth. I've put them in the drawing room.'

Kitty looked up in surprise. Callers were unusual. 'Thank you, Mary.' She rose from her chair, smoothing her hair and straightening her skirt. 'I'll come right away.'

She entered the drawing room to find two strangers awaiting her. One, a little cock sparrow of a man with eyes that looked everywhere except at her, remained seated, while the other, a tall man with a bald head and bushy beard, rose and came towards her.

'Mrs. Barron, I'm Charles Sampson, well acquainted with your late husband. Allow me to offer you my condolences. I was shocked to hear of his untimely accident.'

'Thank you, Mr. Sampson.'

He paused, clearing his throat. I'm here on a somewhat delicate matter. Both Trenoweth and I had some dealings with your late husband.'

Kitty frowned. 'Some dealings, Mr. Sampson?'

'Yes.' He fumbled in his pocket and produced a piece of paper.

Kitty frowned. 'What kind of dealings?'

Without a word he held out the paper to Kitty. When she looked at it she saw it was a note written in William's handwriting. She took it, and as she read what was written there her eyes widened, and her head spun. It was a promissory note, made out to C Sampson, for six hundred pounds. Putting out a hand to steady herself on a chair back, she took a deep breath.

'What is this for?'

'It's a debt your husband incurred while playing cards.'

Before she could reply Trenoweth stood and thrust another paper at her. 'He owes me, too. You better look at this.'

To her horror she read a similar note stating that W Barron owed to P Trenoweth the sum of three hundred and eighty pounds. Both were signed by William, there was no mistaking his signature, and both were dated within the last month.

With a great effort Kitty forced herself to keep calm. 'And is this for cards, too?' she asked.

Trenoweth nodded. 'Yes, that's right.'

'When did William play cards with you?'

'We meet regularly most days, a group of us, and your husband managed to be there most days,' Sampson replied.

'Where did you meet?'

'At the Plough Inn, of course. We have a private room there for our use.'

'He'd been having a bit of bad luck lately,' Trenoweth added.

Kitty clenched her jaw. So this was what William did when he was supposed to be working. He had deceived her, pretending to be working when all the time he spent his time gambling. No wonder he'd not wanted her to enquire into his business activities. And no wonder he hadn't wanted her to mix with the local landowners and their wives. He had been afraid she would learn of his activities. She realised now that this was why he'd withdrawn the money from the bank – it had been to feed his gambling habit.

She stared at the papers in her hand. What was she to do about them? Much as she hated the idea of paying gambling debts, if William had incurred them, they must be paid. However, there was no way she could do so just now.

'I'm afraid I can't attend to these at the moment,' she told them.

'How long do you think we'll have to wait?' Sampson asked.

'They're enforceable by law,' added Trenoweth belligerently.

Drawing herself up Kitty regarded him coolly. She would not allow herself to be intimidated. 'You need have no fear that I will not honour my husband's debts. However,' she riffled the papers in her hand, 'these come to almost a thousand pounds. I will have to make arrangements.'

'So, how long do you think these arrangements will take?'

She would have to allow a month for the timber cheque to arrive. 'Possibly a month. And now, gentlemen, if you'll excuse me, I have business to attend to.'

Walking to the front door she held it open for them.

'Good day, gentlemen. I'll see you in a month.' Her hand trembled as she shut the door behind them.

How could she possibly pay them and still have enough to keep the business running?

## CHAPTER TWENTY TWO

Kitty drummed her fingers on the desk as she wondered how she could pay William's gambling debts. There was only one thing to do, she finally decided, she would have to go down to Sydney and retrieve the diamonds. Then she could sell some and pay Sampson and Trenoweth. Having made the decision she felt better, although the prospect of a trip to Sydney filled her with foreboding. She set her jaw grimly. Rising from her chair, she made her way to the sitting room.

As expected, Bella was sitting there with her needlework. She paused in her stitching and looked up as Kitty entered. 'I heard men's voices earlier, did you have visitors?' she asked.

'Yes. I'm afraid we have a problem,' Kitty told her. She gave her the details of William's gambling activities with her visitors.

Bella dropped her sewing into her lap and listened without interruption. 'Oh, dear. So that's why he was so concerned about the cedar in the storm.'

'Of course. His words make sense now. He really was frightened he would lose the timber, and he knew he needed the money for his gambling debts.'

Bella shook her head. 'How foolish of him. I've known other men to lose their money through gambling, but I never would have suspected William of such folly.'

'It also accounts for the changes in his moods. If he had a winning day he was happy, but if he lost he was ill tempered. Yes, it explains several things. However, it's left us in an awkward situation.'

Bella's fingers flew to her beads, twisting them. 'Oh dear, do you mean that you have to pay them the money William lost? After all, it's not your debt.'

'Perhaps not, but you know how the law works, think back to when Father died. However, even if it weren't so, I'd feel bound to pay them. It's a matter of pride.' She set her lips. 'William had no right to gamble and incur such debts, but he did, and now I must bear the brunt of his weakness. We're going to stay here and take our place in the community, as we should have done from the beginning, and I won't have it thought that I wouldn't honour his debts.'

'Kitty, I know I leave the money side of things to you, because you're very capable in such matters, but you said there's little left in the bank. Will the timber payment cover the debts and leave enough to carry on?'

'Unfortunately, no.' Kitty licked her lips. 'I'll have to go to Sydney and retrieve the diamonds, then sell enough to pay them.'

The colour drained from Bella's face. 'Go to Sydney. But you can't possibly. In your condition, it would be far too much for you. Besides,' she clasped her hands together, 'that dreadful man Craddock might still be there. What if he were to see you again?'

'I've thought it all through. You'll come with me. We won't stay at Adams again; we'll go somewhere else, somewhere small and inconspicuous. Craddock might not still be in Sydney, but if he is, and we should see him, he won't recognise me. I'm still in mourning, and I've been observing the proprieties by wearing black, and while in Sydney I'll wear a heavy veil to my hat as well, so he wouldn't be able to see my face. With my thickening figure...' she patted her stomach with a tiny smile, 'and a loose dress, I'll look quite different to the slim person I was before.'

Bella looked unhappy. 'You seem to have thought it all through, and if you're definite about this foolishness, I'll ask Jack to accompany us.'

Kitty shook her head. 'No, Mother. Definitely not. He'd have to know what we were about, and it wouldn't be fair to him. It would be making him part of what was, after all, a crime.'

Bella took a deep breath. 'I suppose you're right, but perhaps we could put it off until after the baby is born. It wouldn't be so hard for you to travel then.'

'No, then I wouldn't have the extra weight to help disguise me. Besides, I want to pay them and be done with it. We'll leave within the next few days.'

Kitty opened the safety deposit box and untied the handkerchief that contained the diamonds. As they spilled into the bottom of the box they gleamed brightly, even the low light in the room could not disguise their brilliance. Unsure of how many she would need, and remembering the small amount of money she'd received in Sydney from the previous sale, she left one large, particularly brilliant, diamond, and placed the rest in the small pouch she'd brought with her, then retied the remaining one in the handkerchief and locked it in the box again.

'Have you thought about where you're going to sell them?' Bella asked.

'I think we just have to try a few different pawnshops until we find who offers the best price for one, then sell them all there. I know we won't receive what they're really worth, but we don't have much choice.'

'I think I have a better idea. Why not see if Mr. Cavanagh is in Sydney. I'm sure he would know where to take them for the best price.'

Kitty's heart leapt as she thought of Rufe. She remembered their encounter by the river, the morning before he left Redwoods, and the look of horror on his face when she told him of the baby. No, she didn't want to see Rufe again, certainly not at this time.

She shook her head. 'No, I don't want to bother him. Besides, he might well ask awkward questions. And don't forget, he knows Jan van Mayen.'

'Yes, that's true. But when he left us at Redwoods he said he would always be happy to help if we ever needed it.'

Kitty shook her head; she didn't want to talk about him. 'No, Mother.' Her voice invited no argument. 'Come along,' she took Bella's arm. 'Let's start looking.'

After trying four pawnshops with poor results Kitty was feeling tired and dispirited.

'Let's find somewhere to sit for a while and have a cup of tea,' Bella suggested.

'Yes, I could do with a break,' Kitty agreed.

After walking two blocks without finding a tearoom they turned a corner and found themselves outside Petty's Hotel.

'Oh, Petty's,' said Bella with relief. 'We can go in here. My feet are aching. I need to sit down.'

Kitty hesitated. Rufe had rooms here; she didn't want to run into him. But Bella was already mounting the steps, so she followed. Once inside, they both sank gratefully into the comfortable chairs in the lounge and Kitty raised her veil. They were the only customers, and after the waiter took their order, Kitty looked around. It was all as she remembered it. She had enjoyed staying here, but it brought back sad memories of their search for Robert, and of how helpful Rufe had been. Well, that was all in the past. How much had happened since then!

Their tea arrived and as they drank it, Kitty found herself reviewing her life since she had arrived in Australia. She had made a mistake in marrying William, of course. She had been far too hasty. If she had waited, how different her life might be. But it was no use to think of that, no use to look back – now she must think of the future. She needed to sell the diamonds, pay William's debts and return to Bulahdelah, where she would devote herself to the business and making a good life for her coming child.

Refreshed by the tea and the respite she rose from her chair. Smiling at her mother, Kitty held out her hand. 'It's time we moved along. Are you rested enough?'

'Yes, I'm fine now.'

They walked towards the door. They were halfway there when a couple entered from the street. They walked close together, the woman with her hand tucked into his arm and the man with his head bent to catch what she was saying, an attentive smile on his face.

Kitty stopped. The man was Rufe, and the woman, young and attractive with dark hair and creamy skin, was stylishly dressed.

Kitty felt the blood rush to her face and started to turn away, but at that moment Rufe looked up and saw her. He stopped, his body stiffened and his smile disappeared.

The woman stopped talking and swivelled quickly to look, first at him, and then to see what had caused his dismay. Within seconds, Rufe had regained his composure and moved towards them, his companion joining him.

'Why, Mrs. Morland, and Mrs. Barron, what a surprise. I had no idea you were in town. Allow me to introduce my friend, Miss Irene Donovan.'

Irene removed her hand from his arm and smiled as she greeted them, but the smile stopped short of her eyes, which regarded them warily.

Bella replied immediately, her voice warm. 'How do you do, Miss Donovan. And so wonderful to see you again, Mr. Cavanagh.'

Kitty's heart raced, but she controlled her emotion as she inclined her head in greeting, not trusting her voice to speak.

Rufe took up the conversation, his voice smooth. 'It's always a pleasure to see you, Mrs. Morland. And you too, of course, Mrs. Barron. And what brings you to Sydney at this time? Does Mr. Barron have business here?'

'Oh dear, you don't know?' Bella fluttered her hands in dismay.

For the first time Rufe seemed to notice Kitty's black dress. He frowned as he shook his head. 'I've just returned to Sydney, I've been up-country for some time. What's happened?' he asked sharply, looking directly at Kitty.

She bit her lower lip. 'My husband was drowned during a bad storm a short time ago.'

'Kitty, I am so sorry.' Rufe reached his hand out to her impulsively, but then let it fall back to his side. 'Please allow me to offer my condolences. Is there anything I can do for you? Are you here on a matter of urgency?'

Kitty took a deep breath, desperate to accept his offer of help, but uncertain whether she should. She was conscious also of his companion, who stood regarding her coldly. It seemed as if he had found consolation fast enough.

Bella shot a glance at Kitty and seeing her hesitation, stepped into the breach. 'Mr. Cavanagh, there is something we need help with. It is a matter of urgency,' she added, gesturing Kitty to silence as she saw her about to protest.

Rufe turned to Irene. 'Irene, I'm sorry, but would you mind terribly going upstairs without me. I'll be up shortly.'

Kitty noticed a pulse beating at Irene's throat as she replied. 'Of course not, Rufe. But try not to be too long, won't you?' She was smiling but her eyes were hard. Kitty felt them boring into her. Irene was not happy.

'I won't be longer than necessary,' he assured her.

Irene turned on her heel and walked away, her back straight and stiff.

'Now, let's sit down where we can talk comfortably.' He guided them towards a group of overstuffed armchairs. When they were seated he looked enquiringly at Kitty. 'Now, tell me what happened. How did Barron come to be drowned?'

He listened attentively as Kitty related the events of the storm, ending with the recovery of William's body the next day.

'I am sorry,' he repeated. 'But surely it was foolhardy of him to attempt to pull the punt in, it would have safely ridden out the storm, more than likely, and the timber would still be there after the storm.'

'Yes, Kitty tried to tell him, but he wouldn't listen,' Bella said. 'We tried to hold on to him and stop him going further into the water, but he pulled away from us and next thing he disappeared. He just went straight down, and that's the last we saw of him. Some of the men came and dived down into the river but they couldn't find him.' Bella shivered. 'It was horrible.'

'It was a dreadful experience, for both of you.' His gaze flicked back to Kitty. 'And how are you coping now?' he asked, his eyes full of compassion.

Kitty swallowed, his solicitude weakening her resolve to remain strong and self-reliant. Then she thought of Irene upstairs. It was obvious they were together. He had found someone else now and was treating Kitty as he would any woman recently widowed. Taking a deep breath she forced herself to sound composed.

'It was a terrible shock, of course. But, after all, I now have someone else to think of. Redwoods is my child's inheritance, and I'm doing my best to run it capably. I'm fortunate to have Jack Morgan to oversee the men for me.'

Rufe smiled slightly. 'Well, I remember you talked of wanting a business of your own when you first arrived in Sydney. It seems you now have your wish.'

'I wouldn't have had it happen this way. I won't try to pretend it was the happiest of marriages, but I never wished William any harm. However, now I have the business, I intend to make a success of it.'

'And I'm sure you will.' He frowned. 'But I can't see how you need my help. I'm sure you're managing quite well on your own. What I can't understand is what you're doing here in Sydney, at this time. Travelling can't be easy for you.'

'I wouldn't be here if it weren't urgent. We do have a problem. You see, William left gambling debts behind that we had no idea of. He owed nearly a thousand pounds. I had a visit from two of his gambling companions and they brought his promissory notes to me.'

'They're his debts. Do you want to pay them?'

Kitty lifted her chin. 'Yes. I won't have it thought that I won't honour our commitments.'

'And you don't have enough money to pay them. Is that the problem?'

'Yes. William left no money in the bank. Apparently he'd been gambling and losing heavily for some time. However, I have…' she hesitated. How far could she trust him, considering his involvement with Jan van Mayen? Well, she would let him think they were from her family. 'I have some diamonds that I can sell to cover the debt. I had to come to Sydney to obtain them.'

'Ah.' A wry smile twisted his lips. 'Which obviously Barron knew nothing about.'

'Well, no. I hadn't mentioned them to him.'

'Very wise, as it turned out. So what's the problem?'

'Well, you see,' the words tumbled out, 'I've taken them to several pawnshops and they've offered me practically nothing for them. Less than half of what I received in London.'

'To pawnshops? Kitty, that's no place to sell them. Take them to a reputable diamond merchant. Or even to a jeweller. Those places are for dubious deals. They probably think they're stolen.'

Kitty felt her cheeks burn.

Rufe looked at her curiously. 'Do you have them with you?'

Kitty nodded.

'Can I see them?'

She opened her purse and handed him the pouch. He shook the diamonds into his hand and examined them carefully, holding each one up to the light and viewing it from all angles.

He regarded her through half narrowed eyes. 'These are very fine stones. Where did you get them?'

Kitty felt a tremor run through her. 'I…I…you see,' she faltered then took a deep breath. Suddenly she had an overwhelming desire to confide in him, to tell him the whole story. 'It's a long story, and it started several years ago.'

'Kitty.' Bella reached out quickly and put a hand on her arm. 'Careful what you say.'

'Mrs. Morland, whatever Kitty tells me will go no further, I promise you. I would never do anything to harm either of you, believe me.' He replaced the diamonds in their pouch and handed them back to Kitty, who slipped it into her purse again.

'Oh, dear. Kitty, you're not going to…' Bella's voice faded away as she fingered her beads.

Kitty took a deep breath. 'Yes. Perhaps you should leave us for a while.'

Bella looked from one to the other, then rose and walked away.

'This is a long story,' Kitty said. 'Are you sure you want to hear it right now?'

'Yes. Take as long as you need.'

'Then I'll go right back to the beginning. It started back in 1875, when Mother and Robert and I lived in Hampstead with Father, before he died.'

Rufe listened intently as she told him the story. When she told him of going to work for George Arnold he sat bolt upright in his chair. 'The girl at the ball. I knew I'd seen you before, why didn't you tell me?'

'You remember?'

'Of course I remember. Why didn't you tell me?'

Kitty shook her head. 'I couldn't. You'll see why in a minute.'

As she continued Rufe listened intently, yet one part of his mind was recalling how he felt when he saw her as he walked through the door earlier. Her sudden appearance had shocked him and caused the blood to pound through his veins. Then he had noticed her obvious pregnancy and the dark smudges under her eyes, and he'd been overcome by a deep tenderness. Gone was the passion he'd felt for her, he just wanted to cradle her in his arms and soothe her gently. The same protective sensation towards her was still with him.

While she related Mrs. Arnold's false accusations she trembled, and he felt deep anger against the woman. When her words painted a vivid picture of George Arnold, flushed with wine, snoring in his chair, with the pouch of diamonds on the table beside him, he felt as if he was in the room with her, an unseen bystander. He saw her, mesmerised as the stones spilled out on to the table, picking one up and turning it around to catch the light. He felt her loathing for the man who had brought ruin to her family, and been the cause of her father's death. He saw how she fought against the impulse to pocket a handful of the glittering gems, aware they represented the difference between poverty and comfort, and how, suddenly, guiltily, she succumbed to the temptation and fled from the room. He saw her run up the stairs to her tiny room, placing a chair beneath the handle of the door to prevent intrusion, and her indecision as she wondered how to smuggle the diamonds safely out of the house.

After she revealed how she had swallowed them, the spell was broken. He became aware of the agitation dredging up the past had caused her. The stricken look on her face caused him to move alongside her, and take her hands in his own. He chafed them gently, trying to instil some warmth into the cold flesh. Her body shook and her face was ashen as she lived it all again.

'Kitty, Kitty,' he spoke urgently, 'it's all over now. You're quite safe here. No one knows. It's all in the past. You're safe now.'

Kitty's eyes focused again as she came back to the present. She heaved a deep sigh. 'I wish I could be certain of that, but I'm not so sure.' She told him of her meeting with Craddock and his threat to find her. 'For all I know, he might be still here in Sydney. I would never have taken the risk to come again if it hadn't been essential to sell the diamonds.'

Rufe realised he could at least set her mind at rest regarding the sale of the diamonds. 'One part of my business is dealing in gold and diamonds,' he told her. 'I'll buy your diamonds.'

'You don't need to do that,' Kitty protested. 'Just tell me where to go for a fair price.'

So she still had her independent streak. But at least the colour had come back into her face. 'I'll pay market price, no more, no less. Does that satisfy you?' he asked, allowing himself a flicker of a smile.

'Yes. Thank you.' He was rewarded with a look of relief on her face.

'Can I see the diamonds again please?'

She removed the pouch from her purse and handed it to him. Taking the diamonds out, he selected the two finest. 'These two are enough to cover William's debts, but I'm happy to buy them all if you want the extra money.'

She looked hesitant. 'I don't want to take advantage of your kindness.'

'I'm not being kind. I'm simply offering you market value.'

Her face brightened. 'In that case I'll sell them all. The extra money will mean I can meet all my commitments, and have some left over.'

'Good. Now if you tell me where you're staying I'll call tomorrow morning with the money.'

A smile rewarded his words. 'Thank you,' she said. 'This is such a relief to me. And now I must leave you to go up to your friend Irene. She'll be wondering what's happened to you.' Rufe realised he had completely forgotten about Irene.

## CHAPTER TWENTY THREE

Upstairs, Irene paced the floor in her room. It adjoined the sitting room that separated her room from Rufe's. He had insisted that she have her own room, although she wondered if it was because he wanted his own privacy. True, he spent part of every night in her room, but she sensed he was not yet ready for the intimacy that came from sharing a bedroom.

Pausing at the window she looked down at the busy street below, then turned to take in the luxurious appointments in the room. It had been a glorious week. Rufe was an attentive and amusing companion, and everything was going perfectly until they walked into the hotel and nearly collided with those two women.

She realised immediately that Kitty Barron was no mere acquaintance. The look on Rufe's face had been enough to tell her that here could be a real threat to the relationship she'd been working so hard to foster. He dismissed Irene as if she was of no account, even if it had been done courteously enough.

Who was this Kitty Barron that she had such an effect on him? And whose child was she carrying? One would assume it was her husband's, but was it possible it was Rufe's? Could that be the matter of urgency they needed to discuss, now that the husband was dead?

She managed to compose herself and sit calmly. Picking up a newspaper, she turned the pages, reading news items without them registering. But when the door opened, she gave Rufe a welcoming smile as he entered.

'Irene, I'm sorry.' He sounded contrite as he closed the door and came towards her with his hands outstretched. 'It was extremely ill-mannered of me to leave you up here alone for so long.' He took her hands in his. 'I hope you can forgive me.'

Irene smiled as she replied. 'Of course. I'm sure you had a good reason.'

'Mrs. Barron needed some help with a business matter that I was able to assist her with. I'm sorry it took so long.'

'The poor woman. How sad for her to lose her husband at such a time. She must be distraught.'

'Naturally.' Rufe's face was impassive.

'Did you know him too?'

'Yes.'

'I suppose you'd known them for a long time, had you? You seemed to know her well.'

'For some time, yes.' He dropped her hands. 'Now, if you'll excuse me, I must freshen up before dinner.'

Irene watched him go to his own room, her mouth set. During dinner she again brought up Kitty's name, probing gently in a seemingly innocent way, but a mask descended on Rufe's face at the mention of her name and he steered the conversation in a different direction.

She smiled, and responded automatically when he attempted to make small talk in spite of his obvious distraction.

They retired to their suite a little later, and Rufe followed her into her room. That night he made love to her with an intensity and passion that had been missing from their previous couplings. When he gasped and cried out as he shuddered to a climax, she gave a wild cry in unison with him. As he rolled away from her she remained on her back, making little sounds of pleasure. He placed his arm across her and kissed her cheek before moving slowly away from her. A few moments later he left her bed and retired to his own room, as usual. Then Irene drew up her knees and raised her pelvis from the bed, tilting it back towards her. It strained her back but she retained the position for several minutes. From now on there would be no more post-coital visits to the bathroom for her.

Kitty and Bella awaited Rufe's arrival in their small sitting room the next morning, with Bella stitching at her inevitable needlework and Kitty sitting with a book on her knee, lost in her thoughts. She knew she should be feeling happy. She had achieved what she had come to Sydney for; she would soon have the money to pay William's debts, and more. Yet she felt miserable, and she knew it was because Rufe had obviously found solace with Irene. Not that Kitty could blame him – he'd declared his love for her, but it had been too late. She didn't expect him to spend his life pining after her. Nevertheless, she could not help feeling a pang of jealousy as she remembered how attentive Rufe had been towards his young and attractive companion as they entered the hotel.

Pushing such thoughts away, Kitty turned her mind to what lay ahead. Only a few hours more and they could leave Sydney. To her relief they'd not seen Craddock. Was he still in Sydney, and what had brought him here? Kitty had pondered this question many times since their last visit to Sydney but to no avail. However, they only needed to venture out into the streets once more. When they boarded the afternoon steamer and left Sydney behind she would feel safe. The trip back would end the ordeal for her, and once back home she would be able to relax and await the birth of her baby free from anxiety.

A tap at the door brought her out of her reverie. She crossed the room and opened it, knowing it would be Rufe and looking forward to seeing him once more. She stepped back in surprise when she saw he was accompanied by Jan van Mayen.

'Good morning, Mrs. Barron,' Rufe greeted her formally. 'You remember Mr. van Mayen, I'm sure. May we come in?'

Somewhat alarmed, Kitty opened the door wide. 'Of course. Please come in and take a seat.' As she closed the door, she wondered uneasily why Rufe had brought the diamond merchant to see them. She turned around to see that Bella had risen and Jan van Mayen was raising her hand to his lips.

'Ah, Mrs. Morland, how wonderful to see you again,' he said. 'I hope you will forgive me for intruding like this. And you too, Mrs. Barron,' he continued, turning his attention to Kitty. 'I know it is unforgivable on my part, but when you hear what my friend Cavanagh and I have to say, you will understand why we wished to talk to you in the privacy of your rooms.'

Kitty had a sudden fear that it was related to her theft of the diamonds. Had Rufe betrayed her? Turning to look at him she couldn't judge by his expression.

'Perhaps we should all sit down,' Rufe now interjected. 'This could take a little while.' He turned to Bella, who had gone pale. 'Mrs. Morland, please make yourself comfortable, and don't worry. What we have to say need not alarm you or Kitty in any way. Believe me.'

Bella let out a little sigh as she sat down, her fingers seeking her beads. 'I do believe you, Mr. Cavanagh, but…'

Kitty interrupted her. 'But what is it all about?'

Rufe took her firmly by the arm and guided her to a chair. 'Sit,' he commanded, then nodded to his companion. 'Now perhaps you'd better start.'

Jan van Mayen nodded. 'As you know, I'm a diamond merchant. Over the last few years I have been becoming more and more alarmed by the increasing number of thefts and frauds that have been occurring, at first in South Africa and England and lately here in Australia, too. When I heard your story, Mrs. Morland, of how your husband lost a great deal of money, and the sad consequences, I wondered if it could be connected to these other felonies. My enquiries have led me to believe it might well be so.'

Kitty drew a sharp breath. 'You mean George Arnold is involved in the thefts?'

'There are many things that point to his involvement.'

Kitty felt a sudden rush of elation. Was it possible that, at long last, Arnold would be brought to justice? 'Will you be able to charge him with swindling my father?'

Rufe, who had been sitting back with his legs crossed, leant forward in his chair. 'Unfortunately, it's not as simple as that. We haven't been able to discover any firm evidence to prove it.'

Kitty's hopes plummeted. 'But you do believe he robbed my father?'

'Yes, and while we might not be able to prove that, we're certain he's been behind many thefts. We believe he's the mastermind behind an organised crime ring that operates wherever there are large discoveries of gold and diamonds. We also believe his cousin, Thomas Arnold, has set up a similar operation here, under instructions from George.'

'So is that why Craddock was here in Sydney?'

'Yes,' Rufe continued. He's George Arnold's right hand man. When you told me you saw him here in Sydney I immediately told Jan, and we are certain he came out here to help Thomas Arnold further his plans.'

'Then surely there's some way you can prove all this.'

'Would you be willing to help us?'

'Me? How could I possibly help?'

'We need to set a trap for him.'

'A trap? What sort of a trap? And how could I help?'

'We want to create a diamond mine, a very special diamond mine.'

Puzzled, Kitty tried to think how they could do this. 'But you can't create a diamond mine, it's formed by nature.'

'A genuine one, yes. But it is possible to fake one. There are certain signs, or 'footprints' as they're called, that indicate diamonds might be present. These are certain outcrops in rocks, certain shapes that suggest the presence of kimberlite below. I won't go into too much technical detail now, but it's possible to fake these signs.'

Kitty shook her head. 'Allowing for all that, I don't see where I come in.'

'Not you so much as Redwoods. The country surrounding your home is just the type of country where diamonds could be found. You have the river, and Bulahdelah Mountain alongside you with its rock formations. Added to which, you've just had a flood. Which could well have washed away soil covering previously hidden rock formations.'

'So you want to create a fake diamond mine on Redwoods?'

'Yes. A diamond mine that yields several large diamonds. I have some of my own I'll use to salt it with as a decoy. Then we'll leak the information to certain people who are known to be working with the Arnolds.'

'Then what will happen?'

'Then we'll arrange an extremely valuable shipment to be sent down to Sydney, all very secret, and we'll be sure the details reach the right ears. We hope they won't be able to resist a hold-up, and we'll be waiting for them.'

'But surely Thomas Arnold won't be involved himself; won't he just arrange it all and send others to do the actual holdup?'

'Yes. But if we catch them in the actual robbery, the police will make sure they realise they'll hang for it, and it's amazing how the threat of the noose can loosen a man's tongue.'

Kitty shuddered, her own fears well remembered.

Rufe was regarding her intently, an expectant look on his face. 'So,' he asked finally, 'will you help us? Can we use Redwoods? It could be the breakthrough we've been waiting for.'

A picture of her father slumped across his desk, his lifeblood pouring from the wound in his head, sprang into her mind. She remembered her sick horror at the scene as her mother rushed to try and help him, and the sound of her own screams rang in her ears.

Biting her lip, she looked first at Bella, sitting like a statue, then back at Rufe.

'Yes!' The word exploded from her. 'Yes, I'll do anything to help bring that bastard to justice. Just make sure you implicate him, that's all I ask.'

The trip back to Redwoods was uneventful, and a week later Bella and Jack were married quietly in the local church on a sunny Saturday afternoon. Bella looked as radiant as any young bride in a silk dress of pale lavender, with a string of pearls around her neck that was a gift from the bridegroom.

During the ceremony Kitty thought back over the years since her father's death. She had been instrumental in bringing Bella all this way to the opposite side of the world and her chest swelled with gladness to see the look of love on Jack's face as he kissed his new wife. However, she could not help feeling sad as she wished Robert could have been here to see his mother's happiness today. She pushed the thought away. Today was not a day for sadness.

After the ceremony they returned to Redwoods for a celebration dinner, and then Jack and Bella left to spend a week at the seaside village of Forster.

When they returned to Redwoods Jack moved into the house.

## CHAPTER TWENTY FOUR

Patrick Reilly was in love, really in love, for the first time in his life. There'd been plenty of women in his life, too many. All the money he'd gained from the gold fields had been spent on women, fast women and high living.

But he'd never met anyone like Mary. Just being close to her was enough to make him go weak. She was everything he wanted in a woman, pretty, smart, even a bit sassy at times. And he wanted to marry her. But she was as straight as an arrow. And devoted to "her ladies". He had to tell her the truth.

Kitty was surprised to see Mary looking troubled as she entered the sitting room where she and Bella were taking tea.

'Mrs. B, there's something I'd like to discuss with you.'

'What is it Mary?'

'Patrick Reilly has asked me to marry him. And I've agreed. But he's told me a story that doesn't reflect well on him, but he said he couldn't ask me without telling me about his past. And because it's about how he comes to be here, I need to tell you, too.' She took a deep breath. 'It seems he came here to ask for a job because someone asked him to find out what happens here, and to let them know.'

Kitty was shocked. 'Why would anyone be interested in what we're doing here?'

Mary shook her head. 'That's what I asked him, but he didn't know.'

'Perhaps we should ask him ourselves. Will you ask him to come in please Mary?'

Mary nodded and returned in a moment, ushering Patrick into the room ahead of her.

'I believe you have something to tell us,' Kitty prompted him after he was seated.

He twisted his hat in his hands. 'The fact is I've got in with rather a bad lot since I left the goldfields. But I didn't realise they were a gang of bushrangers, not at first anyway.' He swallowed. 'And one day when I'd had too much to drink I took part in a hold-up. Only once, and no one was hurt. The driver laid aside his rifle without a fight when he realised he was outnumbered, and the people inside the coach handed over their valuables soon as they saw the pistols. It seemed like a lark when I was drunk, but once I sobered up I didn't feel good about it, and I've never done it since. And I've told them I won't ever be involved in anything violent again.'

'How does this affect us? How do you come to be here?'

'I know I was a fool, and I'm ashamed of it now, but I was at a loose end and I listened to one of them, a smooth talking fellow, who promised me easy money. I should've known better, but when he told me the boss wanted me to come here and ask for a job, and report back on the household, it seemed like money for jam, and I agreed.'

'And why are you telling us this astounding story now?'

Patrick took a deep breath. 'Because I've met Mary, and I want her to marry me, but I'd told her all my time had been spent on the goldfields, I never mentioned highway robbery, and I don't want us to start a life together with lies between us. So I had to tell her the truth. And I don't want to go back with that gang. I just want to marry Mary, if she'll have me, and earn an honest living.'

Kitty bent her head and pressed her knuckles into her eyes, her mind in turmoil as she went over the incredible story.

'Do you believe Patrick is telling the truth?' she asked Mary finally, lifting her head.

'Yes, Mrs. B. I do.'

'I see.' Kitty knew that Mary's loyalty was not in question, but if this scoundrel had somehow wormed his way into her affections, perhaps her judgement was faulty. After all, he was a self-confessed highwayman.

Bella leant forward. 'I recognise you. Aren't you the man who dived into the water with Mr. Morgan, trying to find Mr. Barron, on the night he was drowned?'

'Yes, Mrs. Morgan, we tried really hard to find him, but he wasn't down there. I reckon he must've been swept away straight off. The current was something fierce.'

Kitty was taken aback that this was the same man. 'It was very courageous of you to do what you did, Patrick.'

Patrick shrugged. 'It wasn't anything. I was nearby when Mary came racing out looking for help. I only did what anyone would have done.'

Kitty warmed to the young man. He hadn't tried to use his actions that night to help him in his present situation. 'It was more than that, but let's leave it for now.' She paused to collect her thoughts. 'I find your story most extraordinary. I'm not going to comment on your activities before you came here, that's between you and Mary. I want you to know I'll be doing nothing about it. Many people make mistakes and it's not for me to judge you.' The picture of herself leaving Arnold's study with a pocketful of diamonds sprang into her mind. 'What I am concerned about is the fact that someone has asked you to report on the happenings in this house.' She paused and shook her head with a frown. 'Why could anyone else possibly be interested in what we do?'

A look of relief came over Patrick's face when he realised she was not going to report him to the police, but he shook his head at her question. 'I've no idea.'

'But who asked you to do this?'

'It was the leader of the gang I was with, but he got his orders from his boss. The big boss.'

Kitty frowned. 'The big boss? You mean there was someone else higher up who gave orders?'

'Yes, sometimes. He bought the stuff from them.'

'Do you know who it was?'

'I do as a matter of fact. He's the one who talked me into joining the gang in the first place.'

'Do you know his name?'

'Only his first name. Eddy.'

'Do you know anything else about him? Does he come from around this way?'

'No, I met him down in Sydney. But he's English. He hasn't been out here very long, he said.'

A sudden suspicion almost took Kitty's breath away. 'You've spoken with him yourself, have you?'

'Yes.'

'What does he look like?'

When he finished telling her Kitty felt faint. His description fitted Craddock. And she remembered Craddock's first name was Edward. It had to be him. So he had traced her after all. But what were his plans? She steadied herself with an effort. 'Can you tell us anything else, Patrick?'

'I'm afraid not. That's all I know.'

'What have you told him so far?'

Patrick shifted uncomfortably in his chair. 'I passed on the news when Mr. Barron drowned. And again that you went down to Sydney, and that you'd come back.'

'And that's all?'

'Yes.'

'How did you get the news to him?'

'One of the boys comes to the bar in the Plough Inn every two weeks and if I've got anything to report I go and meet him there.'

'So you only meet him if there's something to report?'

'Yes, that's right.'

'Thank you Patrick. I needn't keep you any longer. I might need to speak to you about this later. And I don't think we have to mention it to anyone else. I think it's best if we keep it all to ourselves, don't you?'

'Yes, I certainly do. Thank you, Mrs. Barron, you've been most understanding.' He paused. 'I suppose you'll want me to leave now, will you?'

'Do you want to leave, Patrick?'

'No, I like working here. I enjoy cutting the timber.'

'Then you should stay.' She looked across at Mary, who had sat through it all without speaking. 'Do you still want to marry him, Mary?'

Mary nodded. 'Yes, as long as he promises never to have anything to do with anything or anyone criminal ever again.'

'Oh, I do, believe me,' Patrick said emphatically.

That night Kitty wrote to Rufe and gave him a full account of Patrick's story.

A telegraph came from him three days later:

Letter received, will contact you as soon as possible.

It was signed simply 'RC'.

Kitty was on edge, wondering how Patrick's revelations would affect their plans, if at all, and whether she would hear from Craddock. But a month passed with no news. Then, on a day when she felt she could stand the suspense no longer, she heard the sound of horses outside and a few moments later Mary opened the door to the sitting room.

'Visitors for you, Mrs. B,' she announced. 'Mr. Cavanagh and a Mr. Bradshaw.'

Kitty sighed with relief. 'Show them in, please, Mary.' She rose from her chair as they entered the room, feeling ungainly and trying to pretend composure she was far from feeling. 'Mr. Cavanagh, I'm pleased to see you.'

'Mrs. Barron, might I present John Bradshaw,' he replied formally, introducing his companion. 'We're here to carry out the plan we discussed in Sydney.'

'How do you do, Mr. Bradshaw. Please take a seat, gentlemen.' She indicated the chairs but Rufe shook his head.

'If you don't mind, we'll get straight on to choosing the site.'

Kitty stifled her desire to ask him questions. 'Certainly,' she replied, 'I take it you'll be staying overnight?'

'Yes. If that's convenient.'

'Of course. Then I'll see you later.'

When they returned Kitty looked enquiringly at Rufe. 'Have you found what you're looking for?'

'Yes. There's a spot close to the river, in a clearing, that's ideal for our purpose. The flood washed the surface away and left rock formations exposed. It's perfect.'

'So what happens now?'

'We'll work tomorrow to make the site look genuine, then we'll leave, and in a few weeks we'll send a wagon with mining implements and so-called miners. Now, about this letter you sent me. You said you believe Reilly's story?'

'Yes, I do. I can see no reason why he would have made up such a story. And he wants to marry Mary.'

'Is he genuine about that, do you think?'

'Yes. I do.'

'If he's telling the truth, then it makes our plan simpler.'

'In what way?'

'Instead of having to get the news out there, and make sure it reaches the right ears, we simply have Reilly pass the information to his contact, then Craddock will hear it from his henchmen. But first I think Bradshaw and I should talk to him ourselves.' He turned to his companion, who had been silent up to now. 'Don't you think so?'

Bradshaw nodded. 'Yes. Definitely. And it would help if we have someone else on the place working with us.' He turned to Kitty. 'Is there someone among the men that you trust completely?'

'Jack Morgan, my manager.'

'You're sure?'

Kitty smiled. 'Perhaps you should ask my mother.'

A faint flush tinged Bella's cheeks as she replied. 'You can be perfectly sure, Mr. Bradshaw. Mr. Morgan and I are married.'

Bradshaw nodded. 'In that case, I trust your judgement.'

Rufe turned to Bella. 'So it's Mrs. Morgan now, that's wonderful news. I hope Morgan realises what a lucky man he is. I look forward to meeting him and congratulating him.'

'If you'd like to meet him, he'll be here this evening.'

'I look forward to it. As well as meeting him, he might well become an ally in our plans.'

'I'm sure he would wish to help in any way he can.'

'And Reilly?' Rufe turned back to Kitty. 'Can I talk to him without the rest of the staff knowing?'

'I'll find out when Mary is expecting to see him again, she can bring him in then. That way no one will know. They're known to be walking out together.'

'Excellent. Can I leave it to you to arrange? Tonight, if possible.'

'Yes. I'll see to it.'

Kitty organized a meeting for that night between Rufe, Bradshaw, Jack Morgan and Patrick Reilly. Afterwards Rufe professed himself satisfied with both men's integrity and told Kitty their plans were now firmly formulated.

'We'll finish what we have to do here tomorrow, and in a couple of days Reilly will let slip to one of the other men that Mary has told him we've been here to take geological specimens from the site, that there might be diamonds here. All very hush-hush, of course. It'll be enough to cause speculation and might well start a rumour.'

The next day Rufe and Bradshaw went out early.

All morning, Kitty moved aimlessly from room to room.

'Do come and sit down,' Bella admonished her. 'You'll tire yourself out. Remember the baby is due any day now. You need to conserve your energy.'

'Oh, Mother, don't fuss. I don't feel like sitting down. I need to be doing something.'

Bella put down her needlework and looked long and hard at her. 'How are you feeling?'

'I feel fine, just fine. Full of energy, in fact.'

'Hmm. And how is the baby?'

'She's fine, too. Very active, in fact.'

'I see.' She picked up her sewing again. 'You might be closer than you think.'

'I'm just restless, that's all. I really want to be out there, watching what they're doing.'

But it was not until they all sat down to dinner that night that Kitty had a chance to talk to them.

She waited until the two men finished their soup and were waiting for their main meal before she raised the question uppermost in her mind.

'So, did everything go according to plan today?'

'Yes,' Rufe replied, 'everything is now in place for the next stage.'

'Which will be…what?' queried Bella.

'You're going to be invaded by a mining gang. I'll instruct them to disrupt things as little as possible, but I'm afraid it's going to cause some upheaval to your lives. They'll be fairly self-sufficient, but they'll need to clear some land around the site to set up their tents. They shouldn't disturb you too much, because they can go into Bulahdelah for food supplies. In fact, the more people who get to know they're here, the better, we want to spread the word around.'

'Will you be coming back with them?'

'Not at first. But I will come back after they've been digging for a while. That'll be the time to reveal that you have diamonds here. Hopefully to create some interest in the right quarters.'

Kitty's heart beat a little faster with excitement as she thought that perhaps, if Rufe's plan worked, the Arnolds might at last be brought to justice. And also because it meant she would see Rufe again. Not that there was much point to it, for he was obviously in love with Irene. His impersonal attitude to her since his arrival confirmed this. After all, why would he want her, a widow carrying another man's child, someone who had sent him away from her on two occasions? No, he had found solace with someone else. But she would enjoy seeing him again.

She did not sleep well that night, partly from discomfort, it seemed the baby kicked incessantly, and partly because her mind buzzed with thoughts of Rufe and his plan, and Rufe and Irene. She woke the next morning feeling tired, and when she emerged from her room she found the men had breakfasted early and were ready to leave. Bella stood talking to them, obviously saying her goodbyes.

'Thank you for your hospitality, Mrs. Barron,' Rufe said, offering her his hand.

Kitty felt a little chill as she took it; he was behaving so formally towards her, as if the past counted for nothing. 'It's been my pleasure, and I hope our plan is successful,' she replied.

As Rufe and Bradshaw rode away, Kitty and Bella watched from the verandah until they were out of sight, but Rufe didn't turn around.

As she turned to walk inside Kitty felt wetness between her legs and when she looked down a pool of water was forming around her feet. 'What on earth…?'

Bella gasped. 'Your water's broken.' She took Kitty by the arm. 'Come on now, let's get you ready. Into the bedroom. I'll send for the midwife.'

Rufe and Bradshaw separated shortly after they left Bulahdelah, Bradshaw to return to Sydney, Rufe to visit his stores on the goldfields.

Rufe was happy with the salting of the 'mine' at Redwoods. Bradshaw knew his job all right, and they worked well together, and with Jan van Mayen. Their plan had been carefully worked out and he had confidence in bringing it to a successful conclusion.

He knew Kitty longed to bring George Arnold to justice. Kitty. How did he feel about her now? He pictured her as she had been this morning, standing in the hallway to bid him goodbye, with her swollen belly and dark circles beneath her eyes. A surge of tenderness swept through him at the thought. Tenderness, not desire. She was still the same person she had always been, and yet she was not the same. How did he feel about this new Kitty? He sighed. He really didn't know.

And now he was on his way to the goldfields, and Irene would be waiting for him.

He had not seen her since the end of their holiday in Sydney, when she returned to her inn, and he had begun preparations for the planned salting of the 'mine'.

The small group of trusted miners who were going to work there were now also waiting for him, to be told that all was in place to begin their work. Seeing Irene at the same time would be a pleasant interlude. His mind was divided on whether he was being fair to her, continuing to see her, knowing he had no serious intentions towards her. However, he eased his conscience by reminding himself that she was the one who had said, 'no strings attached'. She had set the rules. He enjoyed her company, and sharing her bed even more so, and she seemed happy enough with that situation. After all, she was intent on building up her business. She'd confided in him that she would soon be in a position to sell the inn and move into something better, perhaps a smart hotel in a country town as a first move towards the hotel in Sydney or Melbourne that was her ultimate goal. No, she didn't want the ties of a serious relationship any more than he did.

He patted Banjo on the neck. 'Yes, I'm looking forward to seeing her again,' he told him, 'and there'll be a good feed and a dry bed for you too, old fellow, so we'd better get a move on.'

Irene had fretted for days with disappointment when she realised she was not pregnant after their visit to Sydney, and then lived in a state of apprehension that she might have lost Rufe until she heard from him, telling her when he would be arriving again. She calculated the days and realised that it would be perfect timing. This time she must make sure.

## CHAPTER TWENTY FIVE

Kitty heard the mid-wife's voice through a haze of pain. 'Push, come on now. Harder. Push!'

Panting, she pulled even harder on the leather strap attached to the bed head as she tried to obey the order. Perspiration poured down her body. Bella wiped her face again with a damp cloth.

'And again…you're nearly there…I can see the head. Come on now…another one. Push. Good girl…it's coming. Push!'

Kitty made one more almighty, heaving effort, and suddenly she felt the baby slither out. Thank God. It was over. She lay back gasping. Then she heard a baby's cry, followed by the midwife's voice. 'You've got a lovely baby girl.'

Kitty raised her head and tried to push herself up on her elbows. Bella slipped a pillow beneath her head and pushed her gently back. 'Lie back,' she told her, and before Kitty could argue, the midwife was placing the baby on her chest. Kitty gazed in wonder at her daughter. Red faced and screaming, with her hair plastered to her scalp, she looked the most beautiful thing Kitty had ever seen.

'You just stay there, like that,' came the midwife's voice, 'until I fix the afterbirth.'

A few moments later another pain came, not as severe as before.

'Right. Another push now.' Another slithering sensation, then, 'all over now,' came the satisfied voice of the midwife. 'We'll just clean up and then it's all over.'

Bella took the baby. 'I'm going to wash her now, then I'll bring her back. You just rest for a while.'

Obediently, Kitty let her eyes fall shut, and the next moment she drifted into sleep.

Kitty woke feeling wonderful, totally refreshed. She sat up and looked into the crib alongside her bed. The baby lay there, fast asleep, only her head visible above the covers. As Kitty gazed into her daughter's face, her eyes opened and from her tiny mouth came a loud scream. Bella opened the door and came into the room.

'Oh, so you're awake. How do you feel?' she asked above the noise, moving over to the crib and lifting up the howling baby.

'I'm fine, but there must be something wrong with her to cry like that,' Kitty said anxiously.

Bella laughed. 'She's hungry,' she replied, placing her in Kitty's arms.

The baby turned her head from side to side, nuzzling into Kitty's breast, yelling. As soon as Kitty dropped her night-gown, the baby's screams cut short as she took the nipple in her mouth and sucked energetically.

Bella stood for a moment, watching. 'Well, it looks as if you're managing perfectly well, so I'll leave you alone for a little while to get to know your daughter.'

Kitty watched the baby in awe as she fed greedily. She had heard that nothing could compare to a mother's feelings for her child, but had been totally unprepared for the wave of love that overcame her. Finally the baby, sated, stopped suckling and her head lolled to one side, a trickle of milk dribbling from her mouth. Tenderly, Kitty wiped it away with a bib before carefully unwrapping her and examining the tiny feet and toes, counting to see they were all there. Then she did the same with the fingers. After that, she lifted the dress and the singlet beneath it and examined her carefully from head to toe. Satisfied that everything was as it should be, Kitty wrapped her again and leant back against the pillows, cradling the baby in her arms.

Breathing a deep sigh of happiness, she gently stroked the clean, soft hair and thought she had never felt so content in her life. This little scrap of humanity, so beautiful, so absolutely perfect in every way, was actually hers. Hers alone. How different would it have been if William were alive? Remembering his attacks and rages, she was not ashamed to acknowledge to herself that she could not feel sorry he was not here.

'From now on,' she whispered to the sleeping infant, 'it's you and me, my little petal. I'll see that no one ever harms you, ever. You'll grow up safe and well looked after, and you'll never know what it's like to go without. We're secure and safe here at Redwoods, and here we'll stay. No one can ever take it from us.'

When Bella came back a little later, Kitty smiled happily at her.

'Oh Mother, isn't she beautiful?'

Bella laughed. 'I think she's probably the most beautiful baby I've ever seen.' She crossed the room to sit on the end of the bed. 'With the exception of yourself, of course.'

Kitty shook her head. 'No. Never as beautiful as this.'

'What are you going to call her?'

'Well, I planned to call her Marguerite, after your mother, but she's brought so much joy to my life, that's what I'm going to call her. Joy.'

'Joy?' Bella said slowly, considering, head on one side, then she nodded. 'Mmm…yes. Joy. I like it.'

'Joy Marguerita Barron. How does that sound?'

'I think it sounds wonderful. And I think Joy should go back in her bed now so you can have something to eat. Are you hungry?'

'Actually, I'm starving.' Kitty kissed the top of her baby's head before passing her to Bella.

Later in the day Jack came into the room.

'How are you feeling, Kitty?' he asked, moving from one foot to the other as he stood just inside the door.

'I'm feeling simply wonderful. And have you come to see your new granddaughter?'

Kitty saw a play of emotions cross his face. Surprise, awe, and finally delight.

'My granddaughter.' He spoke slowly as if savouring the words. 'I never thought to hear that.'

'There she is.' Kitty gestured towards the crib.

Jack crossed the room and gazed at the tiny face, topped by a wisp of hair, peeking out from the rugs. A look of such softness came over his face that Kitty felt a lump in her throat. In that instant she knew Jack would be a true grandfather to her child.

Kitty recovered her strength quickly. She felt wonderful. Once she was up and about, her days took on a pattern. After bathing and feeding Joy in the mornings, she liked to put her into her perambulator, weather permitting, and wheel her around the garden, talking to her and telling her about the plants and the birds.

One mild, sunny day, Kitty ventured out the gate and down the track to the riverbank. Four kangaroos, feeding on the green grass a few feet out from the edge of the forest, sat up straight as she came nearer, watching her approach. She expected them to bound away, but they stayed still and alert, watching.

Kitty stopped at the stump, hoping they wouldn't go away, she loved watching them. She lifted Joy from the perambulator and seated herself, cradling the baby on her lap. 'See, my darling,' she said softly, 'those are kangaroos. Oh look, that one has a joey in its pouch; you can just see its head peeping out. When you're a big girl you'll know all the animals here. I'll teach you all about them, and the birds, too. Such pretty coloured birds we have, like those noisy lorikeets and the beautiful king parrots. And you'll hear the kookaburras laughing, we have a pair living in the big gum tree in our own garden, do you know that?'

Joy lay contentedly in her mother's arms, her eyes open, fixed on her face, and Kitty was sure she was listening to her. When she waved one hand in the air, Kitty put her finger out and the baby grasped it tightly and curled her tiny pink fingers around it. Kitty kissed the top of her head. 'Oh yes, my little Joy, Redwoods is a wonderful place for you to grow up. And now that I have extra money from the sale of the diamonds, I have plans to make it even better.'

Kitty decided the time had come to discuss her plans with Jack. 'I think we could build the business up considerably by putting in a mill,' she told him. 'What do you think? Could you manage it?'

'Yes. I've run a mill before.'

'Good. I believe the boat builders down the Myall River are crying out for timber. I'll go and see them and see if we can get their business.'

'You'll go yourself?'

'Yes. If I'm to succeed, then I need to gain their trust as a business person, not as a woman.'

'It won't be easy,' Jack warned her.

'I know that, but I have to try. If they'll just talk to me, I hope I can persuade them I know what I'm doing.'

'Then I suggest you call on Harry Osborne first. He's an approachable man, and he's the biggest boat builder down there. If he takes us on, some of the others are bound to follow.'

Kitty waited until the mill was built, then one morning she dressed with extra care, aiming to present a sober and business-like appearance, and drove the buggy down to call on Harry Osborne. As she drove into his yard, and reined in the horse, a young lad came across and held the horse's head.

'I'm looking for Mr. Osborne,' she told him. 'Would he be about?'

'Yes, missus. He's in his office.' He nodded towards a small building set to one side of the yard, some little distance from where Kitty could see several men working on the hull of a partly built boat. The sounds of hammer and saw filled the yard. Floating in the river at the bottom of the yard, tied up to a landing, she saw another boat, which she judged to be a fishing trawler. Another gang seemed to be putting the finishing touches to that. A busy yard indeed.

Climbing down from the buggy she handed the reins to the boy, and stood watching the activity for a moment or two before heading to the office. Her knock was answered by a voice calling, 'Come.'

Kitty opened the door and stepped inside. A large desk, covered with papers, stood beneath a window, catching the light. The man seated at it looked up from his sketching, then dropped his pencil and rose to his feet as he saw her. Kitty judged him to be in his thirties. He was tall and sturdy, with an open countenance, sandy hair, and side whiskers. Glasses perched on his nose. He removed them as he stood and she thought that, with his strong physique, he would be more at home out in the yard, working on the boats, than here behind a desk.

Kitty took the initiative.

'Good morning, Mr. Osborne. I'm Kitty Barron. I own the timber property Redwoods, at Bulahdelah and we've recently installed a mill to finish the timber on the premises. I'm calling on you today to see if we might be able to do business together.'

Harry Osborne looked startled at her words, but recovered himself quickly and gestured to the chair in front of his desk.

'Won't you please take a seat, Mrs. Barron?'

'Thank you.'

Osborne resumed his seat, sitting back and regarding her. 'I heard of your husband's tragic death in the floods. May I offer my condolences?'

'Thank you, Mr. Osborne. It was, of course, a great shock, but life must go on. Fortunately, I worked with my husband, attending to all the bookwork, so I am conversant with all those aspects of the business. And I'm fortunate in having a very capable manager in Jack Morgan. He's managing the mill for me now, and while we're processing mostly our own timber at the moment, we've also started to receive logs from other estates.'

'I see.' He picked up his pencil and twiddled it in his fingers. 'It's most unusual for a lady to be involved in such a business, as I'm sure you realise, Mrs. Barron.'

'Oh yes. My bank manager made that quite clear to me. He suggested I should sell Redwoods and return to England, to lead the life of a genteel widow in the bosom of my husband's family.'

A smile flickered on his lips. 'And I take it you didn't like that idea?'

'Definitely not. This is my home now. My daughter will be brought up in Australia, where she was born. We both belong here now.'

'Well, I must say you seem very certain about that.'

'I am indeed. And I'm just as certain that I'm capable of running my own business, and I intend it to be a success. Now, Mr. Osborne, if we can discuss what timber you'll need in the next few months, I'm sure I can give you an attractive price, and I promise you my service will be excellent.'

He seemed bemused by her direct approach and tapped his teeth with the pencil for a few seconds while he studied her.

Kitty met his gaze levelly, saying no more. He dropped the pencil, opened a drawer in his desk, and took out a large leather-bound book. Placing it on the desk in front of him he opened it and turned the pages until he found what he was looking for.

'Well now then, let's see what we've got coming up, and you tell me what you can offer me.'

When Kitty left his office she carried with her a substantial order for timber.

As Kitty sat on the verandah with Joy beside her a few days later, a commotion along the track made her look up from the book she held. A wagon and four horsemen approached slowly, with Jack leading the way. They passed the house and headed down towards the river. The horsemen dismounted there and, going to the back of the wagon, returned with axes and saws and began clearing a path through the forest. It was the mining gang.

Kitty wondered if Rufe's plan would work. Would he really be able to implicate Craddock, and, perhaps, even the Arnolds? Now she had Joy it was more important than ever to be free of the danger of her past catching up with her.

Apart from the sounds of pick and shovel, and an occasional miner riding past the house, touching his hat as he passed, the track leading into the forest was the only indication of the miners' presence.

They were on tenterhooks, waiting for something to happen, but had to wait almost two months before Jack brought Patrick home one night so they could both report on progress.

'What's happening?' Kitty asked, once they were all seated in the sitting room.

'Well, quite a bit, really,' Jack told them. 'Our workers all know we've supposedly found a mine, where the flood washed the soil away, and of course they're all agog to know what's happening, what's been found. They've all been told it's out of bounds, but they've all visited the mine on the sly, as we knew they would. And one of the miners let drop early on that it's diamonds they're looking for and that they've found some of decent size. So there have been some nice rumours flying round the town.

Patrick took up the tale. 'Because they know me and Mary are walking out together, they keep pestering me to find out more for them. So I'm dropping little bits at a time, that Mary told me you're all excited about there being diamonds, and she thinks it must be something big. Then, another time, that she overheard you talking about how they've found "the big one," and it's going to be time to send a shipment down to Sydney before too long. And of course I've been telling my contact who comes to the pub the same things, so we know it's reached the ears of the right people.'

Kitty took a deep breath. 'So it's all going according to plan?'

Jack nodded. 'Yes. Providing nothing goes wrong, and I can't see that it will, we're well on track. Jason, the leader of the miners, told me that tomorrow he'll be sending Rufe a cable with a pre-arranged message about goods being ready for delivery any time now. This'll cause a bit more of a stir up here, the postmaster won't be able to keep it to himself, and it'll let Rufe know all's well.'

'Then can we expect things to happen soon?' Kitty asked, suddenly excited.

'Yes. It should soon be all over.'

A few days later Kitty received a letter from Rufe telling her that he would arrive at the end of the month with an escort ready to take their first shipment to Sydney. Excitedly, she passed the news on to Jack.

'Great,' he said, 'I'll let Patrick know, and he can pass it on to his contact. He'll say Mary told him.'

Startled, Kitty sat up in bed, sure she'd heard a gentle knocking. In the dim light coming from the night lamp she looked around. Yes, there it was again. She slipped from bed and put on her wrapper. Picking up the lamp, she hurried into the nursery. Joy was sound asleep. Making her way up the hall she paused as she heard another knock. Someone was tapping at the front door. Who could it be so late at night? Cautiously, she opened it a crack, holding the lamp high. To her amazement, Rufe stood outside.

He put his fingers to his lips. 'Shh, I don't want to advertise my presence here. Can I come in?'

Kitty opened the door wide. 'Of course.'

Rufe entered and closed the door behind him. She led the way into the drawing room, where she pulled the curtains before turning up the lamp and placing it on the mantel.

'No one will hear us in here. Now, what are you doing here so soon? Your letter said you'd be arriving at the end of the month, and that's still two weeks away. And why all the secrecy?'

'I don't want anyone outside to know I'm here. I couldn't trust this part of the plan to a letter, just in case it went astray or was intercepted. The arrangements for the shipment are all in place. However, laying ourselves open to attack at a time and place of the bushrangers' choice, gives them the advantage. So I've decided on a change of plan. We'll get Patrick to tell his contact that this is a particularly valuable shipment so it'll be more heavily guarded than usual. He'll also tell him he's been able to find out where the stuff's being kept on the property, and that he can lead them to it if they stage a surprise raid here instead. They know there are only four miners here. They'll think that'll be much easier than tackling a large, heavily armed escort. Then Patrick can tell us when they're coming and we'll be waiting in ambush for them with the police. Hopefully, we'll catch them without any blood being spilt.'

Kitty felt a stab of fear as she thought of the danger to all those involved. 'Will you be with them?'

'Yes, of course. And possibly Jan van Mayen. There'll also be several armed police.'

'It's still going to be dangerous, for everyone involved.'

'We'll take every precaution, and we'll have the advantage of surprise. Now, do you think it's possible for me to speak to Jack now?'

Kitty nodded. 'Yes. I'll wake him.' She paused. 'Oh, Rufe, I do hope no one's going to be hurt.'

He grasped her shoulders, looking steadily into her eyes. 'You just make sure you ladies stay inside with the doors locked. We'll be all right.'

As they walked into the hall a cry came from the nursery.

'Oh dear, sounds like we've wakened your baby.'

'I'll just go and pick her up.'

'She?' Rufe smiled. 'So you have a little girl.'

'Yes. I've called her Joy, because that's what she is to me.'

'Can I see her?'

'Of course.' Kitty led the way to the nursery. Setting the lamp down on a small table, she picked up the baby, who immediately stopped crying.

Rufe stood watching Kitty cradle her in her arms. Walking over, he gently moved the blanket aside from the tiny face with his finger. The baby immediately grasped it and held on tightly. 'Well, little Joy,' he said softly, 'aren't you a darling. Pretty too. I'm sure you'll grow up to be as beautiful as your mother.' Carefully he disengaged his finger. 'She looks like you,' he told Kitty.

Kitty felt a stab of pleasure.

He smiled at her and touched her gently on the arm. 'And now, if you'll wake Jack, I'll let him know how he can contact me, and he'll be able to tell you our final arrangements. Then I must go. I'm not sure if I'll see you on the night or not, but if I don't, I'll be back as soon as I can to tell you how successful we've been.'

As Rufe waited while Kitty walked down the hall and tapped on the door to wake Jack, his mind whirled with the rush of feelings caused by seeing Kitty again. The sight of her as she answered the door, in her night attire, her hair tumbling about her shoulders, had caused the blood to bubble in his veins. It took all his will power to resist sweeping her into his arms then and there. How had he ever thought his love for her had faded?

## CHAPTER TWENTY SIX

Tonight was the night. Jack came early to warn them and to insist they keep their doors locked at all times, as soon as it turned dusk, no matter what happened.

'You might hear shots,' he warned them, 'but under no circumstances must you unlock the doors unless Rufe, Patrick, or I ask you to. And keep well away from the windows.'

Kitty's heart pumped with a mixture of excitement and fear. 'Are the police here yet?'

'They're nearby but keeping well out of sight until dark, and then everyone'll take their places.'

'Is Rufe here?'

'Yes. Everyone's ready.'

Mary twisted her hands together. 'I'm worried about Patrick. Seems to me he's got a dangerous part to play.'

'We've been through it all, Mary. There're no guarantees, but we hope no one at all will be hurt, least of all any of us.'

Bella twisted the beads at her neck. 'You take care, Jack.'

'Don't worry.' He gave her a quick smile. 'You don't get rid of me that easy. Now, don't forget, don't unlock the doors. And keep well away from the windows.' With that reminder, he left them.

Too keyed up to do more than pick at the light meal Mary prepared, the three women sat together in the sitting room as night deepened. The air was thick with tension as time crept by. Bella stitched her needlework. Mary mended linen. Kitty tried to read. Talk was sporadic.

The sound of gunshots, muffled by the curtains, followed by three more in quick succession, had them all up from their seats.

Kitty hurried to the window. 'Quick Mary, lower the lights.'

She drew back a curtain and peered out into the blackness, Bella and Mary pressing behind her. They could see nothing, but the sounds of shouting came dimly through the closed window. Two more shots rang out, sounding further away this time.

'Oh my God,' Bella cried. 'I hope Jack's not been hurt.'

'Or Patrick,' Mary added.

'I hope all our men are safe,' Kitty whispered.

They stood there, by the window, a silent tableau, listening, for several minutes. But there were no more shots. All was silent now.

At the sound of a horse approaching at a fast gallop Kitty pulled the curtains to, and Mary quickly turned up the lights. Seconds later there was knocking at the door, accompanied by Jack's voice calling out to them. Kitty rushed to open the door.

'Well, it's all over! Eight villains are now being escorted to Gloucester by a group of police,' Jack exclaimed, his voice full of excitement, '

'Tell us what happened. Is anyone hurt?' Kitty asked.

'None of our people. Everything went according to plan. Patrick led the ruffians in on foot, as arranged. Of course the miners were ready and waiting for them. They waited until they'd packed the loot into the saddlebags, ready to take back to the horses, and then they pounced. The scoundrels were taken completely by surprise. Then the troopers came out of hiding. One of the thieves pulled his gun and fired and the captain fired back. Wonderful marksmanship. Shot him in the arm. Then as they were being rounded up, the leader tried to make a break for it, but he didn't get away.'

'Was that the second lot of shots we heard?' asked Kitty.

'Yes. Cavanagh quickly loosed off a couple of shots, pulled him up short.'

Kitty swallowed. 'Mr. Cavanagh wasn't hurt?'

'No. None of our fellows. Only one of the rascals, with a bullet in his arm.'

'What about Patrick?' Mary asked. 'What did he do when the attack started?'

'He just melted away, like he'd been told to, and went straight back to his bed so he can act as surprised as everyone else.'

'And the others?' Kitty asked. 'Where's everyone now?'

'The troopers are taking them off to the lock-up, and Cavanagh and van Mayen went with them, they want to see them safely under lock and key. Cavanagh said to tell you he'll contact you soon.'

Kitty took a deep breath. Did that mean he would come and tell her what happened himself, or would he just write to her with the news?

Days passed without any communication from Rufe, and Kitty could barely contain her impatience. The whole town was buzzing with rumours, according to Jack, and the gossip increased when it was learned that the miners had packed up and left.

When Kitty heard the sound of a horse arriving late one afternoon she rushed to the door. Excitedly, she stepped out onto the verandah.

'Rufe. At last. I thought you'd never get here.'

'Kitty.' He bounded up the stairs and grabbed her, and swung her off her feet, spinning her around, laughing. 'We did it. We did it.'

Kitty clung to him and when he put her down he kissed her full on the mouth. Her arms went around his neck, and suddenly the kiss changed from one of jubilation to deep passion. He crushed her to him. Kitty's heart pounded throughout her body.

Rufe lifted his head. 'Kitty. Kitty.' His voice was thick. 'Why have we wasted so much time?' And with that his lips were on hers again.

A moment later the door behind them opened, and they jumped apart as Bella stepped through. Her fingers sought her beads, her face pink.

'Oh. I…I thought I heard a horse…I didn't know...I didn't realise it was you, Mr. Cavanagh.' She gave a small, embarrassed laugh.

'Mrs. Morgan.' Rufe was breathing heavily but he stepped forward to greet her, kissing her cheek. 'I've come to give you the good news. Our plan was successful in every way.'

Bella clasped her hands together. 'How wonderful.' She stepped back and opened the door wide. 'Please come in. Come down to the sitting room.' She turned and led the way back down the hall.

Kitty tried to pull herself together, tried to still her thudding heart.

Rufe smiled down at her and offered her his arm. 'Caught,' he whispered to her. 'We'll continue that a little later.' His eyes danced. 'In the meantime, I must contain my impatience and tell you what's been happening.'

Kitty took his arm. He squeezed it tightly against his side, and they followed Bella down to the sitting room.

'I'm sorry I've kept you waiting so long to know what's happened, but I wanted to have everything tied up before I came. And the news is the very best. When we reached Gloucester we kept them all separate and questioned them one at a time. The leader of the gang was stubborn; we got nothing from him at first. However, one of his henchmen, when he realised we knew a great deal about the gang's activities, and that he was facing the rope, opened up completely.'

Kitty leant forward. 'Are they the gang that you and Mr. van Mayen have been trying to catch?'

'Yes. There's no doubt about that. When the leader realised one of his men had talked, he knew he was in big trouble. With the threat of the noose dangling over him, he finally told us everything, with the promise that he'd escape hanging.'

'And the police agreed to that condition?' asked Bella.

'Yes. When he offered the name of the person higher up who gave the orders in exchange, they were agreeable.'

Kitty drew in a sharp breath. 'And who was that?'

Rufe regarded her through half-closed eyes, a smile hovering about his lips. 'The name he gave us is Craddock.'

Kitty drew in a deep breath, her pulses racing. She stared at him wide-eyed then let out the breath in a rush. She licked her lips. 'I wonder if…'

Rufe leant over and took her hand in his. 'The best is still to come,' he said, cutting across her words. 'When I learned this, van Mayen and I went down to Sydney ourselves and accompanied the police when they went to arrest Craddock. At first he was all bluster, and tried to deny everything. Finally, he realised how long we'd been watching the Arnolds. A lot of what we suspected turned out to be true and we were able to make him believe we knew more than we actually did. He confessed that he'd been George Arnold's right hand man and that he'd come here to help his cousin employ highwaymen to rob shipments of gold and diamonds. So our friend George Arnold will finally pay the price for his crimes.'

Bella paled as her fingers twisted her beads. 'I always believed George Arnold was lying to us about that diamond shipment being stolen. He is the cause of Kitty's father's death.' She covered her face with her hands and burst into tears. 'Oh Charles. My poor Charles,' she sobbed.

A fierce thrill of exultation ran through Kitty. 'So, at last I'm vindicated.'

Bella looked up, hiccupped and brushed the tears from her cheeks. 'Yes, Kitty, at last I can stop worrying about what you did.' She turned to Rufe. 'I don't know how to thank you. You don't know what this means to me.'

'I think I can guess,' he answered gently. 'Now, no more tears. We should be celebrating.'

Kitty jumped up. 'Yes. We must have Patrick here as well as Jack. They both played a big part in the plan, and they'll want to know how it all ended. We'll have a big dinner to celebrate.'

It was much later that night before Kitty and Rufe were alone together in the drawing room. When all the others had gone, Rufe came to sit beside Kitty on the sofa. She turned to him.

'In all the discussions you and Mr. van Mayen had about the Arnolds, was the matter of the diamonds taken from George Arnold's study ever discussed?'

'No. You need have no fear about that, the incident was never mentioned, neither between van Mayen and me, nor with the police.'

'So Craddock never brought it up, or mentioned my name?'

'No. Craddock had more to worry about than that, believe me. He was fighting for his life. Highway robbery is a hanging offence and he masterminded robberies in conjunction with both the Arnolds.'

'So what will happen to him?'

'Van Mayen and I – and the police – agreed that, as we have sufficient evidence to convict Thomas Arnold and the others here, it was better to take Craddock back to England to testify against George Arnold, against whom we had little firm evidence. He agreed to do so in exchange for leniency.'

Kitty took a deep breath. 'So at last it's all over.'

His eyes, black with intensity, looked deep into hers. 'Yes, Kitty. It's all over.' He picked up her hand that lay on the sofa between them, and played idly with the fingers. 'And now it's time to think about us.'

A pulse beating in her throat almost stifled Kitty. 'Us,' she whispered.

Without a word he raised her hand to his lips and kissed the palm. Then his lips travelled slowly up her arm, dropping little kisses all the way. His mouth moved to the side of her neck. He kissed slowly from side to front, and then down to the tops of her breasts. A wave of heat swept through her. As his hand came up to caress her breast she gasped, and turned towards him. He lifted his head and his lips sought hers, tenderly at first then hungrily, demanding. Passion coursed through her as she responded eagerly.

When he raised his head, his eyes were shining. 'Kitty, my darling, I love you.'

'I love you, too.'

Then his hands were on her shoulders, gently easing her back. He turned her towards him, pulling her to him. As his lips found hers again his hands moved slowly over her body, caressing her. Every pulse in her body throbbed as she moaned with desire.

Suddenly he rose to his feet and pulled her up with him, crushing her yielding body to him. Had it not been for his arms around her she could not have stood. She felt his hard body pressed tightly against her, his breath coming in gasps.

'My love,' he said hoarsely, 'my wonderful, wonderful darling. I love you. I want you. I need you.'

There was nothing else in the world but the two of them. 'And I want you.'

He swept her off her feet and carried her from the room, up the hall into her bedroom.

Kitty stirred and turned over, dreamily wondering at her sense of euphoria, then, as memory came flooding back, she sat up and looked at the bed alongside her. As the moonlight revealed Rufe's figure beside her she smiled, and settled back on her pillow. Rufe put his arm around her, then kissed her lingeringly.

'Are you happy, my love?' he asked softly.

'Mmmm. Deliciously, decadently so.' She stretched in his arms. 'How about you?'

'Never been happier.' His hand caressed her bare arm, then moved to her breast and began tracing a pattern slowly down to her stomach. Suddenly she was on fire again and turned in his arms until they lay body to body. She felt his desire and pulled him fiercely to her.

They made love again as the moonlight slanted across the bed and the hoot of an owl came distantly through the window.

When the first light filtered into the room Rufe leant across and kissed Kitty gently. Sleepily, she lifted her hand and stroked his cheek. 'Mmmm,' she muttered, 'what is it?'

'I'll go to my own room before the household wakens,' he whispered, and slid from the bed.

'Don't go.'

But he was already pulling on some clothes. 'I'll see you soon, my darling.' He bent and dropped a kiss on her cheek. 'Go back to sleep.' He slipped silently from the room.

Kitty slowly wakened. She smiled as she stretched luxuriously. She could hardly believe the wonder of the night. Rufe had roused sensations in her she never knew existed. So this is what real love is like! She he hugged herself, reliving the feelings of ecstasy over again.

After breakfast Kitty took Joy outside and laid her on a rug under a shady tree, where she played contentedly, waving her toys in the air. Kitty sat on a chair nearby, happiness wrapping round her like a shawl. Her senses all seemed highly developed this morning, the air was laced with sunshine, the grass looked greener, the flowers brighter, and the soft daily sounds were a harmonious backdrop to her daughter's gurgles, and the drone of the bees around the wisteria.

Rufe appeared and pulled up a chair to sit beside her. 'I must say you look extremely well this morning, Kitty,' he said with a smile. 'I believe you must have had a good night's sleep.'

'Well, no, Rufe, actually I slept very little,' she answered light-heartedly. 'But I did have an extremely good night. And I am exceedingly happy this morning.'

'I'm pleased to hear that. I'm happy and I, too, had a very good night.'

'Really. Perhaps it has something to do with the fresh country air. They do say it's very healthful.'

He seemed to consider this. 'I think it had more to do with the company rather than the air.' His bantering manner disappeared. Suddenly he was serious. 'Last night was the best night of my life. But it's the forerunner of many more to come.'

'I hope so, my darling.'

He reached over and took her hand in his. 'We have the rest of our lives before us, my love. When we're married, we'll be together every night.'

Kitty's brow puckered. 'Married?'

He raised his eyebrows. 'Of course. Married. It's what people do when they love each other. They marry.'

'But I thought…' her voice trailed off, as confused thoughts whirled through her mind. Joy, Redwoods, their security here that she had worked so hard for...

'What did you think, Kitty?'

'I don't suppose I really thought about it. At all.'

Rufe shook his head slightly. 'Then you need to think about it. I should ask you properly, I suppose.' He took her hand. 'Kitty, my darling, I love you. Will you marry me?'

A jolt of panic struck Kitty. She looked across at Joy, and bit her lip. How could she marry anyone, even Rufe, when it meant that Redwoods, her daughter's legacy, would no longer be hers, but would automatically become her husband's property? She would be betraying her trust.

'Oh, Rufe, I don't know what to say. I love you, but…'

Rufe released her hand, happiness fading from his face. 'But what? Don't you want to marry me?'

'I do. Yes, I do, but, you see, I…I can't.'

'Why can't you?'

'I just can't.'

'What is there to stop you?'

Kitty looked across at the baby. 'Well, you see, it's Joy...'

Rufe frowned. 'Your baby? Why…' he stopped, and his face cleared. 'But she'll be with us, of course. Surely you didn't think I wouldn't want her? I'll treat her as if she's my own child.' He smiled. 'She's the image of you. You need have no fear that I won't love her and take care of her.'

'It's not that.' How could she explain? Nerves caused her voice to falter. 'You see…when William died and Joy was born…well, I decided then that I would never marry again. You see…under the law this property…' she stopped, brought up short by the cold look on his face.

'What are you trying to say, Kitty? Spell it out clearly, please. I need to know what this is all about.'

She took a deep breath. 'It's not you, Rufe. I love you, but I decided I would never marry again. It's too risky. For Joy. Because of the law, that says a married woman has no property of her own. And Redwoods is for Joy. I can't let it go out of my possession.'

The blood drained from Rufe's face. 'And you think I would take the property and leave her destitute. Is that what you think? Is that what you think of me?'

'No, no. It's not like that. But you never know what will happen in the future. And it's the law.' She clasped her hands together. 'I want us to be together, I want to be with you, but I can't marry you.'

Rufe stood and looked down at her, his eyes blazing. 'And what about me? What about what I want? Do you think I'm going to be content to come and spend time with you whenever you call, then go off alone?'

'No, no, of course not. That's not what I meant.'

'I know you never experienced love before. But there's more to love than sexual gratification, Kitty, even if you might not think so at the moment, having just experienced it for the first time. But if that's all you're after, you need a gigolo, not me.'

Kitty jumped up. 'That's a terrible thing to say. That's not what I want at all. You don't understand. I've known what it's like to lose everything, to have no money, nothing. To have to work for someone you hate just to have a roof over your head and enough to eat.'

'I knew there had to be a reason for you to marry Barron, and this is it, isn't it?' He swept his arm around to take in their surroundings. 'You fell on your feet when you landed here. How happy you must have been when he died. Now it all belongs to you.' His lip curled.

'How dare you,' she blazed. 'It's not for me, it's for Joy. It's her heritage.'

'Then far be it from me to take it from her. And now I'll leave you both to enjoy it. Goodbye.' With that he swung around and marched away towards the stables.

Kitty stood frozen, feeling her world crumble around her. She stood watching until she saw him ride away without a backward glance. Then a sob started deep inside her. Pain tore at her heart, stabbed deep, forcing a cry from her.

Joy started to howl, and Mary came rushing from the house. She looked around, and when she could not see Rufe, she put her arm around the sobbing figure.

'There, there,' she soothed. 'Has he gone?'

'Yes.'

'Come inside.' She pulled on Kitty's arm. 'Come on. You're upsetting Joy.'

Kitty raised her head and saw the red-faced baby, her arms thrashing the air. She managed to straighten herself, but as she took a stumbling step, Bella emerged from the house and ran to Joy, sweeping her up into her arms.

'Whatever's the matter?' Bella asked, looking around for the cause of Kitty's distress.

Mary just shook her head. 'I'll get her inside if you look after the baby.' Then she half-led, half-dragged Kitty inside. In her room, she undressed her and put her to bed.

At first Kitty hoped he would come back, or at least contact her, but there was no word from him. She lay in her bed, the clothes pulled over her head, her room dim. She refused to leave the room or allow the curtains to be opened. The food Mary brought her was untouched. She left Joy's care to Bella and Mary. After the first hysterical outburst of grief, there were no tears. Kitty was numb. All that day and the next she laid there, until Bella strode into the room and pulled back the curtains. Ignoring Kitty's protests she threw back the bedclothes.

'Get up,' she ordered. 'You're going to take a bath and get dressed.'

'No,' Kitty protested, turning on her side and drawing her knees up to her chin. 'Leave me alone.'

'No. You're getting up. I don't know what happened between you and Mr. Cavanagh, but you have a responsibility as a mother. You have a baby. She's fretting for you.'

Slowly Kitty straightened her legs and turned on her back. 'You can look after her.'

'She needs you. She's fretting for you,' Bella repeated firmly. 'She won't take her food.'

Kitty took a deep breath. Slowly she sat up.

'Kitty,' Bella said gently, 'perhaps if you tell me what happened, and we talk about it, you might feel better.'

Kitty drew a deep breath. Haltingly, she tried to explain. 'Rufe asked me to marry him, and I said no. But it was because of Joy. I tried to explain to him it was because of the law, because I must keep Redwoods for Joy, I couldn't risk losing it, but he didn't understand.'

Bella sat on the bed beside her. 'Do you love him?'

'Yes.'

'And he loves you?'

'He said so.'

Bella took her hand. 'Kitty, not all men are like William. Your father wasn't. Jack is not. You should have trusted your man.'

'But what if…if something happened…?'

'Surely you believe he's trustworthy. Look how he's helped us. I think you have to trust him. If you write to him, it might not be too late.'

'Do you really think so?'

'I do,' she said firmly. 'I think you should write to him. He's probably mortified that you don't trust him.'

Kitty knew she had handled the matter badly. Perhaps in a letter she could explain how she felt at the time, tell him she knew she had expressed her feelings badly, that she loved him and wanted to be with him, to marry him. If she could make him understand, would he come back? Would he give their love another chance?

She thought about it all day, thinking of what she could say, and then she wrote the letter and mailed it. And waited.

His reply, when it came, was formal. Rufe told her that in the interval since he had left Redwoods, he regretted that his circumstances had changed. I am now married to Irene, he told her. He wished her all the best for the future.

Kitty's hand shook as she reread the letter. It couldn't be true. There it was, the words leapt out at her. Rufe was married to Irene. She crumpled the page and let it fall from her fingers. How could he do this? She felt sick and the air inside the house stifled her. She stumbled outside, down the steps and across the garden. Hurrying all the way through the trees she reached the steep track that led up the side of Bulahdelah Mountain and scrambled upwards, her breath coming in gasps, until she reached a place that overlooked Redwoods.

Panting, she leant against a tree and surveyed her home below. It was for this that she had rejected love. For Redwoods, and for Joy. As she stood there, catching her breath, the shock began to turn slowly to anger. How dare Rufe profess his love for her and then at the first setback rush off and marry Irene? She was well rid of him and his fickle love.

But that night, as she tossed and turned, her anger spent, she went over it all again. Rufe must have left her and gone straight to Irene. How could he have done that?

Had she misread the depth of Rufe's feelings for her? Had she believed his love was as deep and intense as her own when all along it had been merely lust? But if that was so, why had he asked her to marry him? Did he simply want to be married now? When she rejected him, had he decided Irene would do instead? As the tears flowed she knew she didn't have the answer, but she knew she had lost Rufe, and she felt as if her heart must break. Finally, she drifted into a restless sleep.

At the first light of day Kitty rose and dressed, and walked down to the river, shivering slightly in the cool air. The morning mist hung still over the water, its grey silence matching the emptiness inside her. How was she ever going to live, without that love she had known so briefly?

She sat on the stump, a small hunched figure contemplating the lonely future stretching ahead of her. How could she go on when there was only an empty hollow where her heart was meant to be?

When the first golden rays of sun coaxed a little warmth into her she slowly straightened, then stood and walked to the edge of the water. The mist had started to lift. Stretching her arms above her head she stood for a few moments, taking deep breaths of the fresh morning air, and looked around her. Then she turned, all the way around, looking at the grass and the bushes and the tall, straight trees.

Kitty began to walk slowly back along the path. Past the house, through the trees. When she reached the mill, she stopped. The smell of cut wood hung in the air. All was quiet now, but soon it would buzz as the men toiled to transform the waiting forest giants into timber.

Jack's advice had been good. Harry Osborne's patronage had been invaluable. At first, the other boat builders were reluctant to deal with a woman, but when they knew she was supplying Harry, one by one they decided to give her a try. Their orders were small at first, but as she delivered on her promises their orders increased, and the business grew to achieve the success it now enjoyed.

Kitty continued her walk. A group of kangaroos ceased nibbling the grass alongside the path and bounded away at her approach.

A little further on she reached the cutters beginning their day's work and she stopped to watch the rhythmic movements of the axe men. Patrick called a cheery 'good morning' and she raised her hand and returned his greeting. A butcherbird in a nearby tree piped its morning call. Redwoods was coming to life.

When she reached the house she headed for the nursery. As she came level with the dining room Bella called out to her. 'Kitty, are you all right?'

Kitty stopped and looked in at her mother, pushing her pain down deep. 'I'm fine, thank you, just fine.'

In the nursery Joy lay in her cot, and she gurgled and lifted her arms to Kitty as she came into the room.

'Good morning, my darling,' Kitty said as she bent over and lifted her up. Joy's waving hand grasped Kitty's hair. Kitty nuzzled her face against her, inhaling the sweet baby smell. 'We have so much to be thankful for, you and I. We have Redwoods to keep us safe. You have a grandmother and a grandfather, and we have friends. It's time to start a new day, my little one. We have a lot of living to do, and we need to get on with it.'

## CHAPTER TWENTY SEVEN

*Thirteen years later*

Kitty Barron stood on the verandah of Redwoods and wondered at her feeling of dissatisfaction. Why should she feel this way? After all, she had everything she'd ever wanted – hadn't she? It was many years since she had vowed that she would do whatever she had to do, to claw back the prosperity that had been snatched from her family. And she had succeeded.

Looking around, her gaze swept over the large swathe of land that lay between the imposing Bulahdelah Mountain and the Myall River, glinting silver in the sun before her. It all belonged to her, her and Joy. And there was more – the forest of hardwood timber that rang with the sound of the timber cutter's axes and the mill that supplied the timber requirements of the local area and beyond. This was Redwoods. Security for herself, her mother, and her daughter. What more could she want?

Sighing, Kitty turned and went inside, heading to her office where she sat at her desk and pulled a pile of papers towards her. It was time to begin work. There was a quick knock at the door and her mother entered the room.

'Good morning, Kitty. It looks like you're busy already. And so is Joy, I see,' Bella added, glancing through the window to where her granddaughter was busy grooming her horse.

'Yes, she wants to spend as much time as possible with Dancer until she goes down to school in Sydney tomorrow. I'll just finish with these and then we'll have breakfast.'

Bella nodded as she sat in the chair opposite. 'I'm happy that Joy is looking forward to going to St. Catherine's tomorrow.'

'Oh yes, she's excited. She's told me how she can't wait to see "the big world out there away from Redwoods," as she puts it.' Kitty's throat tightened. 'I've told her she won't find anywhere better than here, but she doesn't believe me.'

'It's natural at her age. She's growing up.' Bella gestured at the papers. 'What are you working on now?'

'I'm trying to decide whether to plant more timber or not in the areas where the cutting has finished. I need to look to Redwoods' future.'

'Redwoods' future, yes. But what about you, Kitty? What about your future? I know you never wanted to marry before, because you worried about losing Redwoods but now, since the Married Women's Property Act was passed, there's no danger of that. It's many years since William drowned, and you're too young to spend the rest of your life alone. What about Harry Osborne? Will you consider him?'

Kitty thought of Harry Osborne, a faithful, dependable friend as well as a good customer over the years. He had proposed marriage and she had refused him. Since then, he had often pointed out how it would make good business sense to join their two enterprises, his boat building and her timber mill. But marriage? She didn't think she wanted to marry again.

She shrugged. 'Marriage would mean I couldn't do as I like, when I like. And I've grown used to that, and I don't know I want to give up my freedom. I don't need a husband and besides, although I enjoy Harry's company and value his friendship, I don't love him.'

Bella sighed. 'Well, I know better than to try and change your mind.' She stood up. 'I'll go in to breakfast. Don't be too long.'

'Now then, you won't forget to write and let me know how everything is, will you?' Kitty asked Joy as they said their farewells in the hall of St. Catherine's School.

'No, and don't you forget to write and let me know how everything is at home. And you won't forget to see Dancer has plenty of exercise, will you? You know she's used to me riding her every day. And don't forget, she loves an apple or a carrot when you go to visit her.'

"I won't forget, I promise.' Kitty nodded towards a mistress assembling the waiting girls into groups. 'And now, I can see you have to go.'

Joy picked up her case. 'Bye, Mother. See you in the spring holidays.'

'I'll be here to meet you.' Kitty watched her go with an ache in her heart.

Kitty counted each day until Joy would be home again, but finally it happened, and once again Kitty undertook the trip to Sydney to meet her. She was delighted to receive a good report of Joy's progress, and to see that her daughter was happy in her new school.

The holiday passed quickly, with Joy spending much of her time riding Dancer and then, all too soon, it was back to school again for Joy. This was the pattern of their lives for the next two years. Kitty's business prospered during this time, and she was glad her daughter had adjusted so well and happily to life at St. Catherine's.

Kitty met Joy as usual when the autumn holidays arrived in the third year of her schooling. On the way home Joy chattered happily about school and the other girls, and especially about her best friend, Lily.

'Lily's father has horses,' she told Kitty. 'He breeds them. They sell most of them, but any really good ones they keep. Just imagine having loads of horses on the place.'

Kitty smiled at her enthusiasm. 'You'd think that's wonderful, wouldn't you?'

'Oh, wouldn't it be? And Lily knows loads about looking after them and their bloodlines and all that sort of stuff. It's really good business,' Joy said seriously. 'Her father makes a lot of money from them. We have all those empty paddocks where the timber's been cut. Perhaps we could use them to breed horses.'

Kitty frowned thoughtfully. 'I think you probably need special knowledge, but I could make some enquiries.'

'Then you will look into it?'

Kitty nodded. 'Yes, I will. Horses are certainly more appealing than sheep or cattle, and we have to do something with those empty paddocks. But I can't promise anything definite will come of it.'

Again the holidays went too quickly, and it was time for Kitty to escort Joy back to school. As the cab came to a halt outside the main door, Joy jumped out and held the door open for Kitty.

'Do you want me to wait?' the driver asked, as Kitty paid the fare.

'No, thank you.'

'You needn't stay,' Joy told her. 'I'll be all right. I can see some girls I know.' Her face brightened. 'Here comes Lily. Now you'll be able to meet her.'

A slim girl about Joy's age with long, dark hair was walking towards them.

After introductions Kitty spoke to Lily with a smile. 'Joy's told me lots about you. She's hoping you can come and stay with us some time. Perhaps next holidays if you'd like to, and if it's all right with your parents.'

Lily's face lit up. 'Oh, I'd love to come. I'll have to ask my father, but I don't think he'll mind.' She turned to look across the school yard. 'Oh, here he comes now. He had to find a place to leave the trap.' She waved and called out. 'Father, I'm over here.'

Kitty's heart lurched, and she felt the blood rush to her face as she saw that Lily's father was Rufe Cavanagh. With a racing heart she stood watching as he approached them, noticing even in her state of shock that he had not lost his good looks or his upright bearing.

Rufe's step faltered as recognition crossed his face, and he stood still for a few seconds, but resumed walking towards Lily as she hurried to meet him. Taking him by the hand she pulled him back with her.

'Father, this is my best friend, Joy, and this is her mother, Mrs. Barron, and they want me to go and stay with them for the next holidays. That'll be all right, won't it?'

Rufe looked pale, but he answered calmly enough. 'Lily, where are your manners? That's no way to introduce me to your friends.'

Lily's hand flew to her mouth. 'I'm sorry. This is…'

Rufe interrupted her. 'As it so happens, Lily, I have met Mrs. Barron. And Joy too, although it was a long time ago.' He turned to Kitty. 'How are you, Mrs. Barron? I'm pleased to meet you again after so many years.'

Kitty swallowed at the ball of nerves that seemed to be filling her throat. 'Why, Mr. Cavanagh. What a surprise. Yes, it is many years. Sixteen, I believe.'

'Sixteen years,' exclaimed Joy. 'Oh, we would've both been babies then.'

'Perhaps I wasn't even born,' Lily chimed in. 'After all, you're seven months older than me.'

Something sharp and painful twisted inside Kitty as she struggled with the implications of the girl's remark.

'As often happens, you're quite right Lily,' Rufe told her. 'No. You weren't born then.'

'Can I please go to stay?'

'Are you still at Redwoods, Mrs. Barron?'

'Yes.'

'Then if it suits Mrs. Barron you might go, but Mrs. Barron and I will have to discuss it first. Now, you two had better go inside and settle in. We'll let you know when we've decided.'

Rufe put his hand on Kitty's arm when the girls left. 'How are you, Kitty?' he asked softly, his eyes searching her face.

Kitty felt a rush of anger as she remembered that this was the man who had professed his love for her, and then stormed off after a quarrel, and married someone else immediately.

'I'm fine, thank you,' she told him, lifting her chin. 'And you?'

'Fine.'

'And how is Irene?'

'I really have no idea.'

Kitty's stomach flipped. 'What do you mean?'

'What I said. I have no idea how she is. I haven't seen her since Lily was three years old.'

'But…'

'Look, we can't stand here talking, let's go someplace where we can. There's a nice little tearoom down by the beach. Do you fancy a cup of tea? Although I must say seeing you again has made me feel more like a stiff drink than tea. But it's a bit early for that.'

Kitty hesitated, her insides churning. 'I don't know that we have anything to discuss. After all, anything that was between us ended all those years ago.'

'Please Kitty. Give me a chance to explain.'

'What is there to explain? You chose to marry Irene.'

'There's more to it than that.' He took her by the arm. 'My trap's close by. Please come with me.'

Kitty hesitated, her mind in turmoil. What did Lily's age mean? Had Rufe left her bed and gone straight to Irene's? But no…the timing wouldn't fit. So, what had happened? She took a deep breath. It wouldn't hurt to find out, and then at least she would know.

'Very well. I'll come.'

They had no further conversation until they were seated in the tearoom overlooking Bondi Beach and the waitress had taken their order.

Rufe sat back and looked at her. 'The years have been kind to you. You're still as beautiful as ever.'

'You don't have to flatter me.'

'I'm not. I'm telling the truth. Now, tell me how everything is with you – you're still at Redwoods, then?'

'Yes, I am. But I'm wondering why you haven't seen Irene for so long. When your letter came, I realised you'd gone straight from me to her. '

'Don't,' he said sharply, frowning. 'First, I'd like to know, are you married again? I know Lily called you Mrs. Barron, but that could be assumption on her part.'

'No, I'm not married.'

Rufe leant back in his chair with a sigh. 'When I left you at Redwoods after we quarrelled, I went straight back to Sydney. When I arrived I found Irene waiting for me. As you know, I'd spent time with her in Sydney when we all met at Petty's Hotel that time and then I saw her again when I visited the diggings after Bradshaw and I salted the mine. And then I didn't see her again until after you and I parted.'

Rufe paused before continuing, his face tight. 'She told me then that she was pregnant and the child was mine.' He ran his fingers through his hair. 'We'd always had an understanding, and I'm not proud of it, that our relationship was not serious. I never had any intention of making it serious, and she'd told me she didn't want any commitment – she was interested in furthering her ambitions as an hotelier.' He paused again, clearing his throat. 'I didn't have to marry her; I could have made other arrangements for her. But you and I had parted. I thought you'd never marry me, so I didn't really care.' He took a deep breath. 'When she pressed me for marriage, to give the child a name, I agreed.'

The waitress brought their pot of tea, and they fell silent while Kitty poured the tea and handed Rufe his cup, her mind in a whirl.

He took a sip before resuming his tale. 'When your letter reached me telling me you'd had a change of heart, I thought I'd go crazy, because it was too late. Irene and I were already married.'

Kitty bit her lip. 'I wish I'd known, I thought you didn't really care about me, that it had been Irene all along.'

He shook his head. 'Perhaps I shouldn't discuss this, but I'd like you to know. You spoilt me for anyone else. It was a long time before I could bring myself to touch Irene – anyone but you. Our marriage was in name only for the first year.'

The last of Kitty's anger evaporated as she sipped her tea. How stupid she'd been. It was all her fault Rufe had left the way he did. Her fault they parted, when they could have had all these years together. And now it was too late. They had moved in different directions. And where was Irene now? Had Rufe met someone else? She roused herself, aware he was watching her. 'So where's Irene now?' she asked him.

'She left us when Lily was three years old. I disappointed her by refusing to buy her a hotel in Sydney. She met someone who was prepared to buy one for her in Melbourne and as far as I know that's where she still is. I haven't heard from her since.'

'And Lily? Does she see Lily?'

'No. She never bothered to contact her. She obviously didn't want the complication of a child in her new life, but I'm happy about that.' His face brightened. 'Lily and I are great friends.'

'I'm glad. That's like Joy and me. And have you married again?'

'No.' He shook his head. 'And now tell me, how's your mother? And Jack Morgan? Are they still both well?'

Kitty smiled. 'They certainly are, and they're very happy together. They live with me at Redwoods. I'm glad of their company, particularly now Joy is at school. Mary and Patrick married, too, and they're still with us. Patrick manages the timber gang now, and Jack's busy running the mill.'

Rufe raised his brows. 'Well, you always wanted a successful business of your own. It sounds as if you've realised your dream. It seems as if you have everything you ever wanted in life.'

Kitty's heart missed a beat. 'I'm not sure I could say that.' She paused. 'And now, tell me what you've been doing. Joy told me you breed horses now?'

'Yes. After our parents died, about six years ago, my brother Edward and I bought a property close to Morpeth. Not so very far from you. It's good horse country, and Morpeth has a deep river port.'

Kitty felt a flicker of anger return. 'That's only about forty miles from Bulahdelah. You never thought to come and visit?'

Rufe looked at her for a long moment before putting down his cup. 'I thought of you often, but I didn't think you'd want to see me. Besides, I thought it likely you'd be married again.'

'Unlikely, don't you mean?' she snapped.

'I'm sure it's not for lack of offers.'

'I've never had the inclination.'

He reached across and brushed her hand with his fingers. 'Don't be angry with me, Kitty.' A half smile lifted a corner of his mouth. 'Please.'

His touch caused a tremor to run through her, and his words made her feel she was being unjust. 'I have no right to be angry.' She sighed.

When he spoke again, his voice was soft. 'I suppose Redwoods is changed now, after all these years. I'd like to see it again, if I'm welcome. And the people there, too. When Lily comes to visit in the holidays, do you think I could come with her?' His warm eyes pleaded. 'Perhaps we could even become...' he hesitated, 'reacquainted.'

Kitty's heart faltered as she looked across the table at the man whom she had loved so desperately all those years ago. Was it possible they could pick up again where they were before they quarrelled? Was there any chance those feelings could ever be recaptured? Sixteen years was a long time. How much would they have changed? Kitty took a deep breath. Unless she gave it a chance, she would never know.

She smiled at Rufe across the teapot. 'I see no reason why not.'

****

Continue reading Kitty's and Rufe's story in Redwoods Book Two, **A Liberated Woman.**

## About Kate

Kate grew up in a beach area in Adelaide, South Australia and after an absence of almost twenty five years, spent mostly in NSW, she has returned to her home town with husband Peter.

She has worked as a freelance travel writer, has had many short stories published and is the published author of four novels, including the Redwoods trilogy, which are stories of historical romance and family sagas and have received 4 and 5 star reviews.

Her books, ***'Inheritance'*** and ***'Black Mountain'*** are published by Escape Publishers and have received 5 star reviews.

Kate now pursues her passions of writing, reading and listening to music, and is working on her sixth novel - ***The Trophy Wife***. Kate now writes Australian contemporary and historical fiction, and as long as you tell her, in reviews and emails, that you enjoy what she writes, Kate will continue doing so. Kate love chocolate, fine wines, dogs, music, and seeing new places.

# A Liberated Woman

***Can love be re-kindled after sixteen years apart?***

This is the dilemma that faces Kitty Barron and Rufe Cavanagh. How much will the years have changed them? And what of their teenage daughters – important parts of their lives – would they accept sharing the love that has always been theirs alone?

While Joy embraces the idea of uniting their families, Lily burns with jealousy at the thought of sharing her father's affection, and schemes to keep them apart. When Joy and Lily go to London for a Season, the heady and exciting world of society London is a mixture of adventures and heartache for both Joy and Lily. They find that beneath the gaiety and excitement not everything or everybody is as it seems. Their romances bring problems that have far-reaching effects for Kitty and Rufe, and their happiness. London turns their world and everyone around them into chaos.

*Love, seduction, intrigue, and greed all play a part in this tale. Part romantic story, part family saga, it sweeps from the village of Bulahdelah in New South Wales to pre-federation Sydney, and to the pomp and ceremony of Queen Victoria's court and a London Season.*

**Praise for A Liberated Woman**

*"Kate Loveday's writing is emotionally touching. The stories as they unfold on the different paths were done in a wonderful way while still tying the main threads together. I must say my emotions did become involved here for one of the story lines was heart rending for it is a portrait of life even in this day and age. The writer has a great way of telling her story in words. A historical romance that is not just Australia or London but a mixture of cultures and countries. This one is a good read for a long night where you wish good company. Only problem... It is somewhat of a cliffhanger!. "* Anna Swedenmom

*"Great reading. Loved the series... Looking forward to the last book in the series. Great stories and the all the people in them."* Amazon

*"Wonderful historical romance with a feel of Australia that makes me want to experience it even though I know it would be different today. This*

*sequel to the awesome An Independent Woman reunites Kitty and Rufe while it focuses on their daughters.*" Alice L Kent

*"A Liberated Woman is a romantic tale of women, young and old, coming to grips with the evolution of a new social order forming at the beginning of the twentieth century. Kate Loveday has penned a story that flows well. Readers of this book will get enjoyment out of seeing how the protagonists overcome the different situations they find themselves thrust into."* Warren Thurston, Australian Author

***

# An Ambitious Woman

***The old ways are changing, but they can't change fast enough for Joy Barron...***

**She wants it all. Love. Marriage. Success. NOW.**

Joy is determined Redwoods will become a successful thoroughbred stud, and dreams of breeding a champion racehorse. When David Cavanagh opposes her ideas she schemes to get her way, determined to make her dream a reality. She continues on her wilful way until tragedy strikes and fills her with remorse. Then Thunder, the big, black stallion enters their lives, and with him comes Josh Frazer.

David believes she is more concerned with Redwoods' success than with him and their marriage, and he goes to America with an open-end return date. Joy is broken hearted by what she sees as David's rejection. Josh is willing to take his place in her affections, but she is unresponsive to his advances. But when the children go missing Joy must turn to Josh for help and comfort, and her feelings change.

Against the heart-stopping background of the prestigious Gold Cup race week Joy must make the most difficult decision of her life.

Can a woman love two men? How can she choose between two loves?

***Praise for An Ambitious Woman***

*"Aussie author Kate Loveday's stories about independent women are wonderful stories. She has many twists and turns and surprises, good and bad, in her stories that a reader doesn't expect. She writes so smoothly it is like the pen in her writing hand touches the pages and the words just flow out of her pen onto paper with such ease. Ms. Loveday's writing is smooth and intelligent. She blends everything together very nicely and tells a wonderful descriptive story of different types of people, some you'll love and cheer on and some you'll dislike immensely. This story was not just a romance novel, Kate has imbedded a wonderful cast of true to life characters and many circumstances they went through. It would make a wonderful movie."* Alice L Kent

"More Please!

I enjoyed reading Ambitious Woman as the last in this trilogy. It concluded the story with an interesting and satisfactory ending and if there was more I would love to keep reading." Wendy...Amazon

****

# The Trophy Wife

**Full of courage and resolve, this is a story about reinventing yourself, and the intrigues of Fate. A story of love, friendship, disillusion and retribution as a woman strives to change her life.**

***It seemed as if it would be a fairy tale existence...***

When young and lonely Erin McDonald leaves Newcastle for a job in Sydney shortly after her mother's death she meets high powered business mogul Giles Brightman. He sweeps her off her feet, and she is thrilled when he proposes. Madly in love she marries him, but she soon realises he wants nothing more from her than to look beautiful and be compliant – ready to accompany him whenever he wishes, charming to his business associates, and ready to accommodate him in bed whenever he feels so inclined.

Slowly Giles' violent side emerges, and after an attack that makes her fear for her life, Erin knows she must get away. With little money of her own, and a platinum Amex card, she develops an audacious plan to give her a second chance in life – at Giles' expense. But Giles won't let her go easily.

When she consults lawyer Aden Marlowe the last thing on her mind is a new relationship. She tries to ignore her attraction to Aden, and throws herself into her efforts to create a specialised high fashion boutique. Aden is captivated from the start, but he has a secret, and must hide his feelings.

Giles tries to sweet talk Erin into returning to him, but when his pleading fails he threatens her and demands the return of documents that he accuses her of stealing. Undaunted by his threats, Erin ignores him and continues with her plans, but her home is ransacked and her store vandalised. Aden suspects a sinister reason behind Giles' actions, and he and Erin work together to find the secret of the seemingly innocuous *Phoebus* share documents.

***Can Erin overcome all the setbacks to find a new life...***

*and a new love?*

***Praise for The Trophy Wife***

***"Second chance novel is too bland a term for The Trophy Wife.***

I love women-of-strength novels and that is one on of the things Kate Loveday does so well. When young and lonely Erin McDonald leaves her home for a new job shortly after her mother's death, she is vulnerable to the practiced machinations of the urbane Giles Brightman and falls completely under his spell. Young, inexperienced, and loving does not equal weak, her love holds up under his growing busy-man routine but when he crosses a line, she walks. The tale of the rebuilding of her life, her soul, is the fascinating journey we travel with The Trophy Wife." *Jeanie W Jackson*

*"Kate Loveday's stories of strong women are wonderful.* Her writing is smooth and intelligent. She blends everything together very nicely and tells a wonderful descriptive story of different types of people, some you'll love and cheer on and some you'll dislike immensely. This story is not just a romance novel, Kate has imbedded a wonderful cast of true to life characters and the many circumstances they go through.*" Alice L Kent*

# Inheritance

***An inheritance is usually a blessing . . . could it also be a curse?***

An Australian rural romance about an unexpected inheritance that sends a city girl down deep into the country...

When Cassie Taylor inherits Yallandoo, a cattle station near Cairns in Far North Queensland, she is shocked.

What does she know about running cattle? But the property has been in her family for generations, and Cassie is not a quitter. She leaves behind her Sydney life and heads to the station, determined to make a go of it.

But a long drought and falling prices mean challenges Cassie doesn't expect. To save her heritage, she's going to have to come up with some new ideas — and fast.

Then the threatening letters start to arrive. Someone doesn't want Cassie to succeed, and they're willing to go to any lengths to stop her...

### *Praise for Inheritance*

"*INHERITANCE is a great romantic suspense story, but also a chronicle of Cassie's life as she grows into a woman. I really liked her characters. I also enjoyed how she incorporated the lore of the Aboriginal people of Australia in the story. Ms. Loveday has created a wonderful setting in Yallandoo. Her characters are wonderfully developed and come alive off the page. This is a great book*!" Romance Junkies Reviewer: Lisa

"*Overall I found Inheritance compelling. Kate Loveday has a wonderful talent for getting into each and every character's head and telling the story from their point of view. The different twists and turns in the story retain the reader's interest. A very believable story; one that draws the reader in and leaves them feeling as though they have not only met these people but have really managed to get to know them all, very well.*" RRAH reviewed by Kay James

"*With her first novel 'Inheritance' ,Kate Loveday has created a fantastic read. I applaud her wonderful talent. Great work! Can't wait for her next book!*" Sarah Cook , Author

# Black Mountain

**An adventure set in the Australian rainforest, where the race is on to discover a precious plant – and an even rarer kind of attraction.**

Elly Cooper's friend Jackson has gone missing – along with a journal that contains her dead father's lifelong work and the recipe for a product he described as the 'fountain of youth', potentially worth millions.

The catch is that the main ingredient is a rare plant found only in the Daintree Rainforest in Queensland. And only her father knew where to find it.

Elly enlists the aid of ex–policeman Mitchell Beaumont to help her find Jackson, the journal and the plant. But someone else is on the trail of the precious plant, and it seems they'll stop at nothing – even murder – to get what they want.

It's a race against time in the tropical heat as Elly and Mitchell battle the perils of the rainforest – and the feelings growing between them.

### *Praise For Black Mountain*

"First time reading this author and thoroughly enjoyed her description of the country, characters and story line. Will be checking out her other books." *Net Galley*

"This is a fantastic short read that is fast pace and exciting. I really enjoyed this story as it was something different and really captured my attention. Elly is in a race against time to find the flower that holds the secret to her father's fountain of youth oil. Only problem is she's not the only one looking for the undiscovered flower. Elly isn't out searching the rainforest by herself.

Spending so much time with Mitchell, Elly might find more than just the flower." *Lost in sweet words*

'I really enjoyed this book as it had a hint of romance and bit of intrigue. Plus I have always found Australia fascinating from afar and for that reason found this read fun, and exciting. There are many unexpected things that happen in the story that you will miss out on if you don't take a chance on this enthralling read. 'Black Mountain' is the place where adventure, romance, and mystery abound; what more could one ask for? I would like to read more books by this author."

*Lady P,Net galley*

"Black Mountain is an exciting and complex adventure focusing on a race between greed and love." *Goodreads*

****

# Connect with Kate Loveday

I really appreciate you reading my book!

The following are my Contacts:

Friend me on Facebook ;https://www.facebook.com/kloveday

Follow me on Twitter:https://twitter.com/LovedayKate

Favourite my Smashwords author page:https://www.smashwords.com/profile/view/PL

Subscribe to my blog:https://kateloveday.wordpress.com/

Visit my website:http://www.kateloveday.com/

__*****__

www.ingramcontent.com/pod-product-compliance
Ingram Content Group UK Ltd.
Pitfield, Milton Keynes, MK11 3LW, UK
UKHW041857190726
13854UKWH00002B/949